THE BUTTE POLKA

THE
BUTTE
POLKA

A Novel by

Donald McCaig

Rawson, Wade Publishers, Inc.
New York

*The author wishes to thank Mrs. George Sarsfield, who
contributed Joe Reau's rum pie recipe, and Ms. Jean McGrath,
who first published it in Butte's* Heritage Cookbook. *This recipe
is reproduced by permission of Ms. McGrath on behalf of the
Butte-Silver Bow Arts Foundation.*

Library of Congress Cataloging in Publication Data

McCaig, Donald.
The Butte polka.

I. Title.
PZ4.M1216Bu [PS3563.A2555] 813′.5′4 79-9405
ISBN 0-89256-133-5

Copyright © 1980 by Donald McCaig

Published simultaneously in Canada
by McClelland and Stewart, Ltd.

Designed by Francesca Belanger

First Edition

For Don McCaig
my brave and gentle father

THE BUTTE POLKA is entirely a work of the imagination, not a history.

"Butte Montana is a place where the Company is too big to beat. Where the house cut is always too steep and where victory, below ground or above it, consists in snatching a draw out of the jaws of certain defeat."
—Nelson Algren

THE BUTTE POLKA

1

I AM JAMES MICHAEL MULLHOLLAND. My father was James Michael Mullholland too. He died February 12, 1946, just five weeks after the morning I puffed and whistled up the Copper Street hill toward my sister's house and her trouble. Eighteen below. Butte is fifty-two hundred feet above sea level and the dry air scorches the back of my throat.

The sand trucks have been by and the dry golden sand lies in careless patches on top of the compacted snow. Copper Street weaves through the whitened mounds of the tailing dumps and the few houses don't have any sidewalks so I stay in the middle of the street. There's no cars to speak of.

Polkas have the same cadence as marches and it's a polka moving my feet up the icy hill. At the top I stop whistling, having done justice to my self-discipline, though not to the song.

My sister's name is Kathleen. This morning, I am afraid of her. I am afraid of people in trouble.

Most of the sidewalks on Jackson Street have been shoveled clear. The houses are frame affairs—small duplexes and smaller one-family homes. There are a few brick houses nestled among them, just below the crest of the Hill.

Kathleen's house was covered with brick-patterned asphalt siding. It didn't really look much like brick but it kept some of the weather out.

No front yard. Her house was drawn up close to the sidewalk. From the front porch you could see the tailing dump across the street. From the back porch, on a clear day like today, you could see much farther; to the saw-toothed Highland Mountains, thirty-five miles away.

White plumes of air rose from dozens of mine air-shafts and stood above the Hill, motionless, fifty, a hundred feet high. The plumes of air were beautiful. The sky was beautiful too; blue, vast and impossibly cold.

A card was Scotch-taped above the doorbell: KANGAS.

I stamped the snow off my galoshes and unbuckled them. The frozen metal buckles clutched at my fingers.

She let me in with no welcome. Her parlor was cold but the kitchen was warmer. The kids' breakfast dishes piled up on the sink. The short brown oil heater pumping out heat and the coffee perking on the stove.

She sat down at the table. She put her elbows on the table and her face in her hands. "Joel hasn't called," she said.

"Have you phoned Ketchel?"

"He has no phone. His landlady says she can't be bothered carrying messages for every mucker who beds down there."

"Joel'll come home," I said.

My sister's been beautiful just once in her life: on her wedding day. Her hair was dark red, so red it was almost purple, and she had the nun's complexion to go with it. Her figure was—ample—and her gait powerful enough to make you wonder what would happen to the man who switched her engine on. But she was too short and her cheekbones were too high—so high, her eyes were squeezed oriental above them. "Black Irish" cheekbones, my father called them, referring to the Catholic half of the Mullholland gene pool. When we were kids, I called her "Chink."

When she was sad, she settled into herself like a black lump; pulling you to her, to the core of her unhappiness—repelling you with her passive, sad compliance. She'd been that way her final year as a novice, before she met and married Joel, and I used to dread the long drive up to Helena to see her: the white plastered room, the black lump seated on the enameled wooden chair, the placid, slow enraged lips.

She had a tongue on her and when she was happy, it laved and gilded and mocked. When she was angry, she used it like a butcher knife. I didn't want to be around when Joel finally came home.

I turned off the coffee. I poured two cups. I put a little milk in hers. I sat down across the kitchen table and watched her not drink her coffee.

Nothing new. Maybe the third time this winter Joel had stayed out all night tomcatting. I didn't have too much patience left. Joel and I had been pals a couple years back, but we weren't so tight anymore and I hated him for making me miss a day of work to sit with his wife and watch her melt into her unhappiness.

In the early afternoon, he'd drag home, talking as fast as he could; his fast mouth under his squinted, black, dynamited eyes. It wouldn't help. Not with Kathleen's tongue calling down battalions of saints to examine the mistake she'd married; inviting them to note his numerous faults: at least those of intemperance, lusts of the flesh, improvidence and communism, that they should pick him out of the crowd at the Last Judgment and punch his ticket for the southbound train.

Then, she'd throw him out of the house.

He'd move in with us, my father and me, and sleep on our worn velveteen couch for a week or so, silent, hardly saying a word to my father who loved arguing with him, until one evening, about five o'clock when he'd take a bath, anoint himself with Wildroot, put on one of my better shirts and my solid green tie and return home with more bravado than repentance in his eye.

He always said he missed the kids. Maybe he did.

The coffee was very hot and very weak and Hills Brothers coffee which I've never cared for.

"This coffee should percolate a little longer."

"There's nothing wrong with it," she said, and proved there wasn't by taking a sip.

The ashtray on the table was filled with half-smoked Luckies. Rings on the red-checked oilcloth where she'd set her coffee cups down all night long. Her kitchen was high ceilinged and the little stove sent most of its heat up to lie under the ceiling where we weren't sitting.

"How're the kids?"

"They're jake," she said. "Just jake." She got up and

went over to the sink and wiped her face on a dish towel. I thought for a moment she'd honk into the dish towel but she was too lace curtain for that.

"Shirley and Carl are off to school," she said.

"Uh-huh."

She whirled around and glared at me like I was Joel's substitute. "Can't he see what this does to them? Mister Know It All." A bitter droop to the corner of her mouth and her red-rimmed eyes like open sores. "Shirley asked me this morning, 'Is Daddy moving away?' Oh, damn! Damn him!"

A tear started down her cheek, and soon enough another one joined it. "I'll call the plant," I said. "Maybe they've heard from him."

Joel worked the graveyard shift at the old Missouri River Steam Generating Plant on top of the Hill. A soft job. Him and his partner sitting on wooden chairs, nipping on their thermoses, and from time to time one of them would get up and check the gauges that monitored the steam hissing from the big boilers out to the changing rooms in the mines, the shaft houses, and the Company offices downtown.

One of these jobs that makes you middle aged. The two of them sitting there eight hours. I asked Joel once what he and his partner talked about all night; Joel being pretty mouthy and Ketchel, his partner, as quiet as a Protestant at a wake.

"Communism," Joel laughed.

Joel hadn't punched in last night. Ketchel'd called Kathleen at one A.M., to ask if he was sick or sumpin'.

And Kathleen had called the plant twice to see if the wandering boy had showed up.

"No."

"No."

Maybe the day shift would know something. I dialed. "Hello. My brother-in-law, Joel Kangas, works the graveyard there. Did he come in yet?"

"This is the day shift, Mac."

"Who'm I talking to?"

"Frank Bick. I ain't seen him. When I got here there was only that Indian here."

"Ketchel."

"Yeah. The Indian."

"Look, I'm Jimmy Mullholland, machinist at the Granite Mountain. My dad's a firebug at the Spec. Would you ask your partner if he saw Joel?"

"Jeez, I'm sorry, pal. My partner punched in after I did. Joel wasn't here." He laughed. "Joel's probably off on a tear."

I shook my head at Kathleen. She poured me a fresh cup of coffee I didn't want. I didn't want to be in the Kangas kitchen, a sitting duck, waiting for the master of the house to come home, hungover, unrepentant, and ready to lay into me—"Brother-in-law, hell! Buttinski!"

I wished I was working on the hoist motors at the Granite Mountain. Unlike my family, they were crisp and logical.

Kathleen must have seen something in my eyes because she said, "I'm sorry, Jimmy. Joel's done some boozing, oh, I can't deny that, but he's never missed a shift before."

I said, "Uh-huh."

We were going out that year. Everybody knew it. The last strike was in '34 and we were long overdue.

About the strike, Joel and I differed. He was IWW. I counted my change.

During the War, wages were frozen. The Company's profits had multiplied a couple hundred percent—all those copper shell-casings and tank radiators and hydraulic lines and posthumous medals—and the Company'd passed zero on to the miners.

The union hadn't helped. When John L. Lewis struck the United Mine Workers, the coal miners in West Virginia got some of their due, but the Mine, Mill and Smelter Workers Union had been more patriotic.

We bought a lot of liberty bonds too.

We'd been without a contract since October '45. Every month since then, at least once, the Company'd hold one of its famous one-hour bargaining sessions: fifty minutes for the Company to lay it on the line; ten minutes for the union to make them mad enough to declare the session closed.

Tempers were hot. Single miners were pulling up stakes for Coeur d'Alene, Bisbee, or Wallace, and the married men were counseling prudence. Me too. Since my father and I were both working, there were two Mullholland paychecks. I made $7.80 a day and he made forty cents more. No car—we depended on Joel's when we needed one. I had three hundred fifty dollars in the bank. Life wasn't bad and was going to get better.

Joel was a feisty little fuck. Sam Curnew and the other union bigwigs couldn't seem to decide what they wanted. Joel had gone up to the Hall last night, to light a fire under somebody's ass. Well, that's thirsty work, and I figured that after the meeting, with a couple of highballs under his belt, Joel might have translated his generalized animosity toward the Company into a particular determination to give his goddamned shift a miss. I coughed. "Have you called the drunk tank?"

"My husband's never been in the drunk tank in his life and you know it perfectly well. And if that kind of suggestion is all the help you're meaning to give, it would be better if you went off to work like you want. Me and the children can get along quite well without you though apparently the damn Company can't."

"Kathleen," I said, "we have to check."

"I will not," she said. "I have never yet called the police to ask if my husband has been arrested in the night and I won't start this morning."

So I phoned.

She called the Murray Clinic and St. James.

She washed the morning dishes. I drank more coffee. It got on toward noon. "Maybe he's left me," she said, quite calmly.

"He wouldn't do that."

A car on the street outside. It went right on by.

"A lot you know," Kathleen said. "A lot you know about women and . . . their men. You still goin' with the whores down the Line?" Before I could open my mouth, she was wagging her finger at me. "I seen you, Jimmy. Don't you deny it. Every damn Saturday night, all dressed up and stinkin' from cologne like you been to the whorehouse already. You ever have a woman you didn't pay for? Anybody who loved you more than five dollars' worth? Oh, Jimmy, I'll bet you're a real prince of a fellow!" Her eyes got a little softer. She looked away from me to whisper, "A lot you know. . . ."

"Sure," I said. "Sure."

She washed our coffee cups. I swiped at the kitchen table with a dishrag. She opened the kitchen curtains. She closed the kitchen curtains again.

The kids, Shirley and Carl, came home for lunch. Two cups of Campbell's tomato soup. Two peanut-butter-and-jelly sandwiches on Eddy's bread. Best behavior. Polite as sticks. They ate quick and got out of there.

The afternoon light came from the west where the

sun lay small and cold, close to the horizon. It slipped through the curtains and lay on the kitchen table like an eviction notice. My sister was twisting her wedding ring. No diamond. The family had been scandalized by Joel's choice of a plain gold wedding band. A diamond chip was traditional—an omen of good times to come— the last pawn for the wife whose husband was killed down the hole.

I picked up the Montana *Standard*. One Joseph McCarthy, an ex-marine, was going to replace LaFollette in the Senate. Crime was on the increase. Pictures of one or two rather meek criminals, guarded by lawmen who could have snapped them in half like twigs. The Montana *Standard* worried that communists were going to take over the world. I thought they'd have to do better than the Japs.

My father phoned. "No," I said, "Joel hasn't shown. You should be sleeping. You ought to try to sleep."

"You're too young to be my mother," he said. "And you've got the wrong equipment. I'll call your Aunt Edith. Maybe she can bring some supper over."

My father's willingness to call in the family was a recent development. As the Mullhollands—he and his sister Edith—had edged toward respectability and sav-ings accounts and real Rogers silverplate, they'd drawn apart, become proud of their independence. That was before Jim Mullholland learned he had the Con. Now, he urged family unity on all sides, hoping that with a little practice, we'd be ready when his time came.

"Have you called the Hall?" he asked. "Some of the boys might know something."

"No," I said. "I haven't wanted to get anyone— oh, you know—why get everybody talking about our affairs?"

"Joel isn't the first son of a bitch in the Mullholland family and he won't be the last." My father hung up.

I came back in the kitchen, hungry, hoping Aunt Edith would hurry with her provisions. I said, "The old man's calling Edith. Maybe she can help out with the kids."

Kathleen lifted her eyes to mine, her green eyes murky. "He's left me."

She was quite ready to face up to the facts. She had steeled herself. If she'd been told that Joel was moved in with the most notorious hooker on the Line, it wouldn't have jolted her. "It's time you understood something," she said.

I didn't want to understand. I had an idea that whatever she wanted to say she was going to regret and I knew I didn't care to hear it.

"You know how men are," she said.

I didn't think I did.

"You know. They get, well, *wearied* of a woman. And what she used to do to please him, it doesn't mean so much anymore and . . . the edge is wore off. You understand?"

"Sure," I said. "Sure, Kathleen. Don't worry, he'll come home. He's just sleeping it off somewhere."

"You really think so, Jimmy? You really think so? As God may strike you dead?"

"Sure, Kathleen," I said, "sure, I think so."

"He would have taken the Milwaukee," she said. "He always wanted to go back to Seattle. He liked it out there. This town was always too cold for Joel. And he liked the Milwaukee Road—the trains. Call them, Jimmy. Oh, call them. Ask and see if a Mr. Joel Kangas, or . . . a Mr. and Mrs. Joel Kangas made reservations last night. Seattle. For Seattle. That's where he'd go."

"Kathleen!"

"Please call them, Jimmy."

I called.

I had no more than hung up before she was back at me again—pacing the small kitchen. Jostling her chair every time she passed. "He had been in Salt Lake City. Do you know how big Salt Lake is, Jimmy? It must have a hundred thousand souls. There'd be work there for a man like him. He's always found work, despite his unionizing. He said the Mormons were worse than the Nazis."

I called the Northern Pacific.

"Spokane," she said. "Spokane. Maybe they've got work in the woods."

"Kathleen," I said, "Joel wasn't on any train leaving here last night, going anywhere. Not using his own name."

"Are you saying he wouldn't use his own name?" she said. "A man like Joel using some 'alias'? You think my husband's a sneak?"

"How about the Greyhound?"

"And he wouldn't be takin' no damn bus either!"

The kitchen tap was dripping. It dripped for half an hour or so. I got up to turn it off. I brushed against her. "Excuse me," I said.

And the light: a nervous, pale sort of light that put up no resistance. I called Sam Curnew at the Hall. Sam was recording secretary of Local #1. One of the old hangers-on answered the phone and it took him a while to find Sam.

"Curnew. What do you want."

"Sam, this is Jimmy Mullholland. Have you seen Joel?"

"Kangas? Not since last night." He held the phone too

close to his mouth and his breathing sounded awful: short and raspy.

"Joel never came home. Never punched in for his shift either. Kathleen is real worried."

"Oh, hell," Sam said. "I suppose you heard he made a big speech last night."

I hadn't, but said I had.

"Yeah," Sam said, "Portal-to-Portal. He was red hot for it."

I didn't think we'd ever get Portal-to-Portal pay and I guess Sam didn't either. Some shifts had to hike for an hour underground before putting in their eight hours. Ten hours total. The Company paid for eight of them.

"He gets the boys all fired up," Sam complained. "One day Joel's gonna land us all in the shit."

I didn't want to argue the point. "Do you know where he went after the meeting?"

"Him and a bunch of hotheads left about ten o'clock. Maybe they were going to tie one on. Knowing Joel, he's probably sleeping it off down the Line somewhere."

"Well, maybe."

"I didn't see your dad last night," Sam said.

"He's coughing."

"Say, I'm sorry to hear that. Old Jim's a good man. How does he like bein' firebug?"

"Sam, he remembers you in his prayers."

"Well then, Jimmy, that's fine. It's good to have a place in the hearts of the religious. I'll ask some of the boys if they seen Joel. I suppose you're still happy workin' topside?"

"Next Wednesday meeting, Sam."

"Be lookin' for you, Jimmy."

Getting on to three o'clock and the kids due home

from school. I was hoping Edith beat them here. They had trouble too and I sure didn't know how to handle it.

"What does a man want?" Kathleen asked me. And her hands folded primly on the table and her head cocked so she wouldn't miss a word.

I shrugged.

"No, Jimmy," she said sadly, "I know no other man who would tell me. What does a man want?"

And the funny thing was, I had an answer to give her—one I gave myself too often. "What I wanted" and "What I was going to do" was a crazy litany that chattered through my mind half a dozen times every day and the words never varied. But I was embarrassed, somehow found out, and the words I believed left my mouth bad: "A man wants to make money. He wants to buy things for his family so they don't lack for anything anymore. A man wants to be someone other men can respect. A man wants to improve himself, learn things, keep trying. A man wants a woman who . . . who will stand by his side." I was blushing, angry at myself, unable to go on. I sounded like a travesty.

"I don't understand," she said. She wrinkled her brow like she was trying to find some small part of what I'd said to give her comfort. "I don't understand." She unfolded one of the cigarette butts in the ashtray and lit it. "I have no more cigarettes," she said.

The front door latch: quiet click, smooth as glass. Both of us stood up. It was the kids and we scared them, I guess, the two of us standing there so expectantly. Shirley began to cry.

Though Shirley was a year younger than her brother, Carl, she was bigger than he was by an inch or two. Normally she was a self-contained kid, happy in her world. Carl was thin, blue-eyed and painfully shy.

Kathleen caught her daughter in a fierce hug. Carl's lower lip was trembling. "It's all right, honey. It's all right." Kathleen's voice was breaking up. "Hush, dry those eyes."

I tried a smile on Carl but he only had eyes for his mother. I sat and folded my hands in my lap. Carl's coat was dripping on the kitchen floor and his nose was red from sniffling.

A brisk knock at the door gave me something to do. I jumped up, eager to let Edith in. Edith was a heavy woman, about fifty, and right now she was breathless from exertion and cold. She'd lugged her basket of food almost two miles from her home in Walkerville.

She didn't have her coat off before she was restoring order. Thank you, Edith. She blew Carl's nose, checked his mittens and got him out the door. "Lovely sledding on the Copper Street hill and two boys there were asking for you. And they've got one of those Flexible Flyer sleds."

When the phone rang, it was Sam Curnew on the other end. I guess Sam had been doing some thinking. His voice was more worried than it should have been. "Kangas home yet?" he demanded.

I told him we hadn't heard from Joel. I waited for him to tell me something.

"Christ!" A long pause before he mumbled, "That's too bad, Jimmy. I'm awful sorry to hear that."

I didn't know what he was so sorry about. Joel wasn't a Party man like Sam and his cronies and Joel had given Sam plenty of trouble over the years.

"I talked to Duggan just now. You know Duggan? Nipper Duggan? Duggan went with Kangas over to Spillum's last night. I guess they were all stirred up.

Jimmy, we got to have solidarity. If we don't keep solidarity the Company'll crucify us."

"Sure, Sam."

"I've said that many a time to Kangas's face. Anyway, there were a couple Company men at the bar—Walker and that fat blondheaded pal of his, Burke. They're high mucky-muck engineers now, but in '34 they were just working stiffs and they scabbed. Kangas was all for picking a fight with them—wizing off, making with the big talk—but Duggan kept everything cool until Walker and Burke left. Hell, Burke hadn't even finished his drink."

"So? What happened?"

"Nothin'. The Nipper asked Kangas if he wanted a ride up the Hill but he had his own car."

"Joel?"

"Kangas said he was gonna have one for the road. So far as the Nipper knows, Kangas was goin' on shift. He never gave no intention of doin' otherwise."

Through the kitchen door I heard Shirley yell, "He doesn't love us. He doesn't love us at all. I don't care. I don't care at all!" Somebody smacked her, either Edith or Kathleen. Probably Kathleen.

"Kangas and me never did see eye to eye, but I'm sorry." Sam paused and then, in a different voice said, "I been thinkin' Jimmy. I'm a little nervous."

"Yeah?"

Sam whispered, "Frank Little." The hair on my neck stood up.

"Oh, God damn you, Sam! Fuck you! You go to hell with your 'Frank Little.'"

"Don't you ever sell 'em short, Jimmy. Don't you ever do that."

I was mad. "Sam, if they got Joel, they'll be comin' for you next."

Sam was surprised. "Jimmy, I don't want a strike."

His words hung between us like a declaration of bad faith.

"You know I never gave them an inch they didn't take from me," Sam said. "You know that. But I won't fight a fight we can't win. I don't care what anybody says. I'll fight those bastards tooth and nail but I won't destroy the union to do it."

"Sure," I said. It was cold in that parlor and I was shuffling my feet to warm myself. "If you hear anything, give us a ring, okay? I'll. . . ."

"They been watchin' us, Jimmy. Me and Joel and a couple of the others. Oh yes, you can bet they've got their eyes peeled."

"Who?"

Sam chuckled—more for his benefit than mine. "Hell, what are we so worried about. It's only four o'clock. If he was hittin' the bottle hard, he's probably just findin' his way home right now. Say, Jimmy, I want you to do something for me. Joel's got some books—pamphlets—you know." I could hear the shrug in Sam's voice. "You know the ones. We wouldn't want them to fall into the wrong hands."

"Books? What the hell, Sam?"

"Don't give me no grief, Jimmy. Get rid of them."

He hung up and left me staring at the phone.

His master's voice.

I knew where the books were because Joel had given them to me.

The first couple years I was down the holes, I read a lot in the evenings. I hated the work and books were a better world than the one I lived in. Edgar Rice Burroughs's Mars stories; James Willard Shultz's tales of the Blackfoot Indians—anything about anyplace other than here.

I took to Joel even before he married Kathleen, and I guess he took to me. If I had to have a brother-in-law, he was as good as any. We did a little drinking together and more talking. He treated me pretty good though I was just old enough to drink legally at all. Joel'd been a Wobbly out on the coast and he loved to tell stories about those days. I loved to listen too, though I rarely admitted as much. We had some fine arguments.

Joel: "Jimmy, you're a little old man and you ain't even dry behind the ears."

Me: "Hell, Joel, it took you forty years to grow up."

He'd pressed the books on me. A whole box of them. He said men had fought for the ideas in those books. I couldn't see why. Most of them were IWW tracts— little red books, none of them longer than fifty pages. *One Big Union; Joe Hill, Story of a Workingman; Centralia: An American Tragedy.* He had a few communist tracts too. These were impenetrable. I read a few of them, hoping to use them as ammunition against Joel in our arguments. But when I read the account of Wesley Everest's death (he was castrated, shot, and lynched by vigilantes) I'd had enough. I told Joel, "Why should I spend time reading something unpleasant? If I want something unpleasant, I can just look out the window."

Well, Joel was pretty disgusted with me and our friendship degenerated into a mutual tolerance. He never asked for the books back and I never read them again. I went back to Edgar Rice Burroughs but the fantasies that had enchanted me had lost their appeal. When I finally started night school at the Montana

School of Mines, I was glad to confine my reading to the textbooks. At least they'd do me some good.

Shirley was settled down at the kitchen table, smearing a giraffe in her coloring book. Kathleen was clicking her rosary. There was a neat stack of sandwiches—looked like ham, roast beef, and bologna—and a couple of cold pasties.

I picked up a pasty, got ketchup and a bottle of Great Falls Select out of the icebox.

"I'll be pleased to take the children tonight," Edith said. "We'll have a lovely time, won't we? I've got a doll I used to play with when I was a little girl and, Shirley, I'll let you play with it; but you'll have to be very, very careful because it's such an old doll and she's very fragile."

Shirley sensed condescension and turned a bored face on Edith.

The pasty was too dry.

Carl came in. His snowsuit was wet, his face flushed, and it took him a moment to remember the solemnity of the occasion and when he did, his lower lip dropped and he began to cry.

Edith hugged him. "Oh, you poor child. Goodness, you're wet all over. Here. We'll help you out of that wet old thing."

Carl suffered himself to be comforted. Edith handed him a piece of fudge.

"Hail Mary, full of grace, the Lord is with thee. Blessed art thou amongst women and blessed is the fruit of thy womb Jesus," Kathleen said.

Edith said, "Why don't you go lie down, Kathleen?" She made a bundle of the wet snowsuit and gave it to me. I put it on a chair. "When Joel comes home, I'll wake you."

"I'm not tired, Aunt." Kathleen spoke through ghost lips. "Holy Mary, Mother of God. . . ."

"Then why don't I take the children home with me? I'll fix them a nice hot dinner and we can listen to the radio until it's their bedtime."

"I want them here with me," Kathleen said. "I won't hide them away from this."

"Oh, Kathleen. There'll be plenty of time for that when they're older."

"I want them with me." Kathleen set her lips.

Aunt Edith unpinned her hat and sighed. It was a decorous sigh.

"You'll stay, then," I said.

"Until I can talk some sense into Kathleen."

"Good. I want to go look for Joel. If I don't track him down, I'll ask the sheriff to help."

"You will not," Kathleen said. "Not the police."

"Kathleen," I snapped, "it's time we stop *pretending*."

She shook her head; impatient with my thickheadedness.

"No. Joel would not thank me for sending the police after him."

"Good-bye," I said.

And I blew out of there, conscienceless. A wild joy in my heart and the crunch of my galoshes on the snowy sidewalks and the air nipping my ears, and I was twenty-four—in my prime—and I swung my arms a bit and kept my face stern because of my mission; because I was out of that house and the dead light of the short winter dusk lay about my feet, harmless, and I flew above it like a swallow through purgatory.

Spillum's was a sportsman's joint. In the front room you could buy a hunting license or a duck stamp. A rack of new and used rifles behind the counter and a dozen handguns under the counter's glass top. You could cash a paycheck anytime, day or night.

The rest of the place was discreetly curtained off, but the discretion dated from speakeasy days and there was no reason for it now. You just brushed the curtain aside and strolled into the bar.

On the back wall, a floor-to-ceiling green tote board, with the basketball games, the races, the high-school football, the weights of the heaviest cutthroat trout, the biggest elk rack, according to season.

The room was crowded with small metal tables. If you wanted some grub, there was a lunch counter against one wall. If you needed something to cut the dust, the bar was ready to oblige.

In the back room, the same tinhorns played stud or jacks-or-better all afternoon and most of the night. They spoke code.

I sat down and ordered a draft.

My father emerged from the poker room and stood beside me.

"You sittin' in?" I asked.

"Nope." He ordered himself a whiskey and ditch. He coughed after he downed his shot and that embarrassed him and he wiped his mouth on his sleeve.

My father had been a cowboy near Red Lodge before he went into the mines and he still had a horseman's build: no ass, wide shoulders (the shoulderbones were prominent by now), and the slight bow in the legs. He used to say: "The only thing dumber than a dumb miner is a smart cowboy."

"You hear anything?" I asked.

"Nobody's seen him. You?"

I shook my head.

"Kathleen?" he asked.

"Edith came over. Kathleen's not doin' too good, but Edith's a help."

He took a careful sip of water. He eyed the cigar boxes behind the counter with regret.

The bartender came over and stood before us, big smile on display. I didn't know the guy.

The bartender said, "Jim. Jesus. Jim Mullholland. How long's it been? I didn't hardly recognize you. Jesus, Jim, you don't look so hot. Let me set you up."

"Who the hell are you?" my father asked.

The bartender paused with his jigger in the air. Hurt. "You don't remember me? Papsi Maroni. The Tramway. Remember? Jeez, must be seven, eight years."

"Oh yeah. Sure. The Tramway."

"I was a powderman."

"Yeah, yeah. I remember you now. You still got all your parts?"

"Damn rights. And I got out of the hole while I still had 'em too."

"That's fine. Were you behind the bar last night?"

"Yeah, sure. Until midnight. I don't like the late hours like I used to."

"Joel Kangas—my son-in-law—was he in here?"

"He was. Whatsa matter? Old lady checkin' up on him? He's on the graveyard, you know. He comes in regular, before he goes on shift."

"He never made it to his shift last night. Nobody's seen him."

"Well, he just probably decided to skip a shift and raise some hell. You know what they say about a bad penny." He laughed. Big joke.

My father spoke to me. "I never met a bartender who didn't have a sloppy mouth."

"Jeez," Papsi said. "Jim, that's no way to be."

My father gave him the eye.

"Well," Papsi said, "Mister Walker and Mister Burke was in here last night. They was takin' bets on the Vargas-Ketchel fight. They had a few drinks, sure. You know how they are—they'll give you hell one minute and buy you a drink the next. Joel comes in with Nipper Duggan."

"And got into an argument with Walker and Burke about the strike," I said.

"Yeah?" Papsi was unimpressed. "Who told you that?"

"Duggan."

"Yeah. Well you know how the Nipper is. He'll tell you anything he thinks you want to hear." Papsi gave my father the eye. "Just like some bartenders I know."

My father's ears got a little red, but he didn't say anything.

Papsi said, "Oh, it started with the strike, I guess. They were talkin' about the strike. Joel had heard that Walker and Burke was up to the Granite Mountain garage. And they'd got the tarps off the Company's armored cars and took them down off the blocks and got 'em ready to roll. Joel was talkin' to Walker. He said, 'You know the Company ain't bargainin' in good faith. You know we're goin' out. And Walker, you know you was a scab in '34 and you're gonna be a damn scab in '46 again.' "

(Good goin', Joel. Walker's a decent enough guy, but any time he feels like it, he can pull your rustling card, and you won't work for the Company no more, and where else are you gonna work, you with a wife and two kids?)

"So?" I asked. "What'd Walker do?"

"I dunno. A couple stiffs were wantin' drinks at the other end of the bar and I didn't hear what went on next. When I came back, Joel was still mad, but it wasn't about the strike."

"Ketchel," my father said.

I didn't understand. I guess Joel was different to my father than he was to me and they talked about different things. I don't know why that's funny to think of, but it is.

"Yeah," Papsi said. "You guessed it."

My father said, "Give me another drink. Have one with me."

Papsi brought the bottle and poured. He banged his glass down and collected. "Burke asked Joel if he was backin' Ketchel in the fight. Ketchel bein' Joel's working partner and all. Well, that set Joel off. If the Nipper hadn't been hangin' onto his arm, I think Joel would have smacked Burke, he was that pissed. He said, 'First you drive some poor son of a bitch crazy, then you take bets whether him or some other crazy son of a bitch is gonna beat each other to death?' "

"Joel always did have the gift of gab," my father remarked.

"What's this all about?" I asked my father. Papsi Maroni brought me another beer and another shot for my father though he hadn't finished his. Papsi got himself a drink and was all ears.

"Hell," I said, "what you hangin' around here for? You already know everything there is to know about Kooteney Ketchel. How much you got bet?"

And Papsi smiled at me, false, and said, "Hell, everybody in this damn town knows everything about Ketchel. And what they don't know, that cocksucker, James Sly—he'll tell them."

"Beat it," my father said.

Papsi did. He didn't want to, but he did.

"Last Sunday morning, Joel came by. You wasn't home. You was still off whorin' somewhere."

"My business," I said.

"Yeah. You coulda been home. It wouldn't of hurt you." When my father sipped his drink, he coughed again. "He came by and talked about goin' back down the hole. He said he didn't want no more surface work. He said he wanted to go down where the real working-men are."

"Oh, bullshit."

"Yeah. He was worried about his drinkin' too. And Ketchel. Hell, the two of them on that shift—Joel spent more time with Ketchel than Kathleen. It was okay so long as they got along good. But ever since Ketchel's been fightin', he's been gettin' crazier and crazier. The Indian would just sit there, I guess, and mumble crap at Joel. Politics. You know Ketchel never gave a shit about politics before. Joel thought something was gettin' to Ketchel but he couldn't figure what. So Friday night, Ketchel asked him something. Ketchel ain't no big talker, you know that."

"Yeah," I said. I didn't want the rest of my beer and pushed it away.

"Ketchel asked Joel if he could name the countries the Reds took over."

"Uh-huh."

"Ketchel said they were Poland, Latvia, Lithuania, Estonia, East Germany, Yugoslavia, Albania, and Ketchel said there was one more but he never could remember it right."

2

KOOTENEY KETCHEL wasn't the toughest man in town, but he had his backers. He was one of those short, fat men who aren't fat. He'd go 250–260, I suppose—most of the weight in his iron paunch, his drooping buttocks, his huge forearms and shoulders. Kooteney's sleek black hair was always brushed straight back—like he was wearing a hairpiece or as though a small black beaver was lying on top of his skull. He had Indian features— one type of Indian features anyway—plump cheeks, broad splayed nose. His mouth was straight and not particularly thin but not particularly thick either. He'd got his eyes from his father: Stanley Ketchel; and they were very light gray—almost colorless. His eyes were cold and startling and once you noticed the girth of him, you'd notice his eyes next.

He was by way of being an historical figure. His

father, Stanley, was called "The Michigan Assassin,"
and Stanley had been Butte's darling boy. When Stanley
Ketchel was just another teenage punk, he left Michigan
and rode the rods west in search of something. Whatever it was he was searching for has not been determined and asking Ketchel-the-punk wouldn't have
brought enlightenment; though maybe later, when he
was lying on that tawdry cot with a bullet in his head,
he might have ventured an answer. (When his manager
heard Ketchel was shot, he sent a telegram. It said:
"Ring a bell. He'll get up.")

Stanley Ketchel was a terrific middleweight, fast and
mean. Sometimes he fought as a heavyweight. He fought
middleweights and heavyweights alike and won most of
his bouts because of his genes and ferocity. He even
fought Jack Johnson once, when Johnson was in his
prime. Ketchel knocked Johnson down too; flat. It was
a fix. Johnson couldn't get any fights with white heavyweights and when Ketchel came along and said, "Me,
me," Johnson thought that, hell, half a heavyweight is
better than none, and they agreed to just get out there
and sort of paw at each other in a gentlemanly fashion
until Johnson outboxed Ketchel to take the decision.

But.

When Stanley Ketchel was sixteen years old, he was
the Saturday-night bouncer at the 1,2,3 and the 1,2,3
was where the boys drank who were too tough to get
fights at the Bucket of Blood. In those days, most of the
miners were single. They slept in rooming houses. They
didn't have rooms in rooming houses, they had beds.
There's a difference. You rented a bed for one shift. And
you had one third of a metal locker where you could
keep your clothes. If you overslept, some other miner
woke you up and told you to get the hell out of his bed

because he'd just came offshift at the goddamned
Neversweat and he was tired.

These men enjoyed a good brawl. The sight of a six-
teen-foot, beveled-glass bar mirror toppling slowly forward onto a mob of drunken battlers would move the
more poetic of them to verse. Some of them were pretty
good versifiers too. Here's a verse which has nothing to
do with Stanley Ketchel or fighting but amused me
once:

> *My sweetheart's a mule in the mine.*
> *I drive her with only one line.*
> *All day I just sit*
> *On the dashboard and spit*
> *All over my sweetheart's behind.*

Neil Murphy, the owner of the 1,2,3, had certain as-
pirations he'd stuck to through thick and thin, mostly
thin. Neil's father had been a pub owner in Galway and
his father before him, and to the young Neil Murphy, a
pub was a "warm hidey-hole." Neil set up in Butte. In
time the 1,2,3 lost the special characteristics that make
up a pub and was well on its way to being "just another
joint." Neil'd closed his saloon bar. He'd removed the
dart boards. He'd bricked up the open fireplace and removed the pokers and andirons to a place of safety. His
handpainted drinking mugs—labeled with the regulars'
monikers— Big Jim, Mel, Tom—had been packed away
in excelsior after Mel cracked Tom's skull with Big
Jim's beer mug.

Neil Murphy still had his backbar mirror and a grand
one it was too. Sixty feet long. Six ten-foot sections—
the finest beveled glass, the best silvering. He'd had it
made up in Ogden, Utah, and shipped north.

That mirror was the reason Neil Murphy took on the

teenage punk, Stanley Ketchel, and was the beginning of Stanley's later fame. It was Stanley's job to save the mirror.

Stanley Ketchel's Rules for the 1,2,3

1. When insults are exchanged, put the men out.
2. If a blow is started, intercept it. Put the men out.
3. If a blow lands, put the men out. Be quick about it.
4. If blows become general among the men's friends, put the men out. (In this circumstance, Stanley could count on some help. Murphy and his two bartenders would link arms and press the throng toward the door while Stanley broke up the tougher nuts with his sap.)
5. If a donnybrook starts, get behind the bar and catch ANYTHING that comes at you through the air.

Stanley Ketchel interposed his body between chaos and the remnants of Neil Murphy's dream. And he was damn good. For the year he worked at the 1,2,3, Neil didn't need to order a single replacement panel from Ogden, Utah. Neil bragged him up. "He's a real hooligan, all right," Neil said. "But he's done right by me."

A fight promoter heard about the tough sixteen-year-old and took Stanley on to better things and the mirror got shattered regularly again and Neil Murphy backslid from the Catholic faith.

Stanley became a hero here. He'd fight in Seattle or Boise or Fargo or Hardin and he'd stop by in Butte to have a drink or two with the boys and swap mock punches with the young toughs, cool as a cucumber in his gray suit, his panama, and his gold-mounted elk-tooth watchfob.

When Ketchel got in the ring with Jack Johnson, he was full of piss and vinegar. He'd put on weight to meet the heavyweight mark and he was feeling fine. Sometime in the middle of the twelfth round, he made his play. He hit Johnson with everything he had. Lefts, hooks, jabs, and all his other blows. There's a lovely photograph of that moment. Johnson is lying on his side, braced on one arm, staring at Ketchel. It was taken while Johnson's mind was still on the mat, before the word *"Doublecross"* occurred to it. A moment later, his mind cleared, he got to his feet, and assaulted Stanley Ketchel with a deadly weapon: himself.

So—Stanley Ketchel was not heavyweight champ of the world but he was still middleweight champ, and he'd shown he was something special by knocking Jack Johnson on his can.

Jack Johnson was still the heavyweight champ but that didn't do him much good because no white fighter would take him on. The fighters claimed, publicly, that pugilism was a white man's game and white men should fight white men. Privately, they were scared to death.

But this is all familiar stuff. What isn't familiar is Stanley Ketchel's heart's desire. He always wished he was a train robber instead of a fighter.

Despite his heritage and his size, Kooteney Ketchel didn't become one of the Toughest until fairly late in life — middle thirties? — and he became a contender almost by accident.

The current Toughest Man in Town was a timberman named Vargas. Vargas looked like a fat melted candle and had arms like a seal; marvelous, sleek affairs. He probably weighed about three hundred. Vargas was no boxer. His tactic was belly-to-belly. He'd get right up on his opponent and while all the opponent's blows were disappearing in Vargas's rolls of fat, Vargas would be hitting, hitting, hitting.

Being the Toughest had its good points. Usually you landed a surface job. The drinks were on the house.

When I first met Kooteney Ketchel—'44, '45?—during the last years of the War, anyway—Ketchel was an excessively shy man. He had a private room at the Big Ship and didn't fight. Not even socially.

He dressed soberly in khaki work pants, neatly blacked work boots, and a shortsleeve shirt. The shirt was usually a Hawaiian pattern and was the only splash of color about him. He'd go into a bar—the Yellowstone, say, on a Saturday night—sit down, have three bottles of Butte Special Beer, and go home.

Well, naturally, big as he was, he got more than a few invitations to step oustide. He declined these offers. That made the host testy since nobody likes to invite somebody to a party and have them decline. Kooteney had worked out a couple remedies for these occasions.

The bar's crowded; two or three A.M., the jukebox is playing the "Butte Polka," two drunks are stumbling around the dance floor, each trying to lead. A guy—say, a Norwegian named Larsen—has been making the usual remarks, *fortissimo*, talking about Indians; the only good Indian is a dead Indian, that sort of thing. Ketchel orders his last beer. Larsen moves down the bar, stands behind him, and continues to mine the same vein. The bar gets quiet but not Larsen's voice: "And I don't care two bits about any son of a bitch who won't stand up and fight."

Kooteney signals the bartender. The bartender brings him a beer opener: one of those pointed iron ones, about a quarter inch thick. Kooteney sips his beer. He grunts. He takes up the opener, sets it between two fingers, doubles it over into a U, and straightens it out again. He drops it on the bar, clank. Larsen returns to his chair.

If Larsen doesn't return to his chair, Kooteney fumbles a nickel out of his pocket and ooops, drops it on the floor. Kooteney gets off his stool and bends over to find it.

The bar stools are steel and weigh, what?—eighty, a hundred pounds? Kooteney takes the leg of the bar stool between thumb and forefinger and lifts the stool over his head, the six feet of awkward heavy metal. He wouldn't pick up his nickel. Kooteney was not without dignity. He'd sit down. Nine times out of ten, Larsen would sit down too. Kooteney never said a word while he did his tricks.

Rarely, Larsen was too drunk or crazy to be impressed. If Larsen kept it up, kept pushing, Kooteney, still silent, would finish his beer and go home. Larsen would follow him for a block or two until he got too far from the bar where he'd left his coat.

One day, however, Kooteney Ketchel changed and, for the second time in his life, entered history.

It was a Saturday night in October, already cold, already snow on the ground. Kooteney showed up at the Yellowstone in a blue suit. White shirt. Tie. He should have known better.

Kooteney sat drinking until ten or eleven o'clock— probably eight beers before the inevitable: a fellow name of Lahti. Lahti commenced the Big Talk. Stage One: He moved behind the fat Indian in the new blue suit. Stage Two: He increased the volume and particularity of his remarks. He reached around Kooteney Ketchel and flipped his tie.

And Kooteney Ketchel got off his stool and did something dreadful to Lahti.

Commotion. Quite a bit of noise. Real tears came to Lahti's eyes. I guess Kooteney felt regrets because he handed Lahti's ear back to him. I don't know what Lahti did with it.

Still, one fight does not a contender make. And besides, half the damn town knew Kooteney Ketchel and they—well, they just couldn't take him *seriously*.

Blondetta ran the fanciest whorehouse in Butte. The house was called Irish World. Blondetta's name was not really Blondetta. She had *become* Blondetta when Irish World got to be the number one house in town. The chief madam here is always called Blondetta.

Anyway, this particular Blondetta was a woman of some imagination and a finely tuned business sense. She'd installed crystal chandeliers and flocked wallpaper and real brass beds, and during Prohibition she never served a drink that hadn't come in from Canada. A class joint.

But other houses up and down the Line had chandeliers too, and anybody could buy flocked wallpaper and plush velvet settees.

Blondetta had made the western hooker circuit— Reno to the south, Fargo to the east, Seattle to the west and Calgary to the north—and she knew what a hard-rock miner wanted.

"Forget the whips and boots," she said. "Forget all that crap. A good, simple, healthy fuck," she said. "But *INTERESTING.*"

"Interesting"—well, the answer had to be the girls, but that wasn't as simple as it sounds—you could go wrong. One of Blondetta's competitors, Jew Kate, had the brilliant idea of importing young colleens from the

Auld Sod, thinking the miners would like nothing better than a little piece of the familiar.

The colleens arrived, via New York and Chicago. And though the crop had been skimmed some, the remaining busty eager lassies were enough to make any madam proud. Turned out, the miners were a little uneasy about the new girls from the start because communications being what they were between Montana and Ireland—they never knew whose relative they were screwing. No man likes to be uneasy in bed. Somebody accidentally left a pile of burning trash by Jew Kate's back wall. They left it there three times before her house went up.

French Irma, on the other hand, failed from over-estimating her clientele. She and two thin-faced girls introduced the fine art of fellatio to her brothel. It soon became the rage. One day, a mucker by the name of Hendricks, excited to the point of no return, yelled "Go to it, girl!" and whacked the girl on the back of the head with predictable results. French Irma hopped a train to Wallace, where, barring accidents, she hoped to do better. She left none too soon.

Blondetta's mind functioned pretty much like yours and mine. She was, by turns, romantic, shrewd, very lazy, and very quick. She'd decided to make Irish World the most famous whorehouse in the whole damn state of Montana and she never looked back.

Her first cautious step was cornering the market in Latin girls. Mexican girls (Spanish señoritas!) she had shipped up from Chihuahua. French!! girls from Montreal. A good clean healthy fuck but *INTERESTING*. And that policy was her success. She insured it by bringing in five young Boston whores. The miners thought their accent meant previous wealth and high station. So they schtupped the hell out of them. With the Latin girls they were gentle and romantic but the Boston aristocrats had cystitis so often, Blondetta arranged a quantity rate at the Murray Clinic.

No nigger girls. No chinks.

Blondetta was a great reader of ladies' magazines. She was *très* sophisticated. She could sense a trend. One afternoon, while thumbing through the pages of *Woman's Home Companion*, she noticed a society belle wearing heavy silver and turquoise Indian jewelry. Something struck a chord. She stared at the picture. She went around the house gathering up magazines. She noted a number of pictures of Indian girls—usually tragic, prepubescent waifs just barely old enough to do it.

Little Morningstar.

Blondetta knew she was onto something.

She and her bouncer, Jim Sly, took the Great Northern up to Kalispell the next day. They booked into the hotel.

In 1839, the Kootenai Indians sent a delegation thousands of miles back east to speak to the Great White Chief. They were received with some astonishment. They said, "We have heard of the God of the Whites and would like to hear more about him."

The Great White Chief said, "Sure. If you want to." And one Father De Smet was sent to found missions he called St. Mary's and St. Ignatius.

That was a lucky break. While Indian tribes all around them were being killed and pillaged, the Kootenai, protected by the Jesuits, were left almost untouched. Also, their land wasn't worth stealing.

Kalispell had plenty of Kootenai whores but none of them were Little Morningstar, so Blondetta and Jim Sly rented a carriage and drove the dusty roads out to Ronan. They talked to the people in the bars. The bar owners were bitter because they had to sell the Indians liquor illegally, and they didn't like feeling like crooks. That's an American trait.

Blondetta soon learned of a poor family with a beautiful daughter. The information was accurate. She was beautiful. A small girl, scarcely five feet, good body, graceful, a fine-boned face, and those black Indian braids pulled back from her forehead.

Blondetta thought: "That's her."

The girl's father was dead and her mother was in the Galen Sanatorium as a typhoid carrier. Her grandfather didn't understand what was going on. They told him they were from Woolworth's and wanted to hire the girl. They gave him two bottles of Old Overholt. He thought that was all right. He told her, in Kootenai, to go with them and so she did, willingly enough. All the way back to Kalispell, Jim Sly fingered the revolver in his pocket. It was a Smith and Wesson .44 Russian. He was afraid of Indians.

Blondetta never learned the Indian girl's given name since she didn't need to. Little Morningstar.

But when Blondetta got the girl back to Irish World, installed in her best room at the top of the stairs and outfitted in the softest Indian costumes the Jewish tailors could turn out on such short notice—that's when she discovered she had a problem.

Virginity. Not eidetic virginity. Blondetta didn't give a damn who the girl had or hadn't screwed while on the reservation. Specific virginity; that was the problem. Morningstar did not want to fuck the men who came up the stairs to her room. None.

Jim Sly hobbled back down the stairs with a bruised thigh and mysterious inner complaints.

An unsuspecting miner Blondetta sent to the girl

swore that "As soon as I had me pants down around me knees she came at me like a wildcat, scratchin' and endangerin' me personals."

Blondetta was not without resources: starvation, beatings, a stint in the basement for a couple weeks in the coldest month of winter. "This girl is more virgin than the Virgin Mary," Blondetta said.

Blondetta gave up. She put the girl in the kitchen where she cooked a terrible fried egg and wouldn't speak English.

When Stanley Ketchel came home that spring, he was given a hell of a welcome. He'd fought Kid LeRoy in Twin Falls and put him away in four rounds easy as pie. Local boy made good—the town couldn't do enough for him. West-side homes—the big places with the ballrooms—opened their doors to him (though not to his entourage). Plenty of champagne. Businessmen talked about Montana the land of opportunity. Stanley was polite. He seemed to listen. He drank champagne. He got a little drunk. He went down to the 1,2,3. Neil Murphy greeted him with a roar. "Drinks on the house. Nobody's buyin' tonight but me." Stanley Ketchel sat on the stool which had been his nightly perch a few short years ago. The wooden stool felt familiar to him. He did not undo his tie but felt like he had. About one o'clock someone said, "Let's go down the Line!" About twenty of them ended up carrying Stanley Ketchel down Mercury Street to Irish World. He looked solemn, riding above the crowd of drunken men like a conning tower on a submarine.

Stanley Ketchel, sipping champagne in the parlor at Irish World. It was fancy, but nothing like Polly's in San Francisco. And he'd already had French girls (from

France) and Spanish girls (from Spain). He smiled distantly. He'd had better champagne.

Upstairs the joint was jumping. The girls tripped back downstairs, rearranging their hair and smiles. Behind them the miners came, more slowly, grinning a little, rolling a bit. One pats his girl's behind. Good Sport.

Blondetta was flushed with excitement and the busiest night she'd had in a month. She sidled over to Stanley Ketchel and admired the figure he cut. She poured his champagne with her own hands. She tried to form an alliance of THOSE WHO'VE BEEN ELSEWHERE AND ARE ABOVE THESE PROCEEDINGS. But Stanley Ketchel had been more elsewhere than she had and smiled distantly. He rubbed his knuckles.

She had a thought. "Say, Stanley," she said, "I got a little problem you could help me with." Politely, he inclined his ear.

Blondetta sent a girl to the attic to get Morningstar's costume. "It's in the leather steamer trunk."

She sent for Morningstar. The men and girls stopped parading up and down the stairs. It got very stuffy. Irish World's parlor was not large and the big crystal chandelier made it seem smaller. If you'd been there, you would have wanted to go outside for a breath of air. Morningstar wanted to, but James Sly had a good hold on her.

The costume was a skimpy buckskin vest, a beaded buckskin shirt, beaded moccasins. The moccasins had little bended teepees on each toe.

"Put it on."

Morningstar looked at the miners. She shrugged. She paid no attention to Stanley Ketchel, who was leaning indolently against the wall.

She unfastened her gingham shift and let it fall to the floor. She unhooked the heavy brogans she was wearing. She put the moccasins on.

There was a stillness in honor of her body. Her breasts, jet black hair, her eyes like glacier lakes high in the Rockies where it's too cold for fish to live.

While she dressed, they kept quiet. The rustle of soft buckskin over her soft skin.

"Mister Ketchel."

And Stanley Ketchel smiled and Blondetta felt herself welcomed into the circle of the blessed.

He smiled his small smile and put his champagne glass down on the table. His elk-tooth watchfob gleamed and gleamed like bone.

Morningstar preceded Stanley Ketchel up the stairs of Irish World like there was nothing behind her.

They waited in the parlor until dawn, all of them. Nobody drank much—even the boozehounds went light. The girls talked about style. The miners talked about mining.

When Stanley Ketchel came down the stairs, the morning light was working at the lace curtains over the windows. His gray suit was soft and elegant. His stickpin was straight and the diamond glittered. He'd taken the time to wash his face and comb his hair.

"Well, ma'am," he said softly, "what do I owe you?"

And Blondetta, for the first time in her life, found herself saying, "On the house, Mister Ketchel." Meaning: "That was for love."

And Stanley Ketchel left Butte and was shot to death a year later.

The next night, Irish World was crowded with men who wanted to try the Indian princess. Some offered twenty dollars. Blondetta was in a rage. She snapped at them. "What kind of animals are you? You think that girl's a two-bit chippy? You think that after who she's been with, she'd have anything to do with the likes of you?" She counseled patience. She said in a couple weeks, Morningstar would be available again.

Which was optimistic. Morningstar had a sprained arm, four cracked ribs, a concussion, and her cunt was bleeding so bad the doctor at St. James thought she'd die. Blondetta slipped him fifty to keep his mouth shut and got the girl on the Helena train with Jim Sly.

It was a month and a week before Stanley Ketchel's woman came back and Blondetta chafing every minute of her absence. Blondetta didn't have a high opinion of men's memories and if Ketchel was to lose his title, Morningstar's price would plummet.

When she returned, she was still beautiful, and docile too. If anything, too docile. One man said, "I don't understand what's so special about her. Or what Ketchel saw in her. Hell, she's a looker, all right, but she don't do nothin'. When you ram it to her, she just lies there. She don't even grunt."

Most men, however, were not so choosy and Morningstar was a premium item.

When the baby came, there was no doubt whose it was. If the timing hadn't been perfect—and it was—those eyes were a dead giveaway. Cold gray like Stanley Ketchel's own.

All the girls were excited about the baby. Jim Sly chucked its chin. Blondetta patted it like she would a dog. The girls looked at the baby and felt very sad like their lives had been wasted. One cried.

Morningstar was indifferent to her child. She did not, one girl explained, understand the great mystery of life. She changed the baby's diapers when it squalled loud enough and gave it the tit when the pacifier failed to work anymore.

"That girl has a savage heart," Blondetta said.

And so, the other girls took over the boy's rearing—except for the occasions when Blondetta would trot him out.

When Stanley Ketchel was shot, Blondetta had an impromptu wake with the baby in his crib against the wall where you'd expect the coffin to be. That night, she asked twenty dollars for Morningstar and had six takers.

Blondetta spared no effort to keep Stanley Ketchel's memory alive. Since Stanley died undefeated, he was easier to enshrine than if he'd taken an unlucky punch before he took the bullet.

The boy's birthdays became important festivals at Irish World—birthday and mass said for the dead. Blondetta'd dress the boy in a miniature Indian chief's outfit and bring him into the parlor. "This here's Stanley Ketchel's only son. Stanley was the bravest man to ever fight in the ring, and the only woman he ever loved is right here in this house. She was an Indian maid. This here is Stanley's boy. He's a real little Indian chief."

Kooteney Ketchel.

During these celebrations, his mother stayed upstairs: $10. Blondetta philosophized, "Nothing opens a man's wallet like sentiment. Unless it's a chance to take something a better man had."

Morningstar's career on the Line was, by the nature of things, bound to be brief. As years went by, the light-bulbs in her room lost wattage. She got plump. Morningstar had become comfortable.

The boy's annual birthday parties brought less and less disposable income to Irish World until, on his tenth, nobody wanted to go upstairs and ravish his ma.

"Shit," one said. "She's just an old Indian whore."

The boy was playing with a new capgun and toy tomahawk. He said, "Woo, woo, woo."

What Blondetta said was not recorded. She did, however, repossess the boy's birthday presents, move Morningstar into the dormitory at the back of the house, and cancel all future celebrations. She had her reasons. One of her old competitors—a cribmate from Silver City, Nevada—was doing business with two fourteen-year-old South Texas girls and the miners were already calling one of them "Blondey." Ominous, indeed.

The boy went to work in the kitchen as a potwalloper. His mother enjoyed the warmth of the whorehouse dormitory four more years. She became a favorite of the railroad men who, on their travels, had learned to appreciate comfortable Indian whores.

One morning, Morningstar vanished.

A couple days later, Blondetta noticed she was gone.

Once more, Kooteney Ketchel was allowed into the parlor. "This here boy is the only natural son of Stanley Ketchel, the middleweight champ," Blondetta said. "And he ain't got nobody in the world except me. I knew his dad. He was standin' right where you're standin' this minute. He went upstairs and fathered this boy. Nobody can say nothin' against Stanley Ketchel under this roof. Let us have a moment of silence in his memory, slain as he was, by a coward's bullet, while still in his strength of manhood and undefeated." And then, quite a few miners went upstairs. "Mourning," Blondetta observed, "will get it up when the best set of knockers on the Line can't produce more'n a fizzle."

But the recycling job she tried on the boy wore out fast and before many weeks, he was back at the potsink again. He decided to run away, and, except for honest human loyalty, he probably would have succeeded. One morning, before dawn, he crept out of Irish World's back door with a bundle he'd wrapped in a large western handkerchief. There's no evidence that his choice of the traditional bindle-stiff's luggage was influenced by Blondetta's magazines. It was the zeitgeist tampering again in human affairs that made him select precisely the luggage so favored by real hobos and every other boy running away that year.

It was late spring, 1928. He crept around the freight-cars until he found a train heading east. He thought east was as good as west. In that he was wrong, since the eastern route of the Northern Pacific Railroad consisted mainly of a tremendous number of miles. On this, his first escape, he didn't get to enjoy very many of them.

He sat in the open door of the boxcar, swinging his feet. The train shook and shook. It puffed up over the Continental Divide. When it crossed trestles or entered tunnels, the boy pulled his feet back inside. The air was cold but he didn't mind. It smelled good to him. At Three Forks, the sun was up good and it was very green. There weren't many trees where he'd come from because the smelter fumes had killed all the trees they hadn't used as fuel. Kooteney Ketchel smiled. He sniffed the air. He thought copper was an evil metal the world would be better off without. In this he was wrong too.

He was beside the freightcar taking a piss in the weeds when the brakeman spotted him. The brakeman had hoped he was a hobo he could get money from or, failing that, work over with the nightstick he was tapping against his leg. The brakeman was, in short, ready for action. He was feeling his oats because the spring sun warmed his old bones no less than it warmed the

boy's young ones. He said, "I seen you somewhere before." Tableau. The brakeman tried to remember. He
succeeded. He said, "I know. I screwed your ma." This
latter bit of intelligence set the boy running. He ran
through the alders and through the shallows of the little
tributary that is the official geographic headwaters of
the Missouri River. He slipped on a stone, lost his foot-
ing and fell into the creek full face. He got up again but
his ankle gave way. The brakeman caught up to him and
said, "Come out of there, you little fucker, before you
get my dander up." The boy figured he was caught
square and obeyed. The brakeman hit him a few licks.
The brakeman was mad enough to hit him many licks,
but he was winded. He hit him on the back and thighs
and buttocks. He was very skilled and left no marks. He
handed the boy over to the brakeman on the westbound.
This gent put the boy in the caboose and fed him coffee.
The westbound brakeman told him many stories about
railroading: how railroad men were braver than holdup
men or Wobblies; how they weren't paid very much
though they were always dependable; and how, in each
city they passed through, any railroad man worth his
salt had a beautiful woman waiting for him with her
legs open and wet in the cunt. The boy thought it was
possible railroad men were brave and underpaid but the
women who were waiting would want two dollars and
maybe even five. He expressed this thought. The brakeman didn't give him any more coffee or talk and thus,
through a slight misunderstanding, the boy was never
told the Secret of the Railroads.

The brakeman walked him up from the freightyard to
Irish World because he thought Blondetta would be
grateful and let him knock off a Free Piece. She was not

grateful. She said, "It's true this boy is the only natural son of Stanley Ketchel, but he's been nothing but heartbreak to me."

The brakeman said, "Who the fuck is Stanley Ketchel?" and his chances of a Free Piece died as dead as Stanley.

Blondetta whacked the boy and stuck him in the cellar. Her feelings were mixed. She didn't want the boy, but she didn't want anyone else to have him either. The prospect of Blondey taking the boy and billing him as the "Son of the Michigan Assassin" was too much to bear. For three days, whenever she thought of it, she went down to the cellar and cuffed the boy around. Her strength was not as the strength of ten but her heart was pure.

The next time Kooteney ran away, he didn't get out of the boxcar at Three Forks. He was no dummy. He pissed in the corner of the boxcar instead. In this manner, he rode all the way to Billings. The train pulled into the Billings yards after dark and he got off and sought the company of others like himself. Instead, he found a hobo camp. Someone took pity on him, gave up his own tin can and filled it with a dipper of mulligan stew.

About midnight, the sheriff's deputies and the railroad bulls raided the hobo camp looking for Reds. They found a great many of them there and worked them over with their nightsticks and taught them a lesson they wouldn't soon forget. Many of the Reds escaped in the tall grass and waited, hiding out in cells of two or three, for the morning train to Duluth. The boy did not escape. He learned that to be a Red, one had to be fleet of foot.

One of the railroad bulls recognized him and felt

sorry for him. He knew the boy wasn't a Red because he was the son of Stanley Ketchel, who this particular railroad bull had long admired. Once more, the boy was put back in the caboose. Once more, he failed to learn the Secret of the Railroads. Once more he was locked in the cellar. Once more, the brakeman failed to collect the Free Piece. The only variation was the presence of Jim Sly, who came down the cellar stairs at Blondetta's suggestion and beat the boy without once using his bare hands.

It was winter, 1929, when Kooteney Ketchel made his break again. He stayed in the boxcar at Three Forks. He stayed in the boxcar at Billings. He'd learned his lesson. It was very cold as the train rumbled across the Dakotas all night. He pulled the door shut and it locked. He wanted to get out at Fargo and then at Duluth. In Chicago, he wanted very much to get out and he banged on the side of the boxcar and screamed. But the yardmaster had directed that this car should be shunted to siding J-4, and so it was.

When, five days later, they moved the car to a loading dock to be filled with L. C. Smith typewriters for Minneapolis, they found the boy inside. "P.U.," they said, holding their noses. "P.U."

He wasn't quite dead, but nearly. They would have rolled him out to lie beside the loading dock, but, once more, one of the railroad men had been a customer of Blondetta's and remembered. He remembered her, inaccurately, as a woman with a big and sloppy heart. Who else mourned Stanley Ketchel? He got the boy to a clinic on the South Side where they fed him through a tube.

The next night, this Samaritan was chewing the fat in a speak near the stockyards called Cattleman's Rest.

The Samaritan explained how he'd come to find the boy; how he was having him treated at his own expense; and how he was confident of Blondetta's gratitude. As it happened, he was talking to the brakeman from that westbound freight who had so hoped for a Free Piece. The Samaritan was drinking Scotch whiskey. The brakeman laughed at the Samaritan, and called him a damn fool. He delineated the depth, length and stretch of Blondetta's gratitude and found it wanting. He announced that, as for him, from this day forward, he was going to patronize another whorehouse and abjure Irish World and he thought the rest of the railroad brotherhood should do likewise. At this other whorehouse they had two fourteen-year-old girls who waited for you with their legs apart and their cunts wet.

The Samaritan was, well . . . pissed. He ordered a beer. He counted the money in his wallet and it wasn't much. He drank most of it up anyway. The next time he looked into his wallet, he had much less than before. He thought, "What kind of a bum am I? I didn't know about those two girls with their legs spread apart and wet cunts and I don't know nothing else either. There's something wrong with me and *I MUST NEVER BE FOUND OUT.*" He decided to camouflage himself. He'd been in the First War and remembered how the German guns camouflaged themselves to look like a forest. He cried out, "I've been cheated!" in the voice of a man who's never been cheated before. The speakeasy's bouncer hovered over him so quickly it was like magic. It soon became clear, however, that the Samaritan was speaking metaphorically and the bouncer put his knucks back in his pocket. The Samaritan asked his fellow railroaders if they'd heard about Blondetta, who "never treated a railroad man square, nohow." Some had, some hadn't. All were willing to be convinced. The Samaritan formed a five-man vigilante posse and set out to "teach that two-bit whore a lesson."

They set out in an air-cooled Franklin sedan. They didn't speak on the drive to the clinic though it was a long drive and some were tempted. They marched up to the ward; three in the front rank and two behind. The night nurse thought they were the Mob and fainted, though they were dressed wrong for the part. The man who yanked the tubes out of Kooteney Ketchel's arms closed his eyes before he gave them the yank. The tubes shot fluid all over the Samaritan's shirt. "Jesus Christ," he said. Kooteney Ketchel sat bolt upright and got slugged and lay back again. They drove down to the freightyard, where one of the men had the key to the baggage shed. They crated the boy. They labeled him too:

The Great Northern Railroad Company
The Mainliner

        To: Miss Blondetta
               Irish World
               Butte, Montana
      From: Your railroad pals

SPECIAL HANDLING!!   DANGEROUS DOG!!

Then the posse dispersed. None of them felt like doing more drinking though some of them had money left to stand a couple rounds.

In years to come, the vigilantes forgot that night that started at the Cattleman's Rest.

Sometimes, when they chanced to meet in some

railroadman's hangout, they'd get drunk enough to remember.

"I heard that Indian kid—what's his name, Ketchel? —is getting a lot of overtime at the High Ore."

"I seen him one night down in Meaderville—I was in on the North Coast Limited—he's a good lookin' figure of a man."

"I never did get that damn shirt clean."

"We was pretty drunk, but it was a damnfool thing to do."

"Damnfool."

"Damnfool."

"I'm hearin' things are lookin' up for him. Heard he's wearin' a suit now. He's comin' up in the world."

"Well, here's to him."

"Here's to him."

"Here's to him. He was a tough kid."

The boy didn't wake up once on the trip west. If he had, the baggageman would have let him out. He scuffed and moaned, much like a dangerous dog, but he didn't wake up, and the baggageman played solitaire from Bismark, North Dakota, to Butte.

Jim Sly opened the crate to see what kind of dog Blondetta was getting—right on the station platform. Jim kept his hand on his revolver while the baggage handler prised the nails out.

When the crate's contents were revealed, Jim was honestly shocked. In time, many people became shocked. The crate's label caused especial shock because of the power of the written word.

Two days later, the police chief came to Irish World. He kept his pants on. He said the boy in the box made everybody look bad and feel bad too. He said, further, "What are you up to, Blondetta?"

Blondetta said, "The boy is sixteen now. He's old enough to rustle a job."

The chief said, "That's a great idea. I hear Reno is a great town for the whorehouse business."

So Blondetta got on the train for Reno where she did all right but not fabulous; the South Texas teenager became Blondetta and Jim Sly bought Kooteney Ketchel a lunchbox because there were no hard feelings.

When Kooteney Ketchel fought Lahti, nobody paid too much attention—though there were jokes. After the fight, when Lahti walked over town, men took his arm to say, "I hear you're the greatest Indian-fighter since Custer," and, "I knew you was dumb. I didn't think you was deaf too."

Jim Sly was working for Blondetta's successor and when he heard about Ketchel's victory, his ears perked up. He wondered what was up. He'd noted some changes in a man he knew so well: Ketchel's new blue suit, new clean shirt, dapper new tie. Jim Sly wondered what had changed Kooteney Ketchel's life. Was there anything in it for him?

After some thought, he began promoting Ketchel. He reminded the boys about Ketchel's long-dead father. How fierce he was. He told of opening that dog crate. Kooteney, he said, snarled at him—just like a dog.

Nobody paid much attention to Jim Sly. Except L.J. Tyler.

L.J. was from a county in West Virginia he described as "a hillside that couldn't keep from slidin' into the bottom, no matter how it tried." L.J. fought for fun— Dog-eat-dog or Stand-up—whichever.

He was leaving for West Virginia this spring or as soon as he got his Terraplane fixed, and he wanted to punch Vargas in the snoot. A mental picture of his fist superimposed on Vargas's snoot was part of the furniture of his mind.

L.J. worked at Hansen's packing. All day, he heaved beef carcasses from hook to hook and thanks to the weight of these defunct ruminants, he developed a swath of muscles across his back and the arms of Joe Louis.

One Saturday night, L.J. met a bus in the Intermountain terminal—the midnight bus from Great Falls. "I can lick any sucker in the damn . . . on the goddamned bus." He said these words and he was wearing a blue watchcap set at a jaunty angle when he said them. And he scuffed his feet in the gravel and glowered at the dozen or so pale faces peeking out of the bus windows. Nobody took him up on his offer. They were the poor and unemployed and didn't want to make trouble.

He did better in the bars Saturday nights. In some places, when he came in roaring, "I can lick any damn man . . ." half the bar stood up and formed a line.

He was a believer in the "Blackpowder-pistol" school of fighting. If you get close enough to a man with a blackpowder pistol, even if you miss him, you'll set his clothes on fire. L.J. closed with his opponent and then simply swarmed all over him. He was only six feet, a hundred ninety; but he was fast and willing. And when he lost (and sometimes he did), he'd come back next week bellowing his challenge to the same man who'd put him away. The third time one man flattened L.J. Tyler, the victor was heard to remark, "This boy sure is wearin' on a man."

Vargas wouldn't fight him. "Not yet, Tyler," he'd say. "Work out. You gotta work out." But Vargas liked him and figured to meet him sometime before he got his Terraplane fixed and lit out for parts unknown.

And one by one, Tyler floored the other contenders.

He mounted the stairs of Butte's only black bar and yelled, "Now where the hell did all the Snowballs come from?" In the ensuing fracas, he was thrown back down those same stairs but it took five men to do it.

On St. Patrick's day, he climbed up on the bar in O'Malley's and shouted, "Hey you bunch of dumb Paddies! God save the King!"

And when L.J. Tyler heard about the Ketchel-Lahti fight, he grinned all over his face.

The contenders didn't connect right away. Ketchel would be drinking at the 1,2,3 while L.J. was throwing cops through the big front window of the Board of Trade. While Ketchel was enjoying his solitary beer at Spillum's, L.J. was settling accounts with half of Finntown at the Yellowstone Tavern.

One Saturday night in August—it was a cool night for August—Kooteney Ketchel was drinking at the Main Stope, a little under-the-sidewalk saloon. The joint was quiet. He was wearing his quiet suit, his quiet tie, his brown fedora. He was drinking Olympia beer.

A few minutes before midnight, L.J. Tyler strolled in. A flash of genuine delight spread across his pan. One miner sized up the situation and hurried out to spread the news.

The bartender started pulling bottles off the shelves and storing them in the oak cupboards under the bar.

L.J. took a seat near the Indian, but not too near. He ordered a beer and got it, toot sweet.

A half dozen men crowd through the doorway. They fall silent as soon as they're inside.

Ketchel orders another Olympia. It costs him a dime though the price has gone up to fifty cents for everyone else.

Tyler moves a few stools closer. Everybody notices except Ketchel.

Twenty more men shoulder into the bar. They don't bother to lower their voices: "Ten on the redskin," "I'll take Ol' L.J., four for five."

When Tyler sits down right beside the Indian, Ketchel is rolling his beer bottle around in his hand. This excites one or two of the spectators. They nudge each other. They think the bottle has potential as a weapon and determine it won't be used that way. Not by no fuckin' Indian, anyway.

L.J. grins. Flashy grin. He talks loud though it's so quiet in the bar, you could hear a boot squeak. "Where I come from, they ain't no fuckin' Indians. Nary a one. Fuckin' Andy Jackson—Old Hickory—that's why. You look empty. Let me buy you a beer. Barkeep!"

Two beers delivered and poured.

L.J. grinned his grin. "Now like I was sayin' about Old Hickory. My daddy's daddy fought alongside him in his campaign against the Creeks. And Ol' Andy, he had the right idea. First you kill off all the ones strong enough to fight, then you march the weak ones off to Florida. Oh, a couple thousand miles on pisspoor rations, that ought to do it."

Then, in a spirit of fun, L.J. Tyler removed Kooteney Ketchel's brown fedora and ripped the lining out of it and stuffed the lining into Kooteney's beer glass. The glass overflowed.

Kooteney sighed. He stood up. He commenced.

As a butcher himself, L.J. Tyler should have been expected to appreciate Ketchel's skill. The separation of muscle from bone, exactly along tissue lines, is a difficult and precise art. It's harder still when the animal is alive.

The fight took all of three minutes. One man, the bartender, fainted. The spectators drew back from Kooteney Ketchel, not because they were afraid; though they were. Ketchel went home. L.J. Tyler went to the Murray Clinic where it was touch and go.

That left Vargas.

Vargas let it be known: any time, any place.

L.J. made a few rematch noises but nobody took him seriously because he had parts missing just like his Terraplane which he finally sold for thirty dollars to buy his ticket back east.

Vargas was rather too eager. Ketchel—even his backers conceded—didn't give a damn.

Vargas let it be known he'd be at the Lost Week Inn: midnight; Saturday; December 15, 1945. A crowd showed. Vargas showed. Ketchel never.

Vargas drank pretty heavy until four A.M. He went into the street and stopped a car and hauled the three male passengers out and worked them over pretty good. Vargas's backers apologized to the men later.

The Indian's main backers were a couple young Company men at the Granite Mountain. These two, Burke and Walker by name, had made three hundred dollars betting on the Indian against Tyler. "So what if he was a little rough," they said as they collected their winnings. "L.J. Tyler wasn't no babe in arms." They said that each time a loser balked at paying up. "L.J. Tyler wasn't no babe in arms." And soon, through the magic of simple repetition and euphony, everyone believed that L.J. had got no more than he deserved and started anticipating the Vargas-Ketchel bout.

Ketchel didn't give a damn.

Burke and Walker were so pleased by their winnings, they decided to do something for Ketchel. "He's our boy, now," Burke said. "He's our boy all right," Walker agreed.

One midnight, they hiked up the Hill to the steam generating plant. December, just before Christmas. They had a bottle of Teacher's Scotch, which was fairly rare still, though VE day and VJ day had come and gone.

"Howdy, boys," Burke said.

Joel looked up. Ketchel looked up too and they wished he hadn't. Later, when he talked about it, Walker said, "I never saw a pair of eyes like that before. I seen eyes like that in my dreams, sometimes, but never awake."

Burke was nervous, so he said, "Let me see your rustling card."

Kooteney's rustling card wasn't anything special. Religion? Political affiliations? Family?

None. None. None.

Walker opened one of the boiler furnace doors. A wall of heat. Walker put his hands up and turned his face away.

"You ain't supposed to do that," Joel said. "It fucks up the furnace. Clinkers."

"Sure," Walker said. Walker didn't want to get Ketchel's working partner mad. "That's a hell of a thing, that furnace."

"What do you want?" Joel asked. "You got business with us?"

"You know, Kangas," Walker said. "It's gonna be Christmas soon. If it wasn't for that, maybe we'd transfer you and your buddy back to the hole. You'd make a good shaftman. Maybe you could dig your way to fucking China."

"I ain't his buddy," Ketchel said. His eyes again. "He's a liar. Don't trust him."

"Sure thing, Mac," Burke agreed. He gave Ketchel the bottle of Scotch and said Merry Christmas.

Kooteney set the bottle next to his lunchbox like it wasn't much. He walked over and tapped the glass cover of a steam gauge.

The engineers left. Outside, Walker lit up a smoke and said, softly, "You're welcome, you dumb shit."

Burke said, "He's our boy, all right. Did you see the hands on that ape?"

Joel and the Indian had worked together eighteen months. At first, they got along good. Joel probably razzed Kooteney—he'd do that—but not too much. I wonder what Joel thought when Ketchel showed up in his unlikely new suit. I wonder what he said. I wonder if he cracked wise.

Kooteney Ketchel lived on the third floor of the Big Ship, a miner's boarding house on Galena Street. I'd been there once with Joel.

One Saturday morning, summer of 1945, we were going to have a family picnic down on the Madison River. The kids could go swimming and my father hoped to fool some trout. Joel's fortieth birthday. The picnic basket was ready and the rumble seat of Joel's convertible was open for the kids. Nice morning. Bright sun and the vast Montana sky.

Joel punched out and hung up his hardhat and said, "Let's go pick up Kathleen and the kids. Let's get this show on the road. Wish me a happy birthday, Kooteney. I'm one year older and no wiser today."

Kooteney hung his hardhat beside Joel's. "Oh," he said. "I wish you a happy birthday. Happy birthday, Joel." He brightened. "I'll buy you a beer."

Ignoring me, ignoring the bright sun, ignoring our intended picnic, smiling a smile.

And Joel shrugged at me and said, "Sure, Kooteney. I'll take a beer, but only one. The family's waitin' on us."

We stopped at a grocery store and Kooteney bought a six-pack of Olympia.

His room was neat and white: white walls, white table, white dresser, white bedstead. A blue blanket folded neatly on the foot of the bed. A few pennies and nickels in the *Great Falls Select—Fine Beer* ashtray.

The breeze was blowing the curtains in the windows. I sat on the chair. Joel sat on the bed. Kooteney fussed. He presented us with a bottle of beer each. He opened a beer for himself. He put the opener down beside the ashtray. We drank our beers. Kooteney said, quite solemnly, "Happy birthday, Joel Kangas, and many happy returns."

We said, "Thank you." We left.

Kooteney Ketchel's landlady looked like a velvet pigeon.

I told her I was looking for Joel Kangas. I told her the family was real worried about him. I told her Kooteney worked with Joel and maybe he knew something.

The landlady was a heavy woman in a faded purple dress. She wore her weight pretty well.

She made a noise with her lips, "Puh." She said, "Mister, I wish you luck with that one. He ain't in. I woulda heard him go up the stairs." She turned to point at a spot about halfway up the staircase. "Right there. He smashes into the wall every time he comes home. Right there." She added, "His room stinks."

I asked her if she knew where I could find Ketchel.

"The Mister's not gonna stand for this very much longer," she said. "We don't have no trouble renting the singles."

"Well, I'd sure like to ask him about Joel."

She waved her hand at the door. "There's a couple hundred bars out there. They sell hooch in all of 'em."

I looked for Ketchel at the 1,2,3, the Yellowstone, the Main Stope, Walker's, Spillum's—until the bartender at the Rocky Mountain said I should try the Lost Week Inn.

The Lost Week Inn was a one-room shack perched halfway up the Hill in a hollow formed by the sprawl of the tailing dumps. I knew that under the snow, the earth would be yellow and hard as concrete.

One car parked outside: a low-slung, maroon Buick two-door with snow chains.

At the door, I kicked snow off my rubbers before pushing inside into the warmth.

Long plywood bar. Stools. Tables. That Budweiser poster of Custer's Last Stand on the wall. The jukebox was playing the "Butte Polka."

The bartender brightened when I came in but dimmed when he saw me heading for his other two customers at the far end of the bar.

"H'lo, Kooteney," I said. I asked the bartender to bring me a shot. "Kooteney," I said, "Joel hasn't come home yet."

The Indian was pretty far gone. He sat on the bar stool like that's where he'd fallen. He heard me, though, because he said, sort of soft and squeaky, "Joel? Joel?"

"I didn't catch your handle," Kooteney's buddy said.

A stocky gent, leaning his elbows against the bar for
style and support. He came up straight to look me over.
Eyes so bloodshot it was hard to guess their color:
probably black. His hair was gray and neat and a couple
inches longer than a good barber would have allowed.
And he could afford the barber too. His gabardine suit
fit him like an expensive tailor had given the matter
some thought. The dark furrows above his eyes had
been burned there by hours in the sun. Like he was a
superintendent, maybe, on the section gang or the
highway.

"I'm Jimmy Mullholland," I said. "I'm looking for my
brother-in-law. He works with Kooteney here. Maybe
he can tell me something."

The gent never took his eyes off me while he patted
Kooteney on the shoulder. "He'll do," he announced.
"He's got sand in his craw."

His jaw was square. His arrogant nose started high
on his forehead and broke his face into two steep planes.
His weatherbitten skin was kind of pale and booze-
greasy.

Kooteney lifted his heavy head to stare at his buddy.
I don't know what he saw there. He looked back down
at the bar.

"Kooteney. Do you know where Joel is? Kooteney?"

A muscle jumped on Kooteney's cheek but he kept
mum. His buddy moved in front of him and stuck out
his paw. "Name's Devlin. Durstin Devlin. Dust, for
short."

I took his hand because I couldn't think of a reason
not to. His broad, splayed fingers had worked with a
pick and shovel a time or two, but his skin was soft; like
it had been a while.

He smiled at me—an easygoing smile, a little sloppy

at the edges. He shook his head, but not the smile. "Ol' Kooteney's a little under the weather," he said. His headshake deplored the fact. "They just can't handle the sauce. It fucks up a white man's balance, but with the Indian, it goes straight to the brain." He winked at me. "Best damn buck I ever met. And," he added, "I have met a few." He made it sound like the "few" was the whole damn Sioux nation.

I guessed him for fifty. His low-heeled stockman's boots were squaretoed and plain. "Maybe I can bring him around," I said, reaching past him.

Devlin grabbed my arm. He must have hit a lucky nerve. I was pretty damn strong but I sure couldn't move my arm. I started to twist free for a brawl. "Let go," I ordered.

"Sure, pal." He released me just like we'd never had that little trial of strength. "Let me buy you a drink."

"I ain't thirsty."

"And I don't give a damn for a man who won't drink with me! Barkeep!" His bloody eyes raged at me.

I shook my head, stubborn as a schoolboy. "I ain't drinkin' tonight," I said. "I got to find my friend. I ain't drinkin'."

The bartender arrived with that look of expectancy. Devlin clapped me on the shoulder and beamed. "Well that's all right, then," he said. "Just fine." To the bartender: "What the hell you want? Go on, son. Fade out."

"Thanks, Mac." The bartender's sour remark came from his retreating back.

I inclined my head at Kooteney. "You know him long?" I asked.

"He'll do," he said, with drunken pride in his voice. "He'll damn well *do*."

"You know anything about Joel Kangas?"

His smile exposed most of his teeth. "Why, sure I do. Joel Kangas. He's a communist." His head bobbed up and down like he'd consulted himself and been handed good answers.

"Oh, fuck," I said. "Bullshit."

Dust's teeth were brown with tobacco stains. He showed them all to me again. "Son," he said, "Commies are my hobby." And then, very quick, his hand dipped into his coat and came out with a thin morocco wallet. He flipped it open for a glimpse. The righthand side of the wallet was stuffed with cards—membership cards, for a guess. The other flap had a couple badges pinned to it; one above the other. The big one underneath was an old-fashioned, five-point, silver star. The lettering said something about the Cattleman's Association.

The other badge was acorn shaped. Either gold or brass. He stabbed at it with his forefinger before he snapped the wallet shut. "Attorney general's office," he said. There was a note in his voice that said the badge was an honor he'd never expected. "Subversive investigations," he added.

"You a cop?"

He spread his hands out wide. "Me? Hell no. You might call me a . . . negotiator."

"For the Company."

"Oh, hell, kid. You know how it is. I love Butte. Fine town. It's like a second home to me. I'm from Helena, myself. Got a nice little spread out toward Lincoln. You don't want to be mixed up in this. It's a security matter. National security. It ain't none of your business and you can't help anyway. Go home." His hand rested behind his back above his kidneys like he had something convenient to rest it on back there. Like a gun, maybe.

"I got some questions," I said.

Kooteney's head was down on the bar. A bubble of spit at the corner of his mouth.

"So ask." Devlin laughed. "Hell, I been askin' questions all my life and I never found out a damn thing."

His smile was infectious. I resented it. I shook Kooteney pretty hard and slapped him a couple times but he was limp. Only his face on the bar kept him from sliding off the stool.

Devlin watched as I smacked Kooteney around and the grin never left his face.

When I walked out of there, Devlin called after me, "Adios amigo." I resented that too. The resentment kept me warm on the long walk down the Hill to the sheriff's office.

3

Solidarity forever,
Solidarity forever,
Solidarity forever,
The Union makes us strong.
> The Little Red Song Book
> Industrial Workers of the World

JOEL'S FATHER was a Finn lumberjack working out of
Seattle, Washington. Times were hard, and when the
Wobblies showed up—Joel must have been, oh, twelve
or thirteen—Joel's father went to their rallies and sometimes he took the boy along. The Wobblies held their
rallies outside the lumber camps, and sometimes downtown along the skid road, and there'd be half a dozen
men sitting on the platform waiting their turn to speak

and a couple hundred lumberjacks standing around, listening.

The Wobblies all looked fierce and they spoke that way too and the lumberjacks cheered very loud and the finks wrote down as many names as they could.

> Your sons will call their children after us and name their dogs from men you now admire.
>
> Frank Little

1916. Germany was at war with everybody but us. Woodrow Wilson and his pal, Colonel House, were trying hard to make the war unanimous. The Wobblies didn't want to go to war. They said the war was just workingman fighting workingman. "War will mean the end of free speech, free press, free assembly—everything we ever fought for."

The newspapers denounced the Wobblies. They said the Wobblies were liars and awful. "Foreigners," they called them, "aliens."

> The working class and the employing class have nothing in common. There can be no peace so long as hunger and want are found among millions of working people and the few, who make up the employing class, have all the good things of life.
>
> Between these two classes a struggle must go on until the workers of the world organize as a class, take possession of the earth and the machinery of production, and abolish the wage system.
>
> IWW Preamble

Bitterness and misunderstanding on all sides. The owners hired the Pinkerton Detective Agency to infiltrate the Wobbly organization and let them know what was up. Usually nothing was up. Often the detectives said in their reports that something was up. The detectives were paid by the week. The Wobblies knew pretty well who was a Pink and who wasn't. They made jokes about the Pinks and pushed them around a little. The Pinkertons didn't care as long as they got their reports out every week.

This created further misunderstanding.

On October 30, 1916, four IWW organizers got off the ferry in Everett, Washington. They'd come from Seattle. They meant to agitate for free speech, because how can you preach sedition if nobody will let you preach. They planned to read the U.S. Declaration of Independence publicly in downtown Everett. The town of Everett had laws prohibiting *any* public gathering and the reading of *any* material so they hoped to get arrested and make the town fathers look foolish.

They were met, right on the dock, by Sheriff McRae and his deputies. The deputies formed a gauntlet and made the Wobblies run it. They worked them over pretty good with saps and knucks and tossed them back on the ferry.

This made the rest of the Wobblies pretty sore too. For a week they made speeches about the rights of assembly and free speech. They didn't know an abstraction when they saw one.

On November fifth, a couple hundred lumberjacks and Wobblies boarded two excursion boats: the *Verona* and the *Calista*. Joel's father got on the first boat, the *Verona*. He put twelve-year-old Joel on the *Calista*, which was still loading. He thought there might be gunplay.

It was a chilly day, but the loggers were wearing

their mackinaws and they had big kettles with them. They were going to make coffee in the big kettles later at their rally. The *Verona* was almost an hour ahead of the *Calista* when it pulled into the pier. On the docks, waiting, were Sheriff McRae, some deputies and a couple hundred vigilantes. These vigilantes were not members of the capitalist class the Wobblies hated. They were just thoughtless young men out for a bit of fun with the aliens on the boat.

The boat whistle blew *honk, honk, honk,* as the boat pulled into its mooring, scaring a few ducks aloft. The water hissed alongside. The captain of the *Verona* skillfully eased his boat into its berth. The *Verona*'s railing was black with people.

The vigilantes, who were hiding behind crates on the dock, came out from behind the crates. They stared at the aliens, who looked just like lumberjacks.

"Who is your leader?" the sheriff called out.

"We're all leaders!"

"You can't land here!"

"The hell we can't!"

The Wobblies started to pour off the boat and this struck terror into the vigilantes' hearts because they knew Wobblies ate thoughtless young men and made up packages of their bones which they shipped back to Norway, Finland, Poland and Russia as the main ingredient in "Thoughtless Young Man Soup."

The man who shot Joel's father didn't mean to and didn't know he had. He'd aimed over Mr. Kangas's head but had a higher regard for his marksmanship than was justified.

A ragged volley. Another. A couple of the Wobblies had pistols and popped away.

Screaming and moaning and silence. The captain of

the *Verona* reversed his engines and the boat backed out into Puget Sound.

A few of the bodies slid off the boat into the water where the tide carried them out and some creatures ate at them until they weren't worth the trouble anymore.

The vigilantes had been shot up a little too.

The *Verona* met the *Calista* out in the middle of the Sound. Joel looked for his father among the wounded (31) and dead (7) but his father had fallen overboard and the gulls ate his eyes.

Dear Bill: I die like a rebel. Don't waste any time mourning—organize. It is a hundred miles from here to Wyoming. Can you arrange to have my body hauled to the state line to be buried? I don't want to be found dead in Utah.

Joe Hill

Influenza killed Joel's mother. Joel waited until she was planted before he got his first Red Card.

He was a fourteen-year-old wage plug and he learned just about what you'd expect: that two men on a cross-cut saw are welded together, body to body; the rich stink of the sawdust; that a crescent wrench can peel the edge off a nut quick as a wink; that a buzzy—the rock drill—leaves you limp and trembling after half a shift.

He was a logger at first. Then he was a quarryman and monument cutter in Baring, Washington. He worked in Baring for five years until the quarry closed and he made up his bindle and hit the road.

He just drifted. He showed his Red Card to the other hoboes so he wouldn't get thrown off the trains and kept it in his shoe when he was asking for a job.

He spent a lot of time in libraries. In the winter libraries are warm. He read some books then.

IT'S ENOUGH TO MAKE ME SEE RED!
by, a miner*

Our old friend Jack Dritzen sent us his dues last month, and we'd heard he wasn't rustling at the High Ore anymore so we went down to pay the Doc a visit. He's gone away to Dentist School, you see, and come back a Dentist. He hasn't forgotten his old pals, and says to say hello to his partners at the High Ore and Leonard.

Doc's got his own office now, uptown, in the Metals Bank Building and a fine one it is too.

He's got his own little Dentist's buzzy and a set of dwarf pinch bars. Doc can fill a drift or open a stope in any tooth in your mouth, so if you need a Dentist, you miners know where to go!

Thanks, Doc, for the dues.

At last, somebody quits the holes alive.

> *Joel Kangas,
> columnist for
> *The Miner's Voice*
> May 18, 1944

Joel had a great shock of coarse black hair, a sallow mobile face and a bum leg. His leg had been broken and set bad. Joel said a wall fell on him at a place called Betea in Spain and probably that was the truth.

While he was on the bum, he got beat up fairly regularly by the Legion boys and the Commies too. He finally made his piece with the Commies but him and the Legion never did hit it off.

Not too long after Joel got his Red Card, the Justice Department started killing off the Wobblies. Usually the local boys did the job. It wasn't a conspiracy or anything—just a bunch of civic-minded citizens acting along similar lines. The Wobblies called it *The White Terror.*

> You haven't got guts enough to lynch a white man
> in the daylight.
>
> Wesley Everest

When the local boys fluffed it, the Justice Department stepped in with the full measure and majesty of the law. The Alien and Sedition Act. When they raided IWW headquarters in Chicago, they found the requisite alien, seditious literature; arrested Ralph Chaplin and Big Bill Haywood and confiscated Joe Hill. After Joe was shot in Utah, he'd been cremated and Wobbly headquarters had his ashes—neatly divvied up in small brown paper envelopes. They wanted to set up Joe Hill memorial urns all over the U.S. All that remains of Joe Hill is somewhere in the basement of the property office of the Chicago Police Department. They should have buried Joe in Wyoming like he wanted.

Joel got to Butte in '34.

After their goons had killed Frank Little, the Company brought in troops to break the Western Federation of Miners. It worked. Later the Company announced, "We will never treat with any would-be organization or association of miners again. We pledge ourselves to a fair day's pay for a fair day's work." For years, the Company made it stick. No miner's union. In 1934, the miners reassembled the fragments of the old WFM, and struck for union recognition. They called themselves The International Union of Mine, Mill and Smelter Workers. Local Number One.

The strike lasted four months. At the end, the Company was still selling copper from its stockpile at the Great Falls Smelter, and the mines were still producing; not much, but enough to get everybody mad.

Each day, the armored cars would roll up Anaconda Road with food for the scabs. They drove right through the picket lines. It was hard to see them go by and not think how much the food in those armored cars would mean to your family.

A couple men threw chains over the electrical cables and pulled them down, but some electricians and a bunch of gun thugs sallied forth and soon the mine was humming again. A few angry miners stood on the tailing dump and threw rocks over the mine fence into the yard until one of the thugs came out, waving his pistol.

Two or three miners talked about tossing dynamite, but they were Pinks and nobody paid them any mind.

One morning, a rumor flashed around town: They'd brought in a new load of scabs to work the Anaconda Mine. A couple hundred miners started up Anaconda Road to see what they could do about it. They passed the Neversweat and the Stewart and High Ore Terrace. The houses along the road were filled with people waving them on. And there were people out on the porches and they were waving too. When they reached the ten-foot plank fence around the Anaconda, someone yelled, "Let's tear that damn fence out of there."

A line of special deputies appeared at the top of the fence. Must have been fifty of them.

Somebody fired the first shot. The men on top of the fence fired most of the shots. The miners ran back down Anaconda Road, past the houses with their porches empty now.

Next day, they settled the strike, but Joel left town anyway. He wouldn't come back to Butte until 1940.

I never thought it was much of a contest between a hungry man's stomach and a bank vault.

Joel Kangas

Before Kathleen met Joel, she'd only had one real boyfriend, Bob Whitehead, and she'd used Bob unmercifully because she didn't want to marry Christ.

She was very unsure about taking her vows and the mother superior had granted her a six-month leave to "search her own mind and conscience." That she did. While she was searching, she took a lot of long drives, went swimming, dancing, and to the movies with Bob.

The summer wore on, Kathleen lost some of her pallor, she began to feel more at ease "outside" and Bob Whitehead, well, he wasn't so necessary anymore. She stopped seeing so much of him.

When Joel and Kathleen laid eyes on each other for the first time, it was something to behold. August it was, August of 1940. Hitler was making war in Europe and everybody figured we'd be dragged into it. A new world was waiting in the wings and I guess we knew it and were trying to enjoy what was left of the old one.

The Miner's Union picnic on Miner's Union Day.

Columbia Gardens. It was picnic baskets and checked tablecloths and carefully tended floral plantings in the nineteenth-century formal gardens: an American eagle in dahlias; in carnations, the crucifix of our risen Lord and Savior. The swings rattled and squeaked, the kids shrieked and yelled, the biplane ride went round and round, a mother in a green dress hunting her missing brood, the men sitting under the big elm trees drinking

Butte Special or Great Falls Select, and hot popcorn and peanuts and the long tables laid out with the macaroni salad, the coleslaw, baked beans, lasagna, the hams, the beer coolers and soda pop for the kids.

By noon, it turned real hot—in the nineties—and everyone slowed down; green grass and the distant clink of horseshoes.

Kathleen never did like the hot weather. She was fanning herself with her long-brimmed floppy hat, and her skin showed the first flush of a sunburn. She had modest little halfmoons of sweat under her arms and she squirmed around in her dress, like it was a hair shirt. Her hair was braided and piled on top of her head and it was red as red gold, but her face was sulky and she was chewing at the corner of her lip. My father was off having "one for old times sake" with a couple cousin-Jacks he'd known from the Alice. I leaned back and watched the light dapple through the leaves: all green and gold, soft yellow and brown.

A distant cheer from the ballfield. The miners' contests had started.

"Let's go see," Kathleen said.

"Hell," I mumbled, "I load orecars five days a week. Why should I go watch someone else do it on my day off?"

"I'm bored," she said.

I rolled up on one elbow and picked a bit of grass off my arm. "That's because you have no inner resources," I said.

"The heck with you," she said. "Please, Jimmy, let's go watch. If I sit here any longer I'm going to crawl right out of my clothes."

"Some might enjoy that," I said. "Not me."

She made a face. She brushed the grass off her dress.

Nodding at the people we knew, we strolled toward the ballfield. I must have been bored too and the prospect of seeing someone do, for fun, work that made my body sore every day seemed a charming prospect—somehow filled with delight.

The mucking contest is simple: A pile of rock. A mine car. A mucker and his shovel. A stop watch.

"Go, Cassidy!" "Go, man, you're doggin' it!" And the smooth arcs of rock flying from the man's shovel like his body was spitting them out and the little grunt—more a gasp than a grunt—each time the shovel engaged the rock and the smoothness of the dip and spin and the will to keep it fast and steady. Cassidy! Cassidy! Cassidy!

"Two minutes, forty-two seconds and a half," the timekeeper said and Cassidy grinned this wonderful wide grin and somebody handed him a beer and somebody else draped his shirt over his sweaty back and they shoved the orecar back and dumped it out again. Load the car. Unload the car. Laugh about it. Have a beer. Not me. I have possibilities!

The singlejack contest was a dying sport. Even then, they used buzzies to drill the dynamite holes and only the old miners remembered how to use the heavy sledge and rock drill. One man knelt, holding the drill, turning it slightly between the other man's blows so it got a fresh bite on the rock every time.

WPA art: two men, bandy legged, long bodied, shirtless, muscled bulkily across their chests. One's got a hammer coming off his shoulder—the other is concentrating on the drill (eighteen inches of tool steel) and neither attends to nor fears the twenty-pound hammer whistling past his head to strike right above his hands and an inch miscalculation would smash his wristbones to matchsticks, and never a thought now—they've worked together so long—never a thought the driver might miss or be weak or fail in the slightest respect.

When the time's half gone, the timekeeper calls out, and they switch: hammer for rock drill; rock drill for hammer; and damned if they don't pick up a half stroke. Whang, whang, whang, whang, whang, whang, TIME!

And somebody sticks a folding rule in the hole they made, until it bottoms in the tough granite, and announces, "Hardesty and Cole: twenty-eight inches and five eights." And Hardesty is shaking his head ruefully and Cole shrugs, What the hell.

"And from the Anselmo, two real miners, Jake Quell and Joel Kangas. Let's have a hand."

Joel's partner bends over, spits on the granite and rubs the spit over the stone looking for a fissure. His face is older than Joel's: wrinkles overlying wrinkles like they meant something. He sets the rock drill just so.

Joel doesn't look too good. He'd been boozing the night before and he'd mixed last night's mistakes with this morning's. His shirt was rumpled—a green work-shirt, bunched where he'd worn it inside his pants and a blotch of sweat in the middle of the back. He took it off and tossed it behind him. And he stretched. And he took a couple short deep breaths, Huh! Huh! And he had one of those bodies that can give of itself utterly until it's stopped. And his body shuddered and he coughed and his head scanned around, birdy, birdy, checking the crowd, and only then, he stood easy. My sister's elbow was touching my side and some little jolt of electricity traveled from her to me. I turned to see her face. She was watching Joel in a way that seemed— well, a little premature. I nudged her. She retracted her elbow and ignored me.

"On your mark. Go!"

And Joel lunged into that hammer like a drayhorse lunges into harness, throwing great spumes of sweat—acrid and bitter at first—a whiff drove me back a step—then hotter and sweeter as he touched his reserves. Precise. Precise. A fast, steady whang, whang, whang.

Joel's partner came up and took the hammer and his blows were maybe a trifle harder than Joel's though he kept the cadence where it was.

When the timekeeper shouted "Time!" the hammer was coming up, rebounding, and he spun around, a pirouette, and let the hammer come down to rest beside his foot. "Shit," he said. And he turned loose of the hammer and dusted his hands and walked off the little platform and Joel stood up and shrugged and let his eyes rove over the crowd. His eyes—Kathleen's. He scooped up his shirt, dropped off the platform and planted himself in front of us, his back heaving and sweatstreaked like a Clydesdale's.

"Twenty-eight and a half," the official said. "Kangas and Quell, twenty-eight and a half."

And Joel said, cheerful as hell, "It ain't the booze that gets you, pal. It's the prayin'."

Kathleen rose to the bait. "Praying?"

"Prayin' you ain't gonna die."

And Kathleen who, to my certain knowledge had never been more than mildly high in her life and had, only recently, tucked away her temperance pledge in the trunk with the rest of her juvenilia, smiled at this startling man and said, "I believe, Mister . . . uh, Kangas? that you could use a beer."

"Miss," he replied, "it is the sight of yourself that gives me all the refreshment I need."

"Why, Mister Kangas—Kangas isn't an Irish name."

"Finn. But you'd be Irish, I'm guessin'."

"My mother. My father's a cousin-Jack."

"Mullholland's the name. Jim Mullholland. My sister Kathleen." I nodded my head stiffly.

He stuck out his paw like a damn Swede and pumped mine. "Nice to know you," he said. "And I'm dyin' for a beer. Come along, let's celebrate my losin'."

"Sure," I said.

"No, thank you," Kathleen said. "Drink makes me giddy." Oh, she was so refined. "I believe I'll go down to the pavilion and have a glass of iced tea." And she smiled her special smile—HER DAZZLER—and off she went.

Joel put his shirt on. "Brrr," he said. "When that wind hits the sweat, it's murder." He was speaking of a zephyr that wouldn't ruffle a baby's hair.

I asked him where he'd learned the doublejack.

"Quarryin'."

I asked him where he worked at the Anselmo and he said, "The fourteen hundred. Contract miner."

I said I was a mucker at the Granite Mountain.

"You didn't enter the mucking contest?"

I said I saw no sense honing a skill I hoped to not practice.

And he said, "Ah. Do you want to raise yourself out of the laboring class, then?"

He pulled a cold beer out of the cooler, opened it and drank deep.

I said I'd already seen the laboring class up close and while I found them the salt of the earth, I wouldn't feel right ignoring another circle of people, to wit: the Rockefellers and du Ponts.

"Ahh," he said. He opened number two beer. "But they're such a bunch of assholes."

I grinned at him. "They got no monopoly on that."

The Commies took the bones of the IWW after the Justice Department was done chewing on them. I've been quoting some of the flashier words the Wobblies wrote because Joel knew the words and they were part of his life. He'd read the Commies too:

> The funerals of workers murdered by police, company gunmen and troops, in strikes and unemployment demonstrations, have become, in this period of great class battles, a powerful means of militant mass mobilization and a method by which the whole struggle reaches a higher political level.
>
> Bill Dunne

That's quite a mouthful.

Joel lost his Red Card on a rattler between Wolf Point, Montana, and Shelby, and he never got another one. He didn't want to join the Party. The Commies were pretty good at creating martyrs but that was about the extent of it. Joel thought there were too many Red martyrs already.

The Company finally recognized the union in '34, but Joel didn't give a shit. For the next three years, he was a thief and a drunk. Him and a chippy ran a badger game in Wolf Point. He jackrolled sailors in Seattle. He drank a quart of Old Overholt whenever he could get it.

Spring, 1937. It was raining in Seattle and though

Joel'd sat around all day at the Hall, hoping to shape for a couple Alaskan fur barges, the job only needed six men and the steward had let him know he was tenth on the list.

Wednesday night. There weren't gonna be too many drunk sailors wandering around on a wet Wednesday night; the Salvation Army'd told Joel not to come back until he learned to control his temper; he had a nickel in his pocket; hadn't eaten since Monday and though he was willing to beg, there weren't any more pedestrians in downtown Seattle than there were drunken mariners.

Seven P.M. A fellow named Hal Smith was talking about Spain in the meeting hall upstairs and it was warm, at least, and dry. Smith said that since the U.S. was neutral in the Civil War, volunteers for the Lincoln-Washington Battalion had to enlist in Paris and then would be smuggled to Albacete in southeastern Spain. Joel didn't care. He'd known some doughboys who'd been in Paris in the First War and none of their stories had made him curious. Hal Smith said the Republicans were winning though only Russia was helping them. He said the motto of the International Brigade was "*Passaramos*" which meant "We shall pass!" He praised the Dagtyarev machine gun. Maybe Smith was a little gun-happy, but his description of the Dagtyarev was loving and technically detailed. Maybe Joel felt the way about machines the way I do. Smith called the gun "the fascist-killer." And Joel woke up.

Why-in-the-hell-ever-not?

You don't have to be a Commie to be a Red.
                                                    Joel Kangas

I finished my beer and nice-to-meet-yous. I went looking for Kathleen.

She was sipping a Coke. "Did you enjoy your beer?" she asked sweetly.

"Never touch the stuff," I said.

"Well, then," she said, "you ought to change your brand of toothpaste. Or forego brushing late at night before you stumble home."

"Squirt, I thought you had one there. A real live one. Isn't he a little old for you?"

"Why learn sex from a beginner?" she asked, sweet as pie.

My sister would have made a rotten nun.

Her face was quite grave, quite beautiful. She had the certainty on her face—that look they paint on cheap figurines of Our Lady. Fatuous, I call it.

And called it. At which point the quarrel started that was to last the whole afternoon. My father was unable to stop our bickering but could not countenance it either, so he stayed with his pals, drinking beer.

Dusk came, tempers cooled and while we were standing at the pavilion, waiting for the bus, Joel pulled up before us in a snazzy blue Plymouth convert. "Want a lift home?"

Sure we did. I, as the least traveler, rode in the rumble seat. Joel'd hosed himself down and picked up a shirt somehow. He still looked like a drayhorse, but a drayhorse wearing an orange, floppy-collared shirt. Sight for sore eyes.

When he pulled up in front of our house, he hopped over the door and came around quick to the passenger side where Katie was opening her own door without his help.

"Oh," he said.

"Thanks for the ride, Mister Kangas," she said.

"Joel's the moniker."

"So I understand."

"I mean—can I come by sometime and pick you up and take you to a movie or something?"

"Thursday night."

"What?"

"On Thursday night there's a double feature at the Rialto. I'd like to see that."

"I'll be here at seven o'clock, then," he said. "With bells on."

"You could skip the bells, Mister Kangas," Kathleen said.

"Hell," Joel said. "Hell, honey. For you I'll be wearing the biggest set of bells in Butte and I'll ring 'em all night long."

And he jumped back in his car and drove off and waved and yelled something more about bells which we couldn't quite make out.

It was not the courtship Kathleen expected, though she may have dreamed it once.

Thursday, Joel drove up swinging an old handbell he'd bought some place. Honking the horn and banging the bell. Kathleen blushed and ran outside with one of her braids still loose and flying behind her, yelling at Joel to stop his foolishness or else.

Or else. He put the bell behind the seat.

And they saw Clark Gable. Next Thursday they saw Spencer Tracy. And Mickey Rooney the Thursday after that.

Kathleen had never been that much of a moviegoer. Either she wanted the traditional movie-date courtship we saw in the movies or maybe she liked to sit with Joel without needing to talk.

Joel wanted to go dancing. "No." Dining? How about the Rocky Mountain? "Nope."

After the movie, they'd come back to the house, sit in the parlor — we'd exchange pleasantries — and then Kathleen would put on a brave movie smile and ask Joel, "Just what terrible event caused you to lose your belief in God, Mr. Kangas?"

My father liked to talk to Joel, but we never stayed fifteen seconds after Kathleen put one of her brave deadly questions.

Thinking back on it, it was pretty funny: the two of them sitting on the floppy overstuffed couch, each with whatever dignity, sitting exactly three feet apart—you could have measured it with a yardstick—and each YEARNING for the other. Electricity. Once Kathleen's calico cat jumped up between them, thinking to enjoy the proximity of so many hands. When he landed on the sofa, his hair shot up, he gave a noise more like an "eeeehh?" than a "me-owr" and got his ass off there.

Sweetly, rationally, for two or three hours, they discussed the undeniable fact that he, Joel, was a Red, while she, Kathleen, was a Catholic. "But Christ was a revolutionist!" Once I heard Joel shout that. I cracked the kitchen door open an inch to hear Kathleen's reply. "Render unto Caesar," she said. Joel coughed. My father grinned at me and opened a beer. I let the kitchen door swing shut.

Of course, Kathleen was enjoying those too long, too careful, too reasonable arguments. After Joel'd leave, often as not she'd be humming; and she'd be flushed in the face and her breasts heaving against her bodice. Kathleen was storing up her memories, enriching her store of sentiment to warm her on cold nights when she was older.

It drove Joel nuts.

A couple years later Joel confessed to me that he'd "leave that damned uncomfortable couch in your damned uncomfortable house and your damn sister'd give me a little smile at the door that was so, well . . . 'promising,' I'd forget I was mad and only remember the ache in my nuts. I'd go on down the Line and have me a girl and once or twice, when I was really burning, a couple of girls. Between seein' your sister and the girls I bought so I wouldn't jump on her, Kathleen was costin' me everything I made. Hell. She knew it too. I swear she knew it."

Two months.

To be fair, Kathleen was taunting herself as much as she taunted Joel. She was starring in a movie of herself: THE PRUDENT VIRGIN.

Joel was the worse for wear. Tensions grew between them. Soon the humor was gone. You can't toy with sex very much. The body takes revenge.

Joel got fed up. On Thursday night, I heard his convertible pull up ten minutes early. I heard the bell. He sat in the front seat of his snazzy convertible ringing that damned cowbell. Clang, clang, clang, CLANG, CLANG, CLANG. Oh, he rang it and rang it and Kathleen rushed out in her blue terrycloth bathrobe and hollered at him and he sat there, grinning, ringing the bell like he was calling in *all* the cows or announcing the arrival of the North Coast Limited.

Pretty soon, the neighbors started to find outdoor tasks.

It was a nice fall evening and many of the neighbors were standing on their porches. Kathleen whipped back into the house, just long enough to get a coat to wear over her bathrobe. My father and I went out onto the porch in a more leisurely fashion.

Joel put the cowbell on the seat, got out of the car and leaned on the fender.

Kathleen: all her spinal members were welded.

And the damn fool grabbed her around the waist, jerked her off her feet and kissed her. "MMMMMMMPH," Kathleen said. And he set her down and he groped behind him in the car until he found this enormous bouquet of flowers. Not roses. Mums. Huge white mums. They would have made a first-rate horse collar. "Miss Kathleen Mullholland," he bellowed, "will you do me the very great honor of consenting to be my wife?"

Now, that took her aback. The neighbors too. Mrs. Ewan began applauding in honor of the romance of it all but her husband put a stop to that.

"Mister Kangas," my sister said, just as loud. "The children, if any. They will be raised as Catholics."

That took him aback. "What?"

"WILL THE CHILDREN BE RAISED IN THE FAITH?"

"Why, no. Hell no! No kid of mine will be raised on that thin nourishment."

"Then, Mister Joel Kangas, my answer is *no*."

Joel gaped.

My sister's jaw looked like one of those jaws on Mount Rushmore.

So he got back in the car and gave her a kind of doggy look, hoping she'd relent, but she didn't, so then he said, rather softly, "Well. Fuck you, Kathleen Mullholland."

And my sister yelled, "And you go fuck yourself, Joel Kangas. Because you sure won't be fucking me."

And he punched the starter and roared off and she came back up the walk, tears running from every eye.

Kathleen moped around the house for three or four days. On Sunday, she went up to visit Aunt Edith, for what I presume was spiritual solace. She came home about four, wearing the mask of "sweet colleen, betrayed by feckless lover." She wore that sweet mask around the house for another couple days and it made me sick. "Would you like a little toast, Jimmy? Sure, a man needs a hearty breakfast." Shit.

Next Thursday night, the doorbell rang. Joel on the porch in his working clothes with a brown paper bag in his hand. "Hi, Jimmy. Old Jim home?"

"Sure," I said. And let him right in.

He went straight back to the kitchen and set two six-packs of beer on the table. "I thought we could play some cribbage before you went on shift."

The old man loved a good joke. "Sure," he said. "Young Jim can take on the winner."

My sister came out of her bedroom, feathers flurried. I intercepted her. "Yes," I said. "It's Joel. He's come to play cards with me and Jim. It's got nothing to do with you."

And her eyes got sort of big and she started breathing quick like she was hyperventilating.

"Kathleen Mullholland," I said. "He's come to visit your father, who has made him welcome, and there is nothing you can do about it."

Joel stayed until midnight when my father went on shift and a good time was had by some.

Next Thursday night, Kathleen played her ace: the Ace of LaSalle. Bob Whitehead's dad was a shiftboss at the High Ore and they had a few bucks to toss around; a nice brick house on the west side; and a blue-and-silver '37 LaSalle with blue velvet upholstery. Old man Whitehead got killed two years later when a rotten ladder broke in a manway, and since he had no insurance, the family lost the house and the car and young Bob joined up. But, for now, they were prosperous: car, house, and son Bob enrolled at the State University in Missoula.

Ten minutes after Joel parked on Thursday night, the LaSalle purred in behind his Plymouth. Joel had just opened the first beer when the doorbell rang. Kathleen hurried into the kitchen in her long formal dress. She had her dowdy cloth coat over her arm.

"That must be Bob," she said, chipper. "Jimmy, would you let him in? Joel, could I ask you to do me a big favor?"

"Sure."

"Zip me."

And she turned her long flawless back to him and his hands touched her and when she whirled away to the door, his hands were trembling.

"We're going to the Tommy Dorsey concert," she announced. "Don't wait up."

The cribbage game wasn't a barrel of fun that night though Joel kept playing. He won too. When my father left for his shift, Joel stayed put and started dealing solitaire.

I was sleepy as hell, but I'd see it out. Slap, slap of cards. He cheated.

About three A.M., we heard the LaSalle pull up. Low, muted throb of the exhaust. Then nothing. It seemed like a long time though I didn't comment on it. Footsteps on the porch. They stayed out on the porch a long time too.

Kathleen made the introductions. Kathleen—mussed and awry. Joel—burning like a fuse. Bob Whitehead—oblivious to it all.

Bob Whitehead had a face like a raisin cookie. Eyes set wide apart and shallow. A small pliable mouth. He probably knew to the penny what his white suit cost but didn't know it didn't matter.

Joel shook his hand. "Where do you work?" Blunt.

"Oh, I'm at MSU. Prelaw."

"I'm at the Anselmo Mine, myself."

Bob grinned at Kathleen. Kathleen grinned at Bob.

"How was the dance?" Joel asked. "They play any polkas?"

"Polkas are old hat," Bob said. "You know how to jitterbug?"

"Can't say as I do."

"You ought to get Kathleen to teach you. She sure knows how to 'shake that thing.'" His smile. Kathleen, bless her, blushed.

"Sure," Joel said. "Say, I hear you drive a LaSalle. Now there's a real fine car. If I had the dough, that'd be the car for me."

Bob Whitehead glowed. "It's a beaut. Finest car in America, if you ask me. Say, why not come out and give it the once over."

Kathleen took his elbow. "Bob, I thought this was *our* date. Just the two of us."

"Oh, Kathleen. Don't be that way. After all—how often does a man get to really show off." To Joel: "You got a car? Maybe we'll look at it too."

"Sure thing." Joel was smiling a fake smile. It fooled Bob.

When they went out, I started working up some coffee. Kathleen slipped into the parlor and watched through the curtains. I heard the LaSalle start up. I joined Kathleen on the front porch to watch the La-Salle's taillights getting small and Joel Kangas coming back up the walk, nonchalant as a shoplifter in the checkout line.

"Joel Kangas," she warned.

"Flighty kid, Kathleen. You shouldn't fool around with these young boys."

"Joel Kangas. What the hell did you do to make him drive off like that without even saying good night."

"Nice car," Joel said. "You know, if I'd been just half smart in this world, I would have had enough money for a car like that. I'm old enough for it."

"Joel." Through her teeth.

"Didn't you know, Kathleen, he ain't no mackerel-snapper either. No more'n me. He don't want to raise no baby Catholics either."

And Kathleen was puzzled for about ten seconds until the tears overflowed. She ran inside.

"You're full of baloney," I told him.

He never said anything to that but Bob Whitehead never called Kathleen again. Not one time.

After a couple of days of hurt pride she called Bob and reminded him how much he'd helped her, just by being around, when she was trying to decide about the Order, and though they'd never had a Red Hot Romance, she'd always valued him as a friend, so why the hell'd he run out on her Thursday night?

He said he was sorry for that. Headache. He said he hoped they'd always be friends. As for him, he had to go back to the university to take some examinations he'd missed during the fall term.

Next Thursday night, Joel showed up at eight sharp for the cribbage game. He had a fresh deck of cards, three six-packs and the kind of expression you usually see on itchy-footed saddle-tramps before they saddle up and ride. He spent a lot of time inspecting his knuckles. He was whalin' the hell out of the beer.

At ten o'clock, Kathleen came out of her room and sat at the kitchen table right across from him. She was wearing her Sunday mass suit. Dark-green coat over dark-green skirt; the coat with zootsuit lapels. She wore her brown hat, pinned to her red braids. She held her gloves. White cotton gloves from the five-and-dime. Three or four glass diamonds in her hat, describing a jaunty semicircle.

"Well, Mister Kangas," she said. "If you're done with your card game, I'll be ready to go."

And Joel leaned back in his chair and set his beer bottle down and said, softly, "Well now, Kathleen— where did you have in mind for us to be going?"

Kathleen's lips were bit white. "To wherever you had intended us to spend our first night together. Honeyman. . . ." She'd meant to say "Honeymoon" but slipped. She rallied. "My overnight bag is packed and at the door. A man of your convictions must know the modern methods . . . ways to keep the babies from coming. I do not wish to have a baby."

Joel sat up straight. "Kathleen."

My father said "Kathleen" too.

I didn't say anything.

Kathleen continued. "Mister Kangas, I will leave my faith for you, but I will not raise children without Christ or any hope of peace. Nor will I marry you."

"Oh, hell, Kathleen. Let's get married."

Her head was as high as my father's face was low down. "I could not marry you. You are an atheist. The Church will not marry us."

He grinned. "We'll lie."

If possible, she raised her head higher. "I will not lie away my immortal soul."

"Just a little lie."

"Joel," she said in a fractured voice, "you are going to have to take me soon. I don't believe I can stand very much more of this."

"Marry me. We'll split the kids. Half Papists and the other half Reds."

And slowly, a big fat tear rolled down my sister's cheek. "All the girls, Joel. They need faith so much more than the boys do."

He inclined his head. "All right. That would be all right."

And they got married in the Immaculate Conception church by Father McDevitt, who was wise enough not to press Joel about his religious convictions. They were married outside the altar rail and both signed the paper that promised the kids' souls to the Church. If Joel had private reservations, he kept them private, and Father McDevitt baptized the girl, and the boy too.

It was a fair hike from the bar where I'd left Kooteney to the sheriff's office downtown. The streetlights were infrequent. It was late. The wind was blowing the snow around pretty good, drifting it into the streets. Occasionally a car would churn by me, tire chains clanking up the hill. My cuffs were frozen stiff as boards and I kept my hands deep inside the sleeves of my jacket.

The courthouse was a marble barn. Years ago, when Butte had a hundred thousand citizens and fifteen mining companies, the courthouse was full of politicians and energy. Now, with half the people and only one Company, the courthouse was mostly empty and the custodian occupied an office once tenanted by an appellate-court judge.

My heels clicked across the dirty marble floor. The ceiling rose far above me like an old joke.

The sheriff's office was fronted by a counter to separate them from us. Big, green filing cabinets filled the gaps between the tall windows in back, only half a dozen desks—mostly unoccupied—and wanted posters on the bulletin board. I studied the posters. I wondered about men so reduced. My cuffs dripped water on the floor. My nose was running and I rubbed it quickly with my glove. I was ashamed to be here.

Someone I didn't really want to see came over to the counter. "Help you?" he asked. "Oh. Jimmy. I didn't recognize you at first."

He'd been an MP in the Army and I had heard he'd signed on as sheriff's deputy when he came home. I suppose I'd hoped he'd be on some other shift.

"H'lo, Bob. How's she goin'?"

Bob Whitehead's shallow eyes had got no deeper, but now they were glazed. He'd been a combat MP and seen a few things. Done a few things too. None of them what he'd wished for. He'd put on a little beef. His arms were heavy and his shirt strained across his chest. His eyes weighed me; neutral and patient. There were two other deputies at their desks and a woman thumbing through a stack of magazines. A smell of burnt coffee from the coffeemaker in the corner.

"I'd like to file a missing persons report," I said.

He didn't blink but his mouth put on a little compassion. "Sure," he said. He got a yellow legal pad and laid it across the counter and said, "Shoot."

"His name is Kangas. Joel Kangas. You met him once. That's K-A-N-G-A-S."

But he wasn't writing any of it down, he was shaking his head. "We already got a report on him," he said. "Your Sis called an hour ago, and then about fifteen minutes after her, somebody else called—your dad, I guess. So we don't need you."

"Oh," I said.

"You got nothin' to worry about," he said. "Those guys always turn up, sooner or later."

What a terrific relief. Joel was one of "those guys" who fill out the routine statistics of the police. Nothing frightening, just a little sordid, a little average. I was ready to abandon all of what made Joel Joel—everything special—to see him home again.

"You usually find 'em, eh?"

"Hell, yes," he said. "What'd you think? A couple days, and they come home, under their own steam, beggin' to be let in the door. I'm gonna get me some coffee. Want some?"

He opened the hinged door in the counter. I wasn't having any trouble picturing Joel as miserable wretch begging to be forgiven. "Oh," I said. "No. No thanks."

"Suit yourself," he shrugged. "I'm gonna look over the report." I followed him into the official section.

The young woman was ticking a pencil against her teeth as she worked through her pile of magazines. She had a plain, sunny face. She wore circular glasses.

Deputy Whitehead asked me a couple questions about Joel's routines but he already knew more than I did. He slurped his coffee. I let my eyes wander over the young woman until she raised her eyes and caught me at it.

"Ninety-nine times out of a hundred, these jokers turn up with a big head and empty pockets."

"Joel wasn't like that," I said.

"We already checked the hospitals," he said. "Nobody like him. It says here he has bushy hair."

"Uh-huh."

"Nothin' like that. We had one guy at St. James, got hit by a car on North Montana, who's the right age and size but he ain't got hair and he wears cheaters."

"Joel never wore 'em."

"Well," he said, "we'll keep an eye peeled. All our cars and the city police too."

"You know a guy named Devlin?"

"Devlin? Who?"

"Fifty, maybe fifty-five. Dresses like a rancher out on the town. Drives a Buick Century."

"Oh him, yeah, sure. Dust Devlin. I didn't put the name together at first. He hangs around with Frank Coad. Some kind of investigator for the Cattleman's Association."

"He says he's with the attorney general's office."

Whitehead's eyes got real interested and he forgot about his coffee for a minute. "Yeah. Well, I never heard nothin' about that."

"He didn't want me to talk to Kooteney Ketchel."

"The Indian? What does he have to do with this?"

I told him I'd tried to talk to Ketchel at the Lost Week Inn. I said I thought something fishy was going on. The Deputy stared at the missing persons report like he hoped it would talk to him or something.

"Devlin said it was a security matter. National security. He said I should butt out."

The Deputy's face was a carefully arranged blank. He picked up his phone. He said, "Excuse me." When I failed to get the message, he shooed me away with his hand. I went over and leaned against the sunny woman's desk.

"Hi," I said.

She raised her head long enough to give me a polite smile but went back to her magazine right away. It was *The New Yorker*.

The Deputy called me back. He had a frown. "Sit down," he said. He shuffled the missing persons report. It was only two pages so the shuffle didn't mean much.

"I hear Mister Kangas is a Red," he said.

I shrugged.

He gave me the old eyeball-to-eyeball. I gave it right back to him.

"So what?" I said.

It was his turn to shrug. "Don't make shit difference to me," he said. "He'll turn up. You can quote me."

"Why is this Devlin interested?" I asked. "I wanted to ask Ketchel if Joel had been restless—if he'd said anything about takin' off. Devlin wouldn't let me ask. He said I'd be interfering with a security investigation. Now what's that supposed to mean?"

"It means: 'Don't ask.'"

"Thanks a lot."

"Don't mention it. We'll keep a looksee out for Kangas."

"I'll bet. You still drivin' that LaSalle?"

"You must have heard we had to sell it. I got me a Ford car. A small one." He made a hand gesture to show me how small it was.

"Kathleen still talks about you," I lied.

"Yeah? I'll be damned." He wasn't really surprised. He was ready to believe the best of himself.

"She says you're quite a dancer."

"Yeah. I used to be pretty fast on my feet. Too busy now, though. Got too much work to do."

"How come you let Joel run you off?" I asked.

That killed his smile. "He never."

"Yeah. Sure. How come you never came back?"

That took him back to a place he hadn't been in seven years and didn't especially want to revisit: Joel, leaning over the fender of that beautiful blue car, tugging at a wire or two, saying, "You know, kid, you're pretty sharp. I could get to like you. It's too bad about Kathleen. I think she likes you too." And the Deputy remembering himself as a punk kid before the war and he was getting a little more perspective on himself than he wanted. His face went red and he tried out a very fast smile on me, but the smile gave up quick and Bob Whitehead stared right through me.

"So why'd you never come back?" I asked.

He opened his mouth. He closed his mouth. Maybe he was breathing.

"Kathleen always wondered. I told you she still talks about you, didn't I?"

"I'm sure she does," he said. Voice like lead. "She would."

"What's that supposed to mean?"

He gave me the old man-to-man. "She had the clap." Einstein couldn't have been more sure.

I'm afraid I grinned at him like somebody dumber than I am.

He ruffled the report. He mumbled. "Hell, he was her boyfriend wasn't he? Who'd know better'n him? He said he'd given it to her himself."

4

"Somebody want to let me in on the joke?" the woman asked.

I couldn't. I was laughing too hard. Laughing at Joel and with Joel and from the delight I took in knowing him better.

And the Deputy wasn't about to. He grunted at the sunny-faced woman like a pig who's been kicked. He covered the missing persons report with his hand. Reflexes.

She was too plain. Her tits were too big and her carefully manicured hands were too small. Her hair was curly, brown and short. "You don't think I have a sense of humor?" she asked.

I shook my head at her because I didn't trust my voice.

"Nothin' for you," the Deputy said.

"Why don't you let me decide that?" she asked in a cheerful voice. The voice, like the rest of her, was eager to please.

"Mullholland," I said. "I'm Jimmy Mullholland. My brother-in-law is missing."

Her smile stayed, but the interest left her pale-blue washed-out eyes. Her glasses, clutched in her hand. Her inexpensive, carefully ironed, light-blue suit.

Bob Whitehead swiveled in his chair. It squeaked. He jabbed a thumb at her. "Meet the newshawk," he said.

She wore an uncut sapphire on a gold chain around her neck. It was a big rough stone, maybe three carats. She stuck her hand out to me. "Gail Stinson," she said. "Stinson like the airplane. I cover the courthouse for the *Standard*."

I gave her hand a quick shake. I was proud of being a machinist, so I said, "I'm a miner."

"That seems to be a real popular occupation," she said, but her smile took the sting out of it. She pulled the report off Whitehead's desk and scanned it. "Another skip," she said.

"No," I said. "Joel Kangas wouldn't run out."

She never looked at me, "How many's that make this month, Bob?"

"What?"

"Skips."

"Three or four. I dunno."

"We couldn't use it anyway. It's news when somebody shoots his wife, not when he leaves her. The editor's a family man." She had a grin for her own cynicism.

I got mad at her. I was mad at me for forgetting Joel in the easy comfort of the statistics. He wasn't *just like* anybody. I snapped at her. "You're pretty damn cock-sure."

She took a cigarette out of her purse and lit it. The smoke made her squint. "I hear Salt Lake is nice this time of year."

"He heard Salt Lake was full of fascists."

"Big word. Denver?"

"No."

"Seattle? Portland? Tacoma? Billings?"

"Maybe he just flew off to Europe in his private B-29. What do you know? You never met him."

"That's true," she said briskly, "I haven't."

Bob Whitehead said, "Don't get in a sweat about it. We'll find Kangas."

"Of course you will, Bob." Sweet bullshit smile. It didn't fool Whitehead for a minute. He shoved his chair back and went off to the coffee pot.

I looked at her face. She'd heard a few hard-luck stories in her day, but that didn't make it easier for me to talk about Joel. "I don't have the words for what I mean," I said.

"Yeah," she said. "I have that problem myself, some-times."

"His wife is nearly out of her mind." I hated using Kathleen that way.

"Sure," she said. "I know how it is."

I thought she probably did.

"She isn't mad at Joel," I said. "They didn't have a fight. She's scared something's happened to him."

When Bob Whitehead put his coffee down on his desk, he slopped some. It made a little pool. It stained the missing persons report. Absently, he wiped the re-port on his pant leg.

"It ain't news anyway," he said. "Kangas is a Red. The attorney general's got his man on him. Nothin' you can use."

"Kangas? Kangas? The union guy?"

"Keep your nose out of it."

Her quick smile came and went. "What time you gonna put the Cheyenne prisoner on the train?"

"He goes out in the morning. Seven thirty-eight."

"There's not many inches in that story," she said doubtfully.

"I know you," Bob Whitehead said. "I told you. Mind your own beeswax."

"Oh, heck, Bob," she said sweetly, "nothin's gonna come out of it. Just another skip."

"I warned you." He shrugged. He wadded up the coffee-stained report and tossed it into the wastebasket. "Tell Kathleen I'm sorry," he said. "Tell her I'll look myself. Personal."

"Kathleen always did wonder what scared you off."

He stood up. He was big. He said, "Get the hell out of here."

"Okey-doke." I got. The newspaper reporter tagged along. She wanted to visit Kathleen. She said she had a car.

Dark outside except for the streetlights and they weren't too much good in the soft, wet, falling snow.

"One day I'll get used to it," she said, groping in her purse for her car keys.

"What?"

"The darn snow."

We got in her car, one of those elephant-back Ford coupes. The businessman's coupe with the long trunk for a salesman's samples and luggage. A new one.

"I've even got some of it paid for," she said.

She was a pretty good winter driver. Four inches of soft snow over ice and the soft jing-jing of the tire chains.

She said she'd been born in the central part of the state: Big Timber. Her daddy was a wheat farmer.

The Kangas porchlight was on: a snowswept beacon for the returning mariner.

The snow on the porch was soft and undisturbed.

I banged on the door.

Some of the snow was finding its way under my collar. When my sister opened the door, she took up very little room in the opening and she'd been a good-sized woman.

"You haven't found him," Kathleen said. She wasn't looking into my eyes. She was staring past me at the swirling snow.

I said I hadn't.

She let her head bounce up and down in what was maybe a nod or maybe something broken. "Good," she whispered. She saw Miss Stinson then. She said, "Excuse me." She said, "Come right in."

We tracked snow through Kathleen Kangas's parlor and it didn't matter because hers was a home no longer.

The kitchen was too hot. I made the introductions. They handled the pleased-to-meet-yous.

My sister's face was white. Her color had been pared away, like you pare an apple.

Gail got right down to business. "You haven't heard anything from your husband?"

Kathleen's jerky headshake, no.

"You'll excuse me, I have to ask: He's never done anything like this before?"

Another mute no.

"A minute ago, on the porch, you were . . . uh . . . glad he hadn't been found."

Kathleen found her voice. It was the voice of dry leaves scattering down a sidewalk. "Yes."

Gail let silence ask her question.

Kathleen said, "Now. If he is found now, so late . . . he will be found dead. I pray he is not found. I pray he has fallen for some slut and run from here. The two of them. Running."

"I see," Gail said. She looked at the linoleum floor. "May I sit down?"

"Oh, I'm sorry. Please do. And you, Jimmy, take off your coat."

"Sure," I said. "I could use a cuppa Joe." Though I didn't much want one.

I unbuttoned my coat in that suffocating kitchen and we sat down and Kathleen turned to the stove and Gail tried to give me a sympathetic glance but I wouldn't let her eyes catch mine because she'd called Joel "a skip."

Kathleen made the coffee step by step. Nothing was automatic for her now. I didn't want to watch her so I talked. I told her about the bartender at Spillum's saying Joel had meant to go to work. I told her about finding Kooteney Ketchel with Dust Devlin. I told her Bob Whitehead was a deputy now and had promised to look for Joel, personal.

She said Edith had taken the kids home with her.

The coffee burbled in the percolator.

"He'll find him," Gail said. "I know Bob Whitehead. He's difficult sometimes, but he's a good deputy."

"Thank you," Kathleen said softly. I was real glad

when she sat down, and when the coffee was done perking, I jumped up and poured it.

"Are you Catholic, Miss Stinson?" Kathleen asked.

"No. I'm a Lutheran. At least my family is."

"I don't know that. . . . I don't know about that. Do you marry for eternity?"

Gail made an awkward face. "I don't know."

Kathleen picked up her coffee. She slurped and said, "Excuse me." She said, "We are of one flesh, Joel and I."

"Kathleen," I said quietly, "I don't think. . . ."

"Ssshh," Gail said. "Let her get it off her chest."

My sister's eyes were swirling, lost in space. "I knew this morning that someone had stolen him . . . stolen me. He was no Red," she whispered. "He was a good man. He wanted to live right and he had been with the Reds, in Spain, you know, but there were so many Reds in Spain."

Gail said, "He wasn't a Red?"

"Yes. He was a Red. There's nothing wrong with being a Red. Except in the eyes of God."

"Sis," I said, "why don't you go lie down for a while."

Kathleen aimed her eyes at Gail. "We were close. There was nothing wrong between us. Do you believe that?"

"Yes."

"Can you find him?"

"I don't know what I can do. I can prod the police a little."

"Could you. . . . Could you put an announcement in your newspaper? Joel Kangas. . . . Husband to Kathleen Kangas and Father of Carl and Shirley. . . . Man Missing! All in big bold type and you could say that anyone who's seen him please call the family. Yes, you could do that!"

"I'll try," Gail said. "My editor has the say-so. I can't promise you. I'll try."

"I'd thank you."

And Gail said good-bye with her face and her voice and I followed her and we shut the front door behind us and Kathleen killed the parlor light and we stood under the small circle the porchlight cast. Across the street the tailing dump appearing and disappearing in the snow. We lit our cigarettes.

"I hate this darn snow," she said.

"Yeah," I said.

She said I should buy her a cocktail at the Finlen. The Finlen was by all accounts the classiest place in town to drink a cocktail.

She drove quickly, carefully.

"How'd you go to work for the *Standard*?"

"I couldn't get a job at the Seattle *Post-Intelligencer*."

"Oh."

"I've been out of school two years. The *Standard* isn't so bad. I get to cover all the courthouse beat; crime, anyway."

She said she was twenty-six. I said I was twenty-four. I said I went to the School of Mines at night and studied mechanical engineering.

The Finlen Hotel cocktail lounge was about a quarter full, eleven thirty Wednesday night.

"I wonder why Kangas went to Spain," she said. "All that seems so long ago."

Our coats were wet so I hung them over the next booth to drip there. Gail wanted a manhattan. I ordered a Canadian Club and beer.

When the drinks arrived, we downed them in three gulps and put the glasses on the waitress's tray. "Another," I said. "I needed that."

"You want a fresh cherry?" the waitress asked Gail.

"No, I'll use this one."

"Joel went to Spain because he didn't want to be dead anymore," I said.

"That's a fine reason to go to war."

"Yeah," I said. I peeled the label off my beer bottle. It came off pretty slick.

"Dust Devlin," she mused. "I'll bet I can find out about him."

A guy at the bar spotted her and waved, real hard. He was drunk.

"You spend much time at the courthouse?"

She spoke very seriously. "I'm a reporter. I'm a woman reporter. I begged for months to get away from the society page. I spend hours and hours at the courthouse because I'm afraid they just might decide a woman can't handle the job." When she wasn't smiling, she looked like a homesteader's daughter: shy, plain, stubborn as hell.

"You like the work, then."

"Sometimes yes, sometimes no. I guess it's good experience. A couple months ago, I covered the Steve Hoar case. He shot his father-in-law and wife before he put the shotgun under his chin. They lived in one of those tenements on East Galena Street. People all over those two-story wooden porches in back and blood all over the walls. My editor made me go into the murder room. I couldn't eat for two days."

The drunk was bearing down on us. He signaled again, hoping to find a safe mooring.

"H'lo, Gail. How's she goin'?"

"Frank Coad."

Blue Kuppenheimer suit. Wide, soft lapels. Round little melon belly. About forty. His thin hair combed forward over his widow's peak. He was the county prosecuting attorney. I knew him by sight but not to talk to.

"Aren't you gonna ask me to sit down?"

"We were having a private conversation, Frank."

He sat down anyway and stuck out his hand. What do you do? I shook it.

"I'm about four belts over the line," he announced. "And I saw you sitting over here and decided I'd come over and say hello. What are friends for? Down the hatch. Waitress! Another round over here. On me."

"I got to work tomorrow," I said. "Thanks anyway."

"Oh hell," he said. "The night's young."

I said, "One of the ball bearings on a hoist motor is big around as a baseball and it weighs fifteen pounds."

"That's all right. No offense. You're in the mines, then."

"Jimmy Mullholland."

"Hi, Jim. Frank Coad." He stuck out his hand again. "We've met."

"Oh?" He retracted his hand. "But it was Gail I came over to see. How you doin' Gail? We miss you down at the club."

"I don't cover society anymore, Frank. You'd see me often enough in the courthouse if you spent more time there." Her smile took the sting out of what she'd said.

He elbowed my ribs. "Not a minute more'n I have to. Shitty old place. S'cuse." He fronted Gail. "I liked it better when you used to come out to the country club.

Little cub reporter, right out of college." To me: "Isn't she cute? Cuter'n a bug's ear?"

Gail said, "Oh, darn."

I started to tell him to beat it but Gail got a funny expression on her face and kicked me under the table.

"Frank," she said, sweet as pie, "you mind if I ask you something? I know you get around."

"Sure, kiddo," he beamed. "Anything I know. Anything you wanna know. All you have to do is ask."

Later on, Gail told me she had three brothers. Poor helpless female in a world of rough men. That was the kind of guile Frank Coad was getting from Gail Stinson when she asked, "Frank, you ever hear anything about a miner named Kangas? Joel Kangas."

Frank's eyes sobered up. His face developed political overtones. He patted her hand. "Well, Gail," he said, "I'd hate to have you go and write up a story your editor couldn't print. I'm feelin' sociable. Now why don't we just have a nice little drink."

He started looking around for the waitress and Gail took his hand in hers and said, "Please, Frank. Off the record." Frank was worried about me so Gail said, "He's my cousin."

"Thanks for the drink," I said.

"Yeah," Gail said. "Thanks."

He clinked his glass with Gail's but ignored mine. He looked off into space. "Oh, I guess Kangas is one of the biggest Reds in Butte. Him, and a few others up at the Hall. Five or six of 'em. They're the leaders. And those poor dumb goons—the working stiffs—they listen to those guys. Can you beat that?"

"How many Reds are there, Frank? Here. In this town."

"In the Party? I dunno. Maybe a hundred." He shrugged. "Could be a thousand of 'em."

Gail said, "That's a lot of Reds, Frank."

"Oh hell!" He waved his arm. "This town's always been a Red town. Biggest Red town west of Moscow." He reconsidered. "They got a lot of Reds in San Francisco too. Seattle too."

"So what's this Kangas up to?" Puzzled little girl Gail Stinson. "What do they want, Frank?"

He laughed, "Hell, how would I know? He's a nut case like the rest." He lowered his voice. He said, "There's people keepin' an eye on him."

"Who?"

He got coy. "Oh, I don't know, honey. Why ask me? Nobody tells me anything."

"Who?"

"Well, put it together. The Reds want a strike. This Kangas is yellin' his head off. Strike! Strike! Strike! Now, honestly, do you think this town needs another copper strike?"

He was staring me right in the face. "No," I said.

"That's right. Same thing all the miners say. It's those fuckin' Reds." He squeezed Gail's hand. "Excuse my language," he said.

"Maybe somebody ought to get rid of the bastards," I said. I didn't feel sick saying it either. I felt real excited somehow and very fast and light. "Like someone got rid of Frank Little."

His sober eyes on me. Cold sober. "Well, kid," he said slowly, "don't get me wrong. I admire your spirit. It's boys like you won the war. We took care of the Nazis and the Japs, and we got plenty left to take care of the Reds too."

"I was deferred," I said.

"Oh, yeah? Well, I tried to enlist but I had a hernia. They wouldn't take me." He smiled the smile of a man with a hernia.

"3-7-77," I said.

Gail found a cigarette and waited for me to light it. "What's that?" she asked.

Frank said, "3 feet wide, 7 feet long and 77 inches deep. The size of a man's grave. The vigilantes signed all their warnings 3-7-77." He drew the numbers in the moisture on the side of his highball glass. "We don't need no vigilantes anymore," he went on. "All we need is good Americans. We let the good Americans know who these Reds are and they'll take it from there. All we got to do is let Americans know who their enemies are."

"Where is he?" I asked.

"Who?"

"Joel Kangas."

He crinkled his forehead. "Hell, I dunno. Try the Union Hall. Try his house. Why?" He got worried and talked fast, "Hey, kid, I didn't mean nothin' talkin' to you. I don't want you layin' a glove on Kangas. There's enough people around interested in him."

"Who's interested?" Gail asked.

"Well," he smiled, "I wouldn't be too unhappy if all the Reds hired a special train to haul them away from here. I don't think the Company'd cry too much. Come to think of it, I don't know anybody who'd miss 'em."

I said, "I heard there was a cop named Dust Devlin. . . ." But Frank Coad had other things on his mind and didn't answer. He slid his body deeper into the booth and had Gail cornered.

"Say, Gail," he said, "you still got that Betty Grable

swimsuit? The low-down one? Why don't you come out to the club next week and we. . . ."

"Frank," she laughed, "it's winter. It's an outdoor pool."

"You like to skate?"

"Excuse me, Mac," I said. "I think it's time you left."

"Now, who the hell are you to tell me whether I should go or stay?"

"I'm Jimmy Mullholland. I've got twenty years on you. I ain't drunk. I work with my hands eight hours a day. I don't like your looks, pal."

"Oh, hell, kid," he laughed. "You ain't got nothin'. You want to work tomorrow?" He put his hand on Gail's arm so I punched him in the shoulder. I hit bone. He blanched. I blanched. My knuckles hurt.

He stood up, white faced, jostling the table and spilling our drinks.

"Please," Gail said. "Please don't."

I smiled at Frank Coad though I wouldn't have shaken hands with him. His eyes glared at me, and from time to time he let go his shoulder and made fists. I didn't care because he was backing away.

The spilled drinks were spreading all over the table and Gail was hurrying to get out.

"You shit," Frank said.

I took hold of the table and shoved it away and the bartender was coming toward us and Frank Coad retreating as I got up. We got the hell out of there.

Outside, it had stopped snowing. The stars were out.

Gail was rubbing her handkerchief at the spot on her suit. She handed me the car keys. "You drive."

After we'd gone a few blocks, I said, "I'm sorry."

"That was ugly in there. It didn't have to be ugly. You

shouldn't have hit him. Frank Coad's an important man."

"I see you're learning already," I said, sourly.

She replaced her handkerchief in her purse and snapped it shut. "I didn't want to fight with you too," she said. The note of determination in her voice meant she wouldn't either.

After a while I asked her where she got the sapphire. It turned out her father was an amateur prospector. He'd found the stone in a placer sluice and given it to her when she was a little girl. "It's flawed," she said. "Just a keepsake."

I beelined toward my home. It was after one A.M. and I'd done as much walking tonight as I wanted to.

Her voice surprised me, it was so quiet and precise. "Kangas. The strike. Dust Devlin. Did you know the Company owns most of the newspapers in Montana?"

"Yeah. I've heard that."

"It's true enough. I like my job, Jimmy Mullholland." Then, after a pause, she said, almost wistfully, "I wonder where Kangas is. I wonder if he's in trouble."

"If he wasn't he'd have turned up by now." I pulled up in front of my father's darkened house. Tonight it looked poorer than usual. "Thanks for the lift," I said.

"Maybe there's a story here I can use," she said. "I just don't know."

"Well, thanks a lot," I said. "Thanks for all your help."

Impulsively she took my arm. "I'll try, Jimmy. I'll do what I can."

So, we left it at that. Her taillights were gone before I had the door unlocked.

At six A.M., my father shook me awake. "On your feet now, Jimmy boy. Jesus Christ."

Right.

The morning was easy enough, though a couple of the other machinists scored laughs off me. I was turning wheel hubs from one of the mine locomotives on the brake-drum lathe. A mound of fine black steel shavings pouring over my shoes.

When the noon whistle blew, I went outside, hunkered down against the shaft house, unwrapped my sorry bologna sandwich and watched Walker and Burke stroll across the mineyard. It was five below and the air rose up out of the shaft and froze on the cages at the shafthead.

"Say," Burke asked. "What is that sandwich?"

"Sure," Walker said, "you should get married, Jimmy. It's a shame for a workin' man to be eatin' a lunch like that."

"A cold pasty, with some salt, pepper and ketchup," Burke suggested.

"Or corned beef, cut thick."

"Or a couple ham sandwiches, thick and greasy."

"So the juice runs over your chin."

I threw my sandwich out into the mineyard. I thought the sparrows would find it and eat it. "Joel Kangas didn't come home," I said. "Nobody's seen him since you boys talked to him last, at Spillum's."

Burke stuck his hands in his pockets. "Yeah, we heard something about that."

Walker lit a cigarette and, as a second thought, offered me one. I took it. "We never saw him after that. He was goin' on shift, that's all we know."

"I don't know no different," Walker said.

"I been thinkin'," I said. "I been picturin' Joel gettin' into his car and drivin' up the Hill and somehow, between Spillum's and the punch clock, he vanishes. No-body's seen him. Not him or his car either."

"Let's go inside," Walker said. "Jesus, it's cold."

I held the door to the machine shop. As Burke brushed by me, he said, "We just *bet* on the Indian, Jimmy. We never were particular pals of his."

I walked over to the brake-drum lathe and flipped the micrometer lever back and forth. The fine black shavings from the morning's work were pooled on the floor like oily black sand.

The two of them lined up behind me. "Don't neglect yourself, Jimmy," Walker said. "Sometimes it ain't too wise to take a punch at the wrong sort of person. If you catch my drift."

"I went through the School of Mines myself, Jimmy."

"It's a good school, Jimmy."

"A man should improve himself. You can do anything if you want to bad enough."

"If you've got a job."

Burke agreed that a job was real important. He said him and me were goin' down the hole. So we climbed into the cage. Burke yelled, "Cut the rope," and the bottom of my stomach jumped into my throat like it always does.

The Speculator Mine was out of kilter. Just slightly. Just enough so we went about our work a little pissed off all the time.

The main hoist-motor clutch was broken—the clutch ring had flown apart—so neither of the main hoists was working. We were waiting for a new clutch ring to get here from St. Louis, but meantime, the Speculator miners had to hike from the Granite Mountain shaft—a good half mile—to the workface in the Spec. We'd hooked up a chippy cage in the small shaft compartment, but it wouldn't hold more than two men at a time and there were four hundred miners working each shift at the Spec.

All the ore came out the Granite Mountain too.

Burke and me were standing on each other's feet as we dropped down the shaft to the 2900.

Gray. We were dropping into the gray. We flashed by the shaft stations, each lit with electric lights dangling from the ceilings of massive gray rock rooms.

Once somebody in the mine office told me we took half a million tons of ore out of the Spec each year and I guess it was true. There must have been fifty mines working on the Hill just then and the Spec was probably fifth or sixth busiest.

When we braked at the 2900, I put my toolbox out on the steel floor of the station before I got off myself and Burke said, "Jesus, Jimmy. Get a move on. You musta really hung one on last night."

"You mindin' my business now?"

He took my shoulder. The light bounced off gray walls and Burke's face was gray too, and his hands.

"They was askin' me about you. A word to the wise?"

"Christ, Burke," I said. "You made your fuckin' point. I heard you."

We hitched a ride on an ore train and rode it a thousand yards down the main tunnel. All the fire doors were closed and Burke rode the head of the train and opened them. I rode the drag and closed them after us. Usually we left the fire doors open so the ore trains could highball, but we were worried about fire. The Gem Mine, south of us, had a fire two months ago and fumes got into the Speculator and killed a couple foremen on the 3100. So a couple crews sealed off the Gem tunnels with concrete bulkheads. For good measure, they sealed off the connecting tunnels to all the other southern mines too. That left the Spec connected to only the Badger and the Granite Mountain. The three mines were the farthest north on the Hill, isolated, lonely outposts.

Burke asked me how my father was feeling. I said he was OK but his coughing was worse. I guess Burke was thinking about fires too. That was my father's job; walking all through the mine, checking for fire. Sometimes fires that were bulkheaded off twenty years ago ate right through the bulkhead and broke out again.

We edged through the narrow tunnel into the main stope. Both buzzies were broke down. Burke left me alone to do my work. I disconnected the compressed-air lines, opened my tool box and got at it. There was nobody hauling ore out of the stope so I had the cavernous cool room to myself. I worked on the buzzies until my shift was done.

After I got showered, I gave Gail a call.

No, the cops hadn't found Joel. Yes, she'd found out something about Dust Devlin.

She said we'd meet after dinner, drive up to the steam generating plant and talk to Ketchel.

I ate with my father. Baked beans. He shredded a hunk of lettuce and poured Kraft Blue Cheese dressing on it.

My father had all his pals asking about Joel, but nobody knew a damn thing. I guess he was pretty upset because he started telling me things about Joel he didn't believe. I guess he was worried for Kathleen and the kids—maybe Joel's absence had stolen something from the orderly, dignified progress of Old Jim Mullholland's dying.

He said Joel had run off with a whore. "A stiff dick ain't got no conscience, Jimmy," he said. "But when you come unstuck and are lyin' beside the floozy, that's when you start rememberin' your kids' laughter and your wife's good grub."

I turned on the radio for the *Telephone Hour*. My father loved the lush music they played.

Gail was pretty quiet as we drove up Anaconda Road. She had something on her mind, but I didn't press her. It'd come out sooner or later.

It was colder, the slush had frozen and her tires were slipping and whining on the icy road.

We drove past the high board fences around the mineyards. RESTRICTED AREA. They still had searchlights inside the mineyards from the war.

"My editor won't print the notice your sister wants," she said.

"Uh."

The car lurched forward every time its tires caught a nice patch of sand.

"He said I shouldn't waste my time on the Kangas story," she said.

I didn't say anything. I didn't want to make it easier for her to quit.

"I'm a very careful person, Jimmy. It pays to be careful. If you want to do anything the least bit unusual, like being a career woman, you have to be extra careful."

The road was full of potholes from the ore trucks. Every pothole was filled with ice.

"I know what you're sayin'," I said. "Because I'm the

same way myself. Not Joel. He takes plenty of chances. He said to me once that that's the only way human beings win anything."

"Politics," she said. The way she said it, politics were about as substantial as candy floss.

"You find out anything about Dust Devlin?"

She wrinkled her eyes against the sun bouncing off the ice. "He's been in Butte before. He's a troubleshooter for the Company. He calls himself a 'labor negotiator,' but he's never been near a bargaining session."

The Missouri River Substation was a brick building, shaped like a boxcar half a block long and a hundred feet high.

A smokestack at each end. Along the long walls, twenty-foot arched windows, floor to ceiling, black with dirt: opaque. You could see the lights were on inside, but that was about it. We parked in front.

"Ugh," Gail said.

The door was steel, framed in dirty brick. I pushed and it swung open.

One big barnlike room: the corners hidden in the dusk, behind the electrical transformers, somewhere in the past, somewhere in the future.

One wall was glass. The arched glass cathedral windows rising above us as slick as black marble.

The facing wall held the gauges: clusters of nickel and brass on the red-brick pillars which separated the low white-brick boilers. Hissing and grumbling.

And the water pipes and the fat steam pipes and the electrical cables and the steady hum of the transformers and the faint stink of ozone.

Kooteney Ketchel was sitting on one of the two chairs pulled back against the wall.

He sat there with his hands on his knees. Perfectly motionless.

I swear our feet didn't make any sound on the slab concrete floor but he turned his head to watch us and I raised one hand in a halfhearted greeting. He just sat there as we approached, until we got close enough to see his eyes. Then he blinked, once.

The two chairs: one full, the other frail, yellow and green, empty.

"Hi," I said. "They haven't found you a new partner."

He was staring at Gail. His stare wasn't exactly rude, but it wasn't exactly polite either.

"This is Miss Stinson," I said. "She works for the Montana *Standard*. She's a newspaper reporter."

"Is this where you punch in?" she asked. Old octagonal time-clock on the wall. A small box for the cards beside it. She pulled out Joel's card and handed it to me. Nothing. Gail put the card back and walked around, inspecting the steam and electrical gauges Kooteney and Joel had monitored. Three of the six boilers were running. The temperature gauges read: 4325, 4400, 4350. The faint hissing of the steam.

Kooteney Ketchel walked over to stand between us. "He never punched in," I said.

The hiss of the steam. The hum of the generators.

I never meant to ask him, but his silence ruined me. "Say, Kooteney," I said, "all night long here, just the two of you. What do you and Joel talk about?"

"Did you know Joel is a Red?" Gail asked.

In the silence, I could hear the mine train shunting ore cars a couple of blocks away.

Ketchel pointed at a furnace. "Joel threw a cat in there once," he said. "Number three furnace. He was already dead."

He pulled a clipboard off the wall and began to check the gauges, noting the readings.

He was staring at the boiler gauges when we left.

Outside was cold, snowy and quiet. I felt giddy, like I wanted to throw up. We got in the car. I slid behind the wheel, but I didn't start the engine. Anaconda Road lay out below us snaking between the mines and the houses. The lights glowing all over the city. I started the motor.

"Well," I said, "what do you think?"

I could only see the profile of her face, white and set. Behind her face, the faint glow from the windows of the plant.

"I think he's in that furnace," she said.

5

HOPE IS A SKILL; the ability to discount the evidence. I'm pretty good at it. I can usually find some thread that looks promising.

But I had this picture stuck in my mind: Kooteney Ketchel with Joel in his arms. Kooteney having trouble stuffing a body through the narrow furnace door. The blast of heat. The sweat. The heart jumping like it wants to lunge out of the chest cavity. In that picture, Joel is already dead. There is another picture where he is still alive but the picture's defective and I can force it out of my mind most of the time. Hope. I can even hope for something that's over.

It was two A.M. before I hit the sack and I didn't get much sleep in the three hours I lay there before the telephone rang. The phone ringing was a relief, like the house lights coming up after watching a movie that's made you sick.

"Jimmy? Is that you, Jimmy?" Gail's voice.

"Yeah. Who'd you expect?"

I was barefoot, padding around the phone in a circle on the cold linoleum floor.

"They found his car. Whitehead just called."

"No shit. Where?"

"Down at the dogtrack."

"Okay." I thought for a moment but kept moving. I had to piss. "I guess we better go down and take a look. Can you pick me up?"

She could and did. Five thirty in the morning and still snowing.

Tick, tick of the wipers. The lightpoles getting farther and farther apart until there weren't any. The purr of the tires. Driving into our circle of light. No better idea of what was real than a horse in blinders.

Gail was tired. Her eyes were nervous. "I guess Whitehead found it himself," she said.

"Uh."

"He said he'd been driving all over town. He said it was easier to find a car than a man. He said he's personally checked out every '38 blue Plymouth ragtop in town. He wants the credit."

"Ah, hell. He found it, didn't he?"

They had the wrecker backed up to Joel's Plymouth and the rear of the car was in the air. Four or five burly, bulky cops stamping their feet and cursing their luck. The light revolving on the top of the wrecker, yellow and red. The muffler belching out puffs of white fog which hung there like frozen cabbage.

They'd broken a wind wing to get into the car.

As soon as Deputy Whitehead saw us coming, he went over to one of the other cops and started up a "don't interrupt" conversation. He was telling another deputy how to search Joel's car. The deputy had searched a few cars in his day and kept saying, "I know. I know."

The dogtrack grandstand was behind us, but I couldn't see the whole of it because of the swirling snow. The snow lashed my ankles.

"You see any sign of Joel Kangas?" Gail asked.

Bob Whitehead finished his instructions and turned to her. He wouldn't ignore her. I guess he was a gentleman.

"No. The search didn't turn him up."

"You check the grandstand?" I asked.

"Yeah, we checked the grandstand."

Gail had her notebook out. She said, "You found him, uh. . . ."

"When I got the missing persons report, I noticed that Kangas had last been seen in his car on his way to work at the Missouri River Steam Generating Plant. You know, a car is much harder to conceal than a man, so I began searching for the car. I drove all through this town and. . . ."

"You already told me that," Gail said. "About knowing the location of every blue '38 Plymouth. . . ."

"I was looking for a blue '38 Plymouth convertible, license Montana 1-4487. I must have inspected every 1938 Plymouth from here to Anaconda." He made a noise like a laugh. He continued, "I remembered that often cars are abandoned out here at the dogtrack, once the track closes for the winter, so I drove down at about one A.M."

I looked around. There was one other abandoned junker, mounded with snow. Come spring, the dog-track manager would have it towed away.

"How long's it been here?" Gail asked.

"I don't make guesses."

The wrecker had the Plymouth rolling now. "From the looks of the snow, it came down here tonight," I said.

"You a cop?" Whitehead asked.

"Naw," I said. "I ain't smart enough to be a cop."

Gail put her question between us. "Did you find any tracks? Could you see any footprints? Tracks from another car maybe? It had to take two men to get the Plymouth down here. One to drive the Plymouth and another to bring him back."

"In case you haven't noticed, it's snowing. Snow covers tracks up. It fills them in."

The deputy kicked the toe of his shoes into the snow and some snow stuck on it and he wiggled his foot until the snow fell off. He stared at my face. I don't know what he was hoping to find there. I arranged my features into a fairly pleasing expression. He snorted in disgust. "Tracks," he said. "Shit."

The wrecker was pulling Joel's car off to the police garage. The car looked like a foolish machine. The other cops were getting into their cars.

"Say," Gail said. "There's something I'd like to talk to you about."

"What?"

She shrugged. "It probably isn't anything important, but. . . . Say, it's awful cold out here. Couldn't we go somewhere a little warmer?"

Bob Whitehead looked at her. He made a face he didn't care if we saw. "I was goin' to get some breakfast," he said. "You got something more to talk to me about?"

"Well, I hope so."

"All right. Spillum's is open."

"I know," I said, but he didn't hear me.

When he got to the plowed pavement again, he turned on his red light and siren, so we were five minutes behind him. By the time we walked in, he had his bacon and eggs in front of him and his coat dripping water over the other chair at his small table.

I pulled up a couple dry chairs. He ate. The clock on the wall said seven, so I told them I wanted steak and eggs for breakfast and they should make me up a lunch. I was due on shift in an hour. Gail just wanted coffee.

Deputy Whitehead ate. From time to time he sprinkled salt and pepper over his bacon, eggs and homefries. Then he ate again.

"I think Kooteney Ketchel killed Joel Kangas," Gail said. "I think he stuffed him in one of those furnaces."

Deputy Whitehead ate. He belched. He wiped his face with a napkin.

"You've got a little egg on the corner of your mouth," Gail said.

"Where?" He dabbed with his napkin.

"The other side. Just at the corner. There. That's got it."

"He never punched in," Whitehead said.

"I know. Maybe Ketchel hit him on the head before he punched in. Then he moved the car. Or maybe he waited until morning to move the car."

Bob Whitehead lit a cigarette. A Kool. "I thought of that," he said.

"Well?"

"Well, nothing. It's not my case."

"You found Joel's car," I said.

"No shit," he said.

"Well?"

He wadded up his napkin and dropped it on the floor. "Just followin' up a missing persons complaint," he said. "Look, I been told. Some very big people are interested in this Kangas."

"So?"

"So let them find him. Besides, they ain't gonna shut down that furnace anyway. I already asked."

Gail was surprised. "You what?"

"I already talked to them at the Company and the word is neg-a-tory. They are not gonna close down all the drys and the Company offices for twenty-four hours while the furnaces cool down on the outside chance they'll find the remains of a damn Commie they'd be glad to be rid of anyway."

"But you could order them to shut down," Gail said.

"Sure, me and a couple divisions of marines."

"How about a court order? You know I'd love to write a story for the *Standard* telling how Deputy Bob Whitehead of the Sheriff's Department stole a march on all the other law-enforcement officers in town to solve a murder. Front page. What a story."

He said, "Don't pull my leg." The look he gave her was a mix of puzzlement and respect. "Ain't you been told to lay off? Hell, kid. You work hard. You're doin' a good job up at the courthouse. You want to throw all that away?"

Gail was folding and unfolding her napkin. I was all ears. "Everybody's got to find out how far they can go sometime in their life," she said. "I might as well get it over with."

He heaved himself out of his chair and inspected her with his little eyes. "Not far," he said, and then he left.

"Could you really put him on the front page?" I asked.

"Jimmy," she said to me, "sometimes I don't like you very much. When you ask questions you already know the answer to, just for the sake of the noise."

So we had a quiet breakfast, the two of us. She said that maybe one of the eastern magazines would run a story on Butte, but none of the Montana papers would touch it with a ten-foot pole. She said she already had job feelers out to the Seattle *Intelligencer* and the Great Falls *Tribune*. "I told you I was careful," she said with a pained smile.

I got to work fifteen minutes early, which pleased my foreman some. It was the last thing I did that pleased him.

All the mine electricians were down the hole, setting up a new transformer station on the 2600. I'm not much of an electrician, but the foreman told me to break down the main fan motor and clean the commutator brushes. I guess he didn't have anyone else to send.

The Speculator was a downdraft shaft. We pushed the clean air down our shaft with a thirty-three horse Aerodyne fan and it circulated through all the workings before it exhausted up the Granite Mountain shaft.

It was damn cold and the wind was blowing and the fan sat in the mineyard beside the shaft and I burned my fingers on my wrenches getting the fan housing off. I pried the brushes open against their springs and wiped the brushes with carbon tet. The carbon tet took all the feeling out of my fingers and I was slipping and bashing my hands.

Walker came over and watched me for a few minutes before he said, "You ought to get some first aid for those cuts, Jimmy."

Well, I wasn't in a mood for him. "Fuck it. Why you so interested in my welfare, *Mister* Walker?"

"Oh, Jimmy—it's because you've got such an interesting mind."

"Somebody tell you to keep an eye on me?"

He grinned. "Now, what do you think?"

I wiped my hands on my pants and left some blood there. "You do anything they want, Walker? When they say 'shit' you say, 'When, sir? Where, sir?' "

He lost his grin. "Take it easy, Jimmy boy. The Company never canned Kangas because the union would have made a stink. Who'd make a stink about you?"

"And what've you got with Ketchel? You interested in his mind too?"

And I guess he was caught between something and something because he stuttered, "I never . . . I just bet. . . . You stay the fuck away from Ketchel. That's the word from downtown, Mullholland."

Well, I was pretty hot too. So I said, real quick, "Maybe you helped Ketchel kill Joel Kangas." I knew better than that, but I said it anyway.

He said, "I'll pretend I never heard that, Jimmy." He even turned to walk away.

He didn't get far. "Why pretend, you dumb son of a bitch."

Well, he turned around at that one. "Let me see your rustling card," he said.

And I reached in my pocket and took out the little card and tore it in half and said, "I'll save you the trouble." And he nodded, terse, and walked away, maybe wondering if I was going to jump him, but I was staring at the two scraps of cardboard in my hand and feeling very tired.

I said my good-byes to the other machinists and collected my personal tools. There weren't too many of them. About thirty dollars' worth, I figured. Somebody said, "You don't have to work for the Company to hold a job," and I said something cheerful though we both knew better. I could be a pump jockey. I thought of that.

Somewhere on the way home, I tossed my lunch into somebody's garbage can because I wasn't hungry anymore. I thought I couldn't afford too many more gestures. You eat what you can, not what you want.

Father McDevitt's Buick was parked in front of Kathleen's house. It had a little sign in the front window. CLERGY.

Father Origen McDevitt had a collection of the worst jokes I ever heard, a mincing, pious manner, a heavy hand with the "Special Collections for the Distressed Among Us," an ignorance so dazzling it shone, a face like the map of Ireland, a great pile of black hair he wore in a pompadour, and the sweet ability to ease pain.

He was in the kitchen with my father and sister. I was glad to see him.

"Hello, Jimmy," he said. "Have you news?"

"No," I said. "Unless you don't know about them finding his car."

"Miss Gail Stinson called us," my father said, underlining "Miss." "You should have called us yourself, Jimmy."

I nodded my head that yes I should have.

"You are drawing away from us," my sister said.

I thought she was probably right, but I didn't want to go into it.

Father McDevitt said, "You look tired, Jimmy."

I said that I was. I stared at them, my sister and my father, the ones I loved. "I've looked," I said.

"It's a terrible thing," Father McDevitt said.

"Joel didn't run off," Kathleen said. A fact. She could have been announcing the weight of a brick.

"No, child," Father McDevitt said. "He never seemed to be a man who would do such a thing."

I rubbed my forehead. Clumsy move of a clumsy old bear. "I quit," I said.

It didn't register. My father's face was waiting for more info.

"I quit my job," I said.

"Now that was a hell of a thing to do," my father said. Then he said, "Excuse me, Father." My father stood up. He again said, "Excuse me, Father," opened the kitchen door, and nodded me through after him. He led me into the bedroom: It was really much too small for the two of us. Our breath intermingling. Each body, in that space, trying to reject the other. "Why did you hand them your walking papers?" he asked.

"It's kind of hard to explain."

He waited. He had all the time he needed.

"I got mad," I said. "Fucking Walker."

"What did Mr. Walker do that would make you give up a paying job with your sister's husband missing and your father barely able to work?"

My father always could put things in a nutshell.

"He went too far," I said. "They're watching us."

"The Company."

I said yes.

He closed his eyes for a moment. His eyelids were

old. They'd die when the rest of him did. "Jimmy," he said after a while, "I went down to the payroll office this morning to get Joel's check. He'd worked three days, you know, before he. . . . So I went down to the payroll office. They said I'd have to go to the fifth floor and get authorization before they could give me his check. That was easy enough, though they made me wait at the counter with my hat in my hands." He coughed. I said nothing. He resumed, "And perhaps it was the waiting, but I started to get a little hot under the collar and I asked one of the girls behind the counter if I could talk to the safety engineer. As luck would have it, he was free. H. P. Lenville. A great man, he is, too, wearing those wingtip shoes with the little holes in the toes. 'Mr. Lenville,' I said to him, 'I am James Michael Mullholland, and I work as a firebug at the Speculator Mine, and I would like to bring something to your attention.' He was so polite, Jimmy, you should have seen it. He complimented me, even, on coming up to the office to talk to him, because, as he said, he liked to keep on top of conditions in the mines. He had an accident chart on the wall. I knew some of the names. Carl Babcock, he was on that list—a fall of rock—and Carl was dead. I have worked with Carl. I looked at the list of this year's dead and it made my heart sick, I knew so many of them. Oh, it's a hell of a thing, getting your living in the mines."

I could see my breath. "Strong back, weak mind," I said.

My father put his eyes on mine. "I spoke about the bulkheads at the Spec," he said. "Mr. H. P. Lenville: safety engineer."

"Oh, Christ! Now, why the hell'd you go and do a thing like that for!"

"Because I been in a couple of fires and you ain't!" he snapped.

"Yeah," I said. "Yeah."

"In '32, the Neversweat. I was working in the discovery stope and I smelled the smoke and I dropped everything and ran like hell. I got out. Jimmy, I don't run so good anymore. Eight men weren't so lucky as me and we had to put on the rescue airpacks and go down and drag them out of there. They were on the 1100. They was red in the face from tryin' to breathe. I knew them all but I couldn't tell who they were because their faces were so twisted.

"If there's a fire in the Spec, we'll all be trapped. The shaft ain't workin' and the bulkheads—all the fire exits are sealed."

"So what? What did Lenville say?"

"He thanked me. Oh, he was nice as pie. He said he had some meeting to go to and so long as the supervisor knew, I'd done my job. He asked why I was coughing. I told him I had the Con. And he asked me if it wasn't unusual for a man to keep on working when he had silicosis. He asked me what would happen if I collapsed one night on duty. He asked me what would happen if there was a fire and I got a whiff of it. He said I'd drop like a stone. I wouldn't be any good to the other miners then."

"Yeah," I said. "God damn it!"

He flushed. "Don't get mad at me," he said. "I'm still bringin' home a check."

"What in the hell did you go bother them for?"

"I got mad. Where in the hell are you gonna find another job?"

"I've got money in the bank. Enough to hold me and get some to Kathleen if she needs it."

"She will."

We glared at each other. We loved each other. He walked back to the kitchen and I followed him.

Kathleen's kitchen was green.

Father McDevitt's suit was black. Blacker and duller than his black pomaded hair.

My sister was black with grief.

They were seated at the table. He was holding both her hands.

Father McDevitt had got her grief out of her heart and into her hands. I don't know how.

She was crying.

We stopped in the kitchen doorway.

All of her blackness flowing along their linked hands along his arms into his dusty black suit.

His lips were moving.

He was saying, "Hail Mary full of grace. The Lord is with thee. Blessed art thou amongst women and blessed . . ."

I had tears in my eyes. I also had a tremendous erection. I was ashamed.

I backed out of there. I patted my father on the back. I wanted to tell him I was sorry; that I loved him; but I didn't trust my voice, so I patted his shoulder again. I think he didn't notice.

Kathleen's face was quite beautiful, quite empty, her life at a maximum and minimum.

I pulled my rubbers on outside. I couldn't see very well, but I could feel the cold well enough.

I thought I'd go home and get some sleep, but that decision wasn't mine to make.

It was waiting for me when I stepped outside: Dust Devlin's maroon Buick Century with scuffed whitewalls and two or three dings in the front fender. It hadn't been washed in months and the mudsplash from its front wheels started at the fenderwells and swooped up over the doors.

When I hit the sidewalk, he unlatched the door and shoved it open. Damn thing blocked half the sidewalk. The motor was running quietly. Devlin's expression was even and calm. "If you ain't gettin' in, I'd be obliged if you shut the door."

"Where we goin'?"

A look of annoyance. "I ain't exactly sure. But we ain't goin' anywhere jawin' about it. If you get my drift." His last words were very like a snarl.

There wasn't anything in my mind except the bright notes of the "Butte Polka" and I wasn't scared of him so I got in and pulled the door to.

"Afternoon," he said.

I nodded my greeting.

He slipped the car into first and turned west on Granite Street. The snow was dancing on the snowheaps beside the road as the wind ruffled them. After a while, he asked, "You hungry?"

"Nope."

"Uh." We crossed town on back streets under the crest of the Hill. He drove pretty quick and ran a couple stop signs. Not much traffic.

We passed the few billboards outside of town and the slagheaps where the smelters used to be.

The road zigzagged up the Divide. Butte sprawled behind us, one blunt hill in a barren white plain. Butte's streets and gallowsframes were black. The rest of the world was white. The works scattered over the Hill could have been creatures grazing on the slopes of an ancient, not entirely lifeless volcano.

The road leveled out on top of the Rockies and ran straight for a while.

The Buick's circular speedometer showed sixty-five and climbing. The road was bare of snow and glare ice except for the wind-tossed snow streamers that chittered over the surface. It was a brilliant dead day; glare and black shadows. The wind thrummed against the windows. The hum of the motor. The buzz of the heater fan.

A couple miles past the Divide, Dust said, "Think of it. If you was to find just the right spot up here, you could spit and half your spit would run into the Pacific Ocean and half in the Atlantic. There's a bottle in the jockey box."

"Nope."

"Reach it for me, then."

I handed him a fifth of Old Crow. Without moving his eyes off the road, he uncapped it and had himself a swallow. "Here's to the workingman," he said.

I didn't know what to make of that so I kept still.

He pushed the bottle at me for a moment and finally leaned it against his leg. "You ain't the most talkative son of a bitch I ever met," he observed.

The steep snowbanks beside the road were flagged occasionally by the tall red poles that guided the snowplows. The sky was a curious navy blue, very intense. I was squinting against it. He kept the speedometer at seventy-five. In the summer this road was two lanes, but now only one and a half. When we passed another car, the Buick was half on, half off the hard-packed snow.

"I heard you tore up your rustling card."

"Yeah."

He had himself another swallow as the car rushed down into the Boulder Canyon; twenty miles of nasty, twisting road. He slowed to fifty-five. The sun hadn't got all the ice here and some of the corners were slick as hell.

"I've known a few muckers who did that," Dust said. "Usually they found it was hard times. Man's belly starts growling so bad he can't hear himself think."

"It got to be a burden," I said. And then got mad at myself for picking up his manner of speaking.

"It says right in the Bible that we was meant to carry burdens," he said. His hands were so light on the wheel it was like he was caressing it. We were going too fast and the dense pines in the canyon rushed past us, black on white. "What do you care about this Kangas?"

"He's my brother-in-law."

"Shit. I had me one of those. George Byrnn. Married my only sister. She's dead now. He was up at Polson working on Kerr Dam. Just a pick-and-shovel man. He was too dumb to be anything else. Made a bet with a couple Mexicans he could jump into the spillway and swim out. He was wrong. I never did bother to go up to Polson to look for him. And"—he patted the steering wheel—"they never did find him, neither."

My sudden rage dried my mouth and stiffened my neck like it was clamped in iron. His eyes were on the road, roving it. His hands were soft on the wheel.

" 'Course," he went on, "I never cared for my brother-in-law so much. Never liked the cut of the man. I suppose you're different."

I whispered, "What do you know about Joel?"

"I know he's a Red." The back end of the car twitched on a slick spot, but he saved it easily enough.

"What else?"

"There ain't much else. When a man's a Red, that's it for them. It's like bein' a priest. Once you know a man's a priest you know most of what's important about him. You know what he's gonna do. Now, your priest ain't gonna murder babies in their cribs or run no whorehouses, or get a whole lot of dumb muckers in trouble. You know where you are with priests. Same as Reds."

I closed my eyes. Joel was slipping away from me faster than the receding landscape. Suddenly, I didn't want to know any more answers. I wasn't going to like them, not one.

"Joel—" I tried, "Joel has kind of a joking way about him. He can hardly do anything without making a joke about it. But it's easy, if you know what I mean, the way he does it. Just as natural as can be."

Dust's "I don't think so" rushed right over the tail end of my words. "I think that's why he joined the Reds. He thinks he's too smart for everybody."

We tore through Basin and Boulder. We drove beside the gravel pits the gold dredger had left behind in the creek bottom. "Kangas never thought the rest of us was worth much. That's why he's laughin', boy, he's laughin' at us."

I insisted Joel could take a joke on himself as easy as he could put one on somebody else. I don't know why I said that.

Dust took another good swallow on the bottle, and waved it at me. It didn't mean anything to me. After a bit, he tucked it against his leg again.

The speedometer back at sixty-five, seventy on the straightaways. He began to hum a song through his nose, like a three-note trombone. "Ain't you curious about where I met him?" he asked suddenly. "Shit, you're curious about everything else."

I figured he'd tell me once he stopped circling around it, and I said as much. He barked a laugh at me. I guess my impudence pleased him. My neck ached.

The road climbed up onto the high plains and stayed there. Long lines of fragile snow-fence kept the snow from drifting across the highway. The ranches we passed were trampled and muddy near the barns but away from them, the snow was unmarked. My eyes hurt.

"It'll do a hundred, just like they claim," Dust volunteered. An affectionate pat on the steering wheel. "Course I never clocked it and speedometers always lie a little but I had her on the pins more than once."

The speedometer was calibrated to one hundred and ten. Even at eighty-five, the Buick rode good, not floating or anything, and the engine hum was constant; maybe a little shriller. He was working his bottle again. I kept my hands folded in my lap. Except for my rigid neck, I was relaxed as a baby.

"Where we goin'?" We'd already covered fifty miles.

"A little ride." He lifted one hand off the wheel and waggled it. "Just thought I'd get to know you better." Then he mumbled something. I think he said, "Everybody has someone to talk to."

When he saw the East Helena smokestack, he brightened, "My old stamping grounds. I been up and down every damn dirt track for miles around."

Helena, the capital, was tucked into a narrow gulch at the base of the hills. Dust slowed to a legal twenty-five and observed all the stop signs as we passed the Gothic-Victorian capitol building. "Copper and cows," he said. "That's what Montana's all about. If you don't understand that, you don't understand nothin'." A note

of scorn in his voice. He tried out his bottle again and it
still worked.

"I thought you might be taking me to see Joel," I said,
as the Buick left town.

"Now how the hell could I do that?" He took his attention off the road and, it's true, his eyes were surprised.

"Somehow I thought you might know where he is."

"Uh." The speedometer crept up again: eighty,
eighty-five, ninety. His whiskey bottle fell over onto
the seat but he didn't notice.

The steep walls and spires of Wolf Creek Canyon.
The road stayed in the bottom beside the creek. More
pines. Black holes in the frozen creek ice where the
boulders pushed through. I wished I had sunglasses.
We passed every car we came up behind, curve or no.
I thought: This man has got to age fifty without a fatal
accident. The thought gave me some comfort.

Dust coughed, politely, summoning my attention. "I
was in Butte the first time during the First War. They
was gonna strike then too. Hell, I was just a kid, twenty-
three, twenty-four."

"That ain't no kid."

He shrugged. Briefly, he looked at me, trying to place
himself at my age. The broken capillaries in his bloodshot eyes looked like roadmaps. His fingertips tapping
the steering wheel and the Buick a little sloppy on the
curves now. Here and there patches of black ice crossed
the road and they were throwing us around some.

"Kid like that thinks he's got plenty savvy. Enough as
the next man, if you catch my drift." He rubbed at his
eyes with the back of his hand. "He figures he's ready to
see the elephant. To do it up proud. And, by God! you

do!" His hand patted across the seat for his bottle. When he found it, he uncapped it and drank a toast to that kid, whoever he was.

"So," I said. "Now you're a whatchamacallit—a 'negotiator'?"

"I've got this little spread out by Lincoln," he said quickly. "Couple hundred head of the damnedest black Angus you ever seen. Some say the Hereford'll put on meat faster, but I don't see it that way."

"You told me about your little fucking spread," I said. "You were with Kooteney Ketchel. I was looking for Joel. I still ain't found him or heard a straight word where he might be."

He was too busy to answer. The Buick howled through the turns and into Wolf Creek. Twenty houses, a cowboy bar, a fancy bar. The car slid to a stop in front of the fancy bar: Frenchie's. Frenchie's was a roadhouse with a couple good-sized front windows and herds of animal heads mounted on the walls inside. As Dust cut the engine, he said, "From time to time, I do a job away from the spread. When I do, my cousin takes care of the cows. You couldn't ask to meet a nicer guy."

Frenchie's was clean and it smelled good. It was warm. Dust picked out a booth for us and sat where he could watch the road, the dark shadows of the animal heads at his back. A burly waiter took his order: burger, fries and a Highlander beer. I asked for a glass of water.

"What's a matter, you ain't hungry?" he asked, chomping into his hamburger.

I drank my glass of icewater and sucked on the ice cubes. The cold calmed my nervous stomach. "Kangas," I said.

He dropped his half-gnawed hamburger onto the plate. "Jesus Christ! What's Kangas to you? It's a nice day. Look outside. Real pretty. They got good·food in this joint. I ought to know. I eat here all the time. All you can think of is this Kangas."

"I never thought about him much before he disappeared," I said. "I thought I had all the time in the world to get to know him. I wish I had it to do all over."

His head was cocked quizzically, like a droll bear's. "Oh yeah," he said, more to himself than to me, "I know what you mean." He banged his fist down on the table and gave me the sort of nervous smile cult members give each other when they meet, by chance, in some foreign land. "Oh yeah." He summoned the waiter, who put a Highlander and frosted glass in front of me. I didn't touch it. "I wonder if you're a Red too?" he mused. That strange, sappy smile never left his face. It gave me the creeps. "Naw," he answered himself, "you ain't a Red. You haven't the stones for it."

"What fucking difference does that make?" I snapped.

He favored me with a knowing look. "Plenty. And you know it too, Mac. You know how many countries the Commies have taken over since the war? There's Poland and Latvia and Yugoslavia and . . ."

"Fuck that. Where's Joel?"

"I only met him the once. It was the morning before he disappeared."

And a wash of relief soothed me, and my neck let go of its ache and I poured myself a glass of beer and it was cold, bitter and good.

Dust had been asked to be a negotiator. No cash involved, nothing like that. He had " a lot of good friends all over the Treasure State and once in a while I do 'em a favor." When I asked what sort of favors, he grew vague. When asked for the names of his friends, very vague; though he did say the Company, the Cattleman's Association and a few of the boys in Helena shared his views. He admitted there were exceptions to every rule and some of the meanest bastards in the state worked for the Company. He said, "I lost out a time or two myself." This, he didn't amplify. When I asked him if he carried a gun he said sometimes he did and so what? There was nothing illegal about that. It depended on the occasion. When I started another question, he cut me off. "I'm gonna tell you a thing or two if you quit yappin' at me."

OK by me. He cleared his throat. His eyes attached to mine in a direct manly stare. I don't believe his eyes heard what his mouth was saying. Weakly, generally, he began talking about the strike: how a strike never did anybody any good. And how a strike never put meat on any man's table. And, for once, the union was being responsible—hell, they didn't want no strike either. It was just a few hotheads like this Kangas. Maybe he could talk to Kangas and straighten him out. Ol' Dust knew how to deal with hotheads, all right.

Dust was staying at the Finlen. Not the fanciest suite in the hotel but not the cheapest either. He figured he'd catch Joel after he came off shift so he left a wakeup call for six thirty, showered, shaved and dressed carefully. He used his badger-bristle hairbrush, because a stiff bristle stimulates the scalp. He stopped at the desk long enough to get his car brought around, went into the coffeeshop and ordered steak and eggs, sunny-side up. The steak was fine but the eggs were bright yellow, no fine white skin covering them. Sunny-side up means a fine white skin covering the yolk so Dust didn't leave a tip. The bootblack who shined his boots had a fine line of patter and his cloth snapped and popped just the way

Dust liked. The shine was twenty-five cents. Dust gave him fifty. The workman must be worthy of his hire.

The Buick was cold and the windshields were frosted over. He drove real slow up Anaconda Road, peering through the holes he'd scraped clear of ice. He wasn't in any hurry anyway. Ketchel always left the plant first and Dust wanted him to be well clear before he talked to Joel. No sense confusing the issue. About five to eight, his Buick slid right in behind Joel's old Plymouth, blocking its exit. Used to be, Kooteney would hitch a ride downtown with Joel, but these days the Indian wouldn't take anything from him, not even the time of day. Dust chuckled. He left the engine and heater on and tipped his hat over his eyes, pretending to doze. It'd have to spook Kangas, Ol' Dust waiting for him that way. It'd be to Dust's advantage and Dust never gave away any advantage, not if he could help it.

But there's times things don't turn out the way they should. A man can give the best damn ride he ever did and still get bucked off.

Kooteney Ketchel came out of the plant, saw Dust's Buick and started for it with a big dumb grin plastered all over his face. Maybe he figured Dust was here to taxi him downtown. Well, Ol' Dust knew him and the Indian shouldn't be seen together too much. Especially not by Kangas. Some of the Reds might start putting two and two together. Everybody in Butte *knew* where he stood. Better they shouldn't know about Ketchel.

So it wasn't surprising Dust was upset. Hell, he figured Ketchel would be long gone. When the big galoot came up to the car, Dust lowered the window and it stuck halfway down, like it always did when the car had been left outside all night in the cold. Like a damn fool, Dust pressed his face at the half-open window and hissed, "Go on, get out of here. Make tracks." Kangas was still inside so he had a few seconds, if only the pea-brained redskin would *move*. "Get the hell out of here. I don't want to see you around here anymore." But Ketchel's grin was slow to fade, like he just couldn't believe what he was hearing and the plant door slammed and Kangas spotted the two of them and Dust leaned back in his seat and said, "That tears it."

Kangas was all buttoned up in a plaid mackintosh. No hat. His thick black hair flopping in the wind. "You gonna move this hearse, Mac? You got me blocked in."

And Ketchel standing there like a bump on a log. He'd lost his grin, but the message hadn't reached his feet.

"This a buddy of yours, Kooteney?" Joel asked.

Kooteney shook his head, violently: no.

"This crazy son of a bitch?" Dust said. "Hell, I was just gonna ask him about the Vargas fight. I don't give a shit for him or any other teepee creeper. I just wanted to put some money on the fight."

Too late, Kooteney got the message. He started off down the Hill, lunchbox in hand. He had a long cold walk ahead of him, but he was used to it.

"You must be Kangas. Joel Kangas."

And Kangas gave him a measuring look, like he was wondering what kind of snake he was meeting and should he stomp it. "Who's askin'?"

"Name's Devlin. I'd shake with you but I can't get this damn window up or down. Every time the motor gets cold it locks up."

Joel shifted his lunchbox to his left hand. "Why don't you move this heap so I can go home?"

Dust had a specially friendly homely grin. He used it. "My friends call me Dust."

"Your friends are gonna be calling you hospitalized unless you give me room to get by."

You take your great athletes, like DiMaggio or Babe Ruth. When they're hittin', they just can't do anything wrong. It's impossible. But put them off their stride and hell, they ain't no more use than sandlot ballplayers. Everybody gets put off their stride one time or another. "I come to talk to you about the strike," Dust blurted.

Joel's mouth got tight. He pushed a lock of hair off his forehead like he was mad at it. "So you're the bastard been blowin' in Ketchel's ear," he said.

"Never met him before. I just asked him about the fight."

"Your name's Devlin. I'll remember that."

"I hear you're the only miner who wants a strike," Dust said.

"You got it right. You're damn right I want a strike. If we don't strike the Company from time to time, they get to thinking they're God Almighty. We ain't had a raise in six years or a contract since the end of the war. We don't get paid enough for the work and the work's too dangerous. We carry their damn rustling cards like they were passports of a sovereign nation."

Devlin tried to catch up to where he should be. "You won't win a strike," he said. "Hell, they got plenty copper stockpiled and the price of copper ain't so hot anyway. Even if you managed to stay off the job, they can get all the copper they need from Chile, now the Nazis ain't torpedoin' the ore boats."

Joel made a fist, but just to blow on it. "You ain't here to say that," Joel said. "That ain't the message you was paid to deliver. We get that message from the Company direct. What makes you so damn persuasive?" And Joel came up real close to the window and stared directly into Dust's smile and when he finally took his eyes away, Dust felt like a man who's been body-searched. Joel's face was tired. "I see," he said.

"You got a nice wife, couple kids. Hell, you ain't no kid yourself no more. You ought to learn to take it easier. Let some of the young bucks speak their piece."

"What's the sweetener?" Joel asked, quietly.

"What?"

"You boys always got two hands," Joel explained like it was old hat to him. "Here, the coast, Spain—same thing. You got one hand that giveth and one hand that taketh away. You're the fucker who made Kooteney nuts, aren't you."

Dust didn't say yes or no. "You afraid of him?" he asked.

Joel laughed. "I been scared so many times by so many men, I wore it out. What the hell do I have to be scared of?"

And Ol' Dust gave him a big smile to let him know who. "You'd make a good foreman," Dust said. "Older man like you."

"Sure. And what does that have to do with it? I just came off shift. I got a wife and warm bed at home. Why don't you move your car?"

"I can't promise you anything. . . ."

"Course you can't promise me anything. You can threaten me. That's what you goons are hired to do, but you can't promise me nothin' because the Company'd have to acknowledge you and they ain't gonna do that. Not ever."

"I'm a cattle rancher, myself. I've got a couple hundred head of black Angus. Blackest scoundrels you ever saw."

"Move the car."

Dust was thinking that maybe he could persuade his friends to make Kangas a shiftboss. He didn't know, but he was willing to give it a try. "What do you want?" he asked.

"Everything. Everybody wants everything but you bastards want more than everyone else. Damn Company owns the state. They take three out of four dollars that get made, no matter who makes it. Did it ever seem funny to you? You got so goddamned much and you're still trying to get at the scraps the rest of us got. Don't that seem funny? You won all the marbles and you still ain't satisfied. Oh, we'll strike you all right. We sure as hell will. If you don't move your car I'm comin' over the top of you."

And before Dust could make his best offer, Kangas was starting up that old Plymouth and it was a good thing the Buick was running because if it hadn't been, there would have been a hell of a crash.

Going down the Hill, with the cold air coming right through the half-open window, Dust was too angry to stop for Ketchel though he saw him clear enough.

Some days it don't pay to get out of bed. Some days, a man had to be philosophical. There wasn't any way to get through life makin' friends with every man you met. You might as well stick to the friends you got. Kangas had guts though, even if he lacked good sense. Like those old boys who hunted grizzly bears up in Marias Pass. Some men just had to go up against the biggest thing there was and annoy it. You had to think high of

yourself to do that. To walk out on a man like Ol' Dust
Devlin when he was just talking sense. Just negotiatin'.

At Frenchie's, seventy miles north of the Missouri
River Steam Generating Plant, Dust Devlin dunked a
french fry in the ketchup. His bloodshot eyes guttered
like a fire somebody's pissed in. "I liked him," he said.
"I would have been proud to call him my friend."

While he'd been speaking, I'd seen Joel as I'd known
him and as I hadn't. The set of his mouth, the way his
hair kept falling into his eyes, the sound of his voice.
Even as I saw him, I knew he was dead. And even dead,
I would know him differently and anew at each turn in
my own life. He had become various. I was his collector.

I felt easy and soft, angry and ashamed. Like I'd been
forced. "Where is he?"

Devlin wiped the beer foam off his lip with his
knuckle. "I only talked to him the once. I ain't seen Joel
Kangas since the morning before he disappeared."

I could have asked more, but he got to his feet, paid
the check and left four bits for the waiter. It would be
dark in an hour or so, and already the wind howling
down Wolf Creek Canyon had a bite to it. I said, "Now
we're going back to Butte."

"Why, sure. Sure we are."

He had another slug from the Old Crow before he
shut the car door behind him. When he hit the starter
button, he kept it whining for a second after the motor
caught and the starter bendix howled like it will when
it's abused.

He revved the motor three times and the oil pressure
had probably hit fifteen pounds or so before he threw it

into gear. A cold engine likes to have a bit more oil than that coating the cylinder walls.

I believe he drove the Wolf Creek Canyon about five miles an hour faster than it could be driven. The drive would have been comfortable at forty. Generally the speedometer hung around sixty-five, and a couple times it got quicker. He was using all the road, sliding from lane to lane on all the bad turns. I kept my hands in my lap, quite relaxed and curious somehow. My existence had passed out of my hands. It had become part of an unspoken pact between Devlin and myself. If he was eager to die, why then, I would die too. I'd go that far with him.

But I would not ask him to slow down.

On the flats outside of Helena, the speedometer trembled at ninety-five. Between the six-foot snowbanks, the road was a bobsled run and that's how he was driving it. The Buick was shaking. If he'd been able to stay on the asphalt, it wouldn't have shimmied that way, but one side or another of the big car was always running on packed snow.

He did keep his eyes on the road. Usually he kept both hands on the wheel, except when he reached for his bottle.

He has to kill him to kill me, I thought.

And, he nearly did. Outside of Boulder, he lost it on a patch of glare ice. The front end wobbled, yawed, and bye bye. I heard myself say, "Here we go, you fucker," as we swapped ends. Kaleidoscope. The windows became a solid bar of blurred white. Dust was wrestling the wheel. The bottle smacked my knee and rolled under his feet. My body was totally thrilled.

When he dared touch the brake, we'd done a couple

180's on the straightaway without touching either snow-bank. We were three hundred yards down the road from where we'd started and facing the wrong way. He braked. He popped it out of gear. He rummaged under his feet for the bottle. He offered it to me, his eyes still on the road where our progress was marked by tire scars like broken stitches on the pavement.

Absently, I took the bottle and started to unscrew the cap. I popped the cap back with the heel of my hand. "Fuck you," I said. My voice sounded like a half-strangled frog.

"You . . . you do know how to hate, don't you, Jimmy. I wish I knew how to hate. I'd be a happier man. Never was able to take things serious, I guess. I'm like Will Rogers. Just like Old Will. Did I tell you I shook hands with him once? It was at the Calgary Stampede. Course he wasn't a humorist then, he was just a trick rope act."

He swallowed a little bourbon, more for form's sake than need, and drove until he found a place wide enough to turn around. He went slower all the way back to Butte.

We came off the Divide toward the lights on the Hill. Saturday night traffic—the streak of the headlights—the faint flicker of the neon. The lights were glittery. Dust geared down for the long grade. "I don't think Ol' Kooteney ever had a decent set of clothes until I bought him one. Damn, I hate to see a man who doesn't care enough about himself to look good."

It started to snow. As we headed toward my father's house, Dust got on the subject of the Vargas-Ketchel fight. He was backing Ketchel. "To the hilt," he said.

6

THE SILVER BOW CLUB had been the millionaires' club before most of them hopped trains, east or west, seeking gentler climes.

The building was about what you'd expect: heavy stonework, hand-carved balustrades and stained-glass windows.

The Silver Bow Club's chef was Joe Reau, who had a sad life. One of Joe's famous desserts was Rum Pie.

Crust:

4 egg whites   ¼ tsp. cream of tartar
1 cup sugar

Mix sugar and cream of tartar and add to stiffly beaten egg whites. Beat. Grease two pie tins and divide the meringue and bake 1 hour and 10 minutes at 275 degrees.

Filling:

1 cup whipping cream	¼ cup milk
2 egg whites	salt
2 egg yolks	2–4 tbs. rum
⅓ cup sugar	½ tsp. vanilla
2 tsp. gelatin	toasted almonds for top

Soak the gelatin in ¼ cup milk for about five minutes. Dissolve over low heat; cool. Beat the yolks and add sugar, salt and vanilla. Add the gelatin and rum. Fold in the beaten egg whites. Add the whipped cream and pour into baked shells. Top with whipped cream and chopped toasted almonds or coconut.

When the Miners' Union bought the Silver Bow Club, most of the miners thought it was ironic. The Company men said it was like a nigger in a Cadillac.

Sam Curnew's office was dusty and bare. His old wood desk, his swivel chair, the coat rack, another wooden chair for visitors, a bulletin board which bore:

two mimeographed sets of minutes

a safety poster that showed a couple of rocks falling down on some cartoon miners, knocking them cockeyed. The message: BE SAFE. AFTER YOU BLAST, BAR DOWN!

three snapshots of people at a picnic: friendly, smiling at the camera

a photo of Sam's wife. She was an unsmiling ascetic woman

and this hymn, typed out neatly on a sheet of onion-skin paper:

DEFINITION OF A SCAB

After God had finished the rattlesnake, the toad, the vampire, He had some awful substance left with which He made a scab.

A scab is a two-legged animal with a corkscrew soul, a waterlogged brain, a combination backbone of jelly and glue. Where others have hearts, he carries a tumor of rotten principles.

No man has a right to scab so long as there is a pool of water to drown his carcass in, or a rope long enough to hang his body with. Judas Iscariot was a gentleman compared with a scab. For betraying his master, he had character enough to hang himself. A scab has not.

Esau sold his birthright for a mess of pottage. Judas Iscariot sold his Savior for thirty pieces of silver. Benedict Arnold sold his country for a promise of a commission in the British army. The modern strike-breaker sells his birthright, his country, his wife, his children, and his fellow men for an unfulfilled promise from his employer, trust or corporation.

Esau was a traitor to himself; Judas Iscariot was a traitor to his God; Benedict Arnold was a traitor to his country; a strikebreaker is a traitor to his God, his country, his wife, his family, and his class.

I set Joel's books on Sam's desk. Sunday morning. The doors were unlocked but there wasn't anybody else in the hall.

I sat on the edge of Sam's desk and listened to the burp and hiss of the radiators, doing less than their damnedest.

I looked out the window. There was a little grocery store across the street.

I got up and walked to the back of the building, to the meeting hall. I was feeling echoes.

It had been the Silver Bow Club's ballroom.

Room for maybe 650 miners—the smoke, the cheers and jeers, the electric smell of us.

Placards on the wall from Bertoglio Electric, Wilson

Motors, the Wintergarden Bowling Alley. The placards said: *Best Wishes* or *Good Luck*—sentiments like that. None of them said *Workers of the World Unite.* Some of the placards were lettered in blue and gold, some in orange and black; some were quite gay.

Frank Little's photograph hung behind the podium. It wasn't very large and though it was the only photograph on that wall, it would be easy to miss it.

It was about eight inches long and maybe six inches high.

Frank Little
"We shall never forget"

There were three photographs in the frame, laid out like a triptych.

The center photograph was the passport photo of a man who'd always have trouble at customs. In this picture, Frank was alive. Frank Little had wary, go-to-hell eyes, a narrow face and chin, and he wore a huge, dashing black hat that Lord Byron might have envied. It was a sail of a hat. The black sail of a black privateer easing alongside some fat complacent merchantman.

"He isn't Joel," I said aloud.

In the other two photos, Frank Little was dead.

In life, Frank Little had been a cripple. He limped. In the lefthand photo, you couldn't spot his deformity, though you could see all of him except his cock and balls, laid out, as he was, on a mortuary table, stripped, with his head back and the rope burns around his neck. I don't know whether he'd been strangled or had his neck broke, though the men who took him out and lynched him from the Milwaukee trestle that night had signed their note "3-7-77" and as vigilantes, presumably, some one of them would have known enough to break his neck with the drop.

They'd nailed the note to his chest, but there was no mark of the nail wound on his chest. They'd shot him a few times, too, because, why not? I could see three or four modest bullet holes in him. His feet were big for his frame and they stuck up straight in the air. His knees were knobby and his elbows too. His rib cage was pretty good size though there wasn't much flesh on it and not too much hair either.

He was wearing bright white boxer shorts. I suppose the photographer dressed him special for the picture and I imagine some miner ran from the coroner's office to Hennessey's to buy one pair of white boxer shorts, medium, so Frank Little could be attired modestly in his death.

Frank Little had been losing his hair. Maybe that's why he wore the hat.

In the righthand picture, Frank was in his coffin and it was a big one—walnut and bronze thing about the size of a two-hundred-gallon tank—and Frank's head resting on the pillow.

He looked like a doll.

The doll's eyes were closed. In the other pictures you could see his eyes, but they weren't burying no live doll, they were burying a dead one and of course they closed the damn eyes.

Sam Curnew stepped up softly behind me. "Poor old Frank," he said. "You know that people come from all over to look at that picture? Last month, it was some kid from the University. He said he wanted to write Frank's history." Sam chuckled to himself. "Now there's one history that won't be written."

I touched his sleeve. "I got something for you, Sam. Like I told you on the phone."

"Oh, I figured you'd be up here to talk to me, sooner or later."

There's ten thousand jobs I'd take before I took a job as a shaftman, bucketing gobs of muck and rock in the sump of a three-thousand-foot hole. When he was a shaftman at the Alice, Sam Curnew's muscles hung in his bones like coils of oiled hemp. He'd been out of the holes for ten years and his muscles were still big but filled with soft water. Sam's stoop made his arms hang out front of him when he walked. His hair was combed forward. Sam always seemed to have too much forehead. The wrinkles were plentiful around his eyes but his forehead was smooth as an alabaster wall. As we headed for his office, he talked over his shoulder. "They put up a plaque to Frank, you know. It's down in the Mountain View Cemetery." Sam flopped his big hand carelessly, like he was drawing the plaque. "I'll bet that thing weighed two hundred pounds. Some hooligans stole it a couple years ago. Sold it for scrap."

Sam left his overcoat on when he ushered me into his office and indicated I should take a seat. I perched on the edge of his desk. He wore a white shirt, unbuttoned at the collar, and no tie. Carefully he uncoiled his spring earmuffs and set them on his filing cabinet below the photo of his wife. "This what you brought me?" He was flipping through the titles in the carton of books. "I didn't mean for you to do that, Jimmy. You could have kept them. Just so they were out of Kangas's house."

"I don't see what's so damn dangerous about those books," I said. "They're just bullshit anyway."

Sam pulled a couple books out of the box and set them aside for himself. "Six Company goons killed Little," he said. "They dragged him out of his rooming house, tossed him in their car, drove him down to the Milwaukee trestle and hanged him. Frank never wrote one of these books. He was a talker. Once you heard him talk, you never forgot it. Twenty thousand miners marched down Montana Street for his funeral. They shut down all the mines too, until the governor sent troops in. I heard Frank speak a couple times. He had a gimpy leg. . . ."

"Just like Joel."

"That's coincidence," Sam said. "Frank Little was dangerous. Kangas, no. We won't strike and the Company knows it."

"That's bullshit too," I said.

"Don't call these books bullshit, Jimmy. They're filled with mistakes and quarrels over things most men can't remember anymore, but they were very expensive. Men died. And you're better off not having them under your bed. Because when the knock comes in the middle of the night, you'd find it easier to explain a case of dynamite in your basement than this box of books under your bed." He chuckled. "You could always say the dynamite was for prospecting out in the hills. And, 'Sure you'll file your claim as soon as you find something worth claiming.'" Again he laughed. Again it was mostly for his own benefit.

"Sam," I said, "I know a dozen men who've already left Butte to look for work. Of course there's gonna be a strike."

"They'll finish us if we do," Sam said, politely, like he was discussing the weather. "What do you care, Jimmy? You pay your dues. I suppose you'll show up for the strike vote but I won't see your face in the Hall until then. You came up here to ask about Kangas."

I was taken aback by his abruptness. "Yes," I said. "I think he's dead."

Sam's eyes were as constant as sealed-beam headlights. "He would have called if he was able," Sam said.

Though I agreed with him, Sam's easy acceptance of Joel's death felt like he was driving a nail into Joel's coffin. "No loss to you, Sam." I created a fairly ugly grin. "He never was one of your precious Party men."

Sam's eyes got tired. "If you think that, you can go home and I can go home. My wife and I wanted to visit her sister this afternoon. I get a kick out of my wife's sister. She's a real card."

"But Joel never joined the Party."

"No! That reckless son of a bitch never did anything he didn't want to. Not once. He'd get up on his soapbox" —Sam lowered his voice to parody Joel's—" 'No Portal-to-Portal. No Retroactive.' Kangas could make a speech, there's no denyin' that. 'Six months without a contract and six years without a pay raise.' Kangas was like a pipe organ. Noisy as hell once you pulled out all the stops."

"You didn't like him."

Sam's voice was clipped with impatience. "Nothin' to do with it. Course I liked him. He was the sort of man everyone liked. But he was doin' his level best to ruin everything I've worked for."

"How?"

I don't think he heard my question, or maybe he did but chose to ignore it. "He ever talk to you about Spain?" He looked off into space like Spain was out there somewhere. "No Passarán," he said.

"Joel told me about Spain. He told me about a lot of things. I wasn't much of a listener. I'm making up for lost time."

"No Passarán," Sam repeated. Apparently "No Passarán" was up in the sky next to Spain because that's where Sam kept his mild brown eyes. "They shall not pass."

"He told me about Spain," I said. "He said Franco cut them to pieces."

"Yeah," Sam said. "I heard him say that. I almost went to Spain myself. My wife wanted us to go. But she was pregnant and I didn't think it was such a hot idea. She miscarried, anyway."

"I talked to a fellow yesterday. Devlin—"

"You ever see that pin of his?" Sam interrupted. "That was given to him by the Friends of the Abraham Lincoln Battalion. When they got off the boat in New York. It was the only thing he got out of goin' over there."

I knew the pin. It was red and green, with a clenched fist on it.

Outside, it was a clear, cold day; last night's snow, a soft virginal blanket, except where the tire ruts cut down to old ice and sand. Sam's window hadn't been washed in years. The little grocery store across the street had a display of foodstuffs in the window and I was hungry. A colorful pyramid of cans and boxes, trays filled with weary hothouse vegetables: reds, greens, faded yellows and browns.

"We were in Seattle once," he said. He cleared his throat. He cleared it again. "Seattle's a good town. There's always work for a man in Seattle. Good union town. We had our conventions there. Us and the Lithographers, the Machinists, and the Longshoremen. The Longshoremen—what a great bunch they were."

"During the war."

"We were stayin' downtown at some railroad hotel, but we'd go up to the Olympic for drinks. You can see all the Puget Sound from this bar they got up there. All blue and green and the islands sticking out of the water. It's beautiful. You ever do any fishin', Jimmy? We used to hire a boat and go out into the Sound, on Sundays, you know. They never held meetins on Sundays."

"I ain't much of a fisherman, Sam," I said. "It's my father who likes to fish."

"They got a bar up there and when you sit up there the whole city is down below you and up the coast you can see the lights from Boeing. There was a lot of work at Boeing."

"Why don't you just tell me what you got to tell me, Sam?"

"I never invited you up here for a little polite chit-chat," Sam said evenly. "It was you who wanted it. I can go home as soon as I get hold of the janitor and have him turn the heat down in the Hall."

"Yeah," I said quietly, "Seattle's a great town."

Sam punched his words out slow, like he'd earned them. "We'd sit up there every night and drink beer and stare down at the city. Me and Joel. We were both walking delegates then. Friends." He took a deep breath. "Adventurer," he said, like he was ashamed of the word.

"Who?"

"Most of the comrades think Joel's an adventurer," Sam explained carefully.

"Christ!" Sam had an uncomfortable looking bulge under his topcoat. I hadn't meant to say anything about it but the "adventurer" bullshit made me mad. "You're carryin'?" I asked.

He drew his topcoat back, absentmindedly. A nickel-plated revolver was stuck under his belt. He coughed. "It's startin' up," he said. "Kooteney Ketchel's an informer. Did you know that?"

"What does he know?"

"Not much. But whatever he hears goes right into Devlin's ears. The Indian's been suckin' after him for months."

"I talked to Devlin. He ain't much."

"Mister Dust Devlin. I know him. Whenever he comes to town, you better watch your back."

"Devlin and Ketchel. . . ."

"Ketchel's his dogbody. Devlin shows up whenever the Company needs a little late-night work. He was a 'special deputy' in '34. He was in Butte when Little was still alive. Somebody pointed him out to me. Him and me are about the same age. He was a kid then, but already he was a goon. Devlin liked to wear thigh-high riding boots. I never saw him on a horse."

"Was he one of the guys who killed Little?"

Sam laughed. "Naw. After it happened he made noises around town that he was one of the vigilantes but he wasn't. He hasn't got guts for that kind of job. The goons who killed Little were out of town on the next morning train. Everybody knew who they were. Devlin was just a punk with big boots and a big mouth."

"Sam," I said, "I could use a drink."

He started to say he didn't have any booze, but he remembered something. He went into his file cabinet and took out a dejected-looking Christmas package. It was bourbon. Old Fitzgerald.

"I was gonna give this to someone last Christmas, but I forgot." He crumpled the card and tossed it in the wastebasket.

I took a stiff jolt and Sam did likewise.

"Here's to him," I said. "And here's to you, Sam."

Sam was looking out his streaky window at a streaky

cold world. Maybe he was looking at the little grocery store. Maybe he was hungry too. He stuffed his hands into his pockets. Maybe he was cold.

"You ought to get out of here and go to Seattle," Sam said. "I heard they pulled your rustling card."

"I tore it up."

"I wish I'd gone to Seattle," Sam said. "It's different there. A man can live. Get out of Butte, Jimmy. That's the best advice you'll ever hear."

I nudged the box of books. "Joel wanted me to read these things. I never cared for them."

Sam picked up the three books he'd selected. When he tapped them on the desk, dust motes flew into the air. "Joel read too much. I used to tell him that. That's how he came to write the column for the *Miner's Voice*. I caught some flak for it. Some of the comrades wouldn't. . . . We couldn't let him on the negotiating committee. He had to speak his piece from the floor like any other worker. We never treated Joel bad. We could have told him to take a hike but we didn't."

I handed him the Old Fitz but he didn't do anything with it.

"Seattle. We were drinking and we were talking. Jimmy, you got to count on the worker. He's the only one you can trust. Top of the Olympic. We were ridin' high." His chuckle again. "The Soviets were holding the Nazis at Stalingrad, us and them were allies. Christ, we were ridin' high. I already had my card. I told Joel he should get one too. Nobody but the Party gave a damn for the working man. Hell, Joel thought the same as I did. I told him we'd never win without solidarity." Sam's face got fierce with the heat of an old, old argument. "That's how the Justice Department licked the Wobblies. The Justice Department had discipline and the Wobblies didn't. Without solidarity, we haven't the ghost of a chance. Joel said he'd go it alone."

"What did he say, Sam?"

"That was a long time ago." Sam paused, gathering his memories. "He talked about Spain. How he hurt his leg. I remember him talkin' about gettin' out of Spain at the end. They were running through the hills at night, trying to reach the border, and the Italian whippet tanks were chasin' after them. The Party was too cold for him, he said that."

"That all?"

Sam waited for his recollections to catch up. "No. He said something about bein' too old to join, but that was just a joke because he was a couple years younger than I was. I asked him a couple times to join but he'd say the same thing; that he was too old. It didn't make no sense."

"And you don't want a strike," I said.

Sam looked at me like I was crazy. "Why, Jimmy? So they can break up the union? They're waitin' for us, Jimmy. It always happens after a war. They got all these generals with nothin' to do so they turn 'em loose on the Reds. Truman won't help us. He's got to keep the Congress off his back. They're gonna pass the Taft-Hartley, you know. No union can get recognition unless it signs a loyalty oath. No communist officers. If we strike now, they'd love it. They'd cut Local #1 into pieces so small you'd never be able to put it back together again."

I reached into the wastebasket and picked out Sam's Christmas wrappings and the card. The card was from Sam to somebody I never knew.

I said, "I hope you know how to shoot that thing," and left the Union Hall and went across the street and bought myself a ham sandwich. The meat was fine and

I suppose the bread wasn't really that dry, but my mouth was and I couldn't eat the damned sandwich.

Gail Stinson's apartment was in the Pennsylvania block, a big rabbit-warren of a place with stores on the street floor and the floors above filled with doctors, dentists, chiropractors and retired merchants.

She wasn't too glad to see me. "Oh. H'lo."

Three room apartment: living room, bedroom, kitchenette. Not too much in the way of nice furniture, but the place was freshly painted (white) and was hung with new curtains (yellow). She had a shelf of books above her couch—Gothic novels, mostly, and poetry, interspersed with her old college textbooks: *Introduction to Economics, Modern Journalism: Theory and Practice.*

The pillow on her couch was sateen with gold embroidery. It had a motto (*The Fighting Lady*) and the illustration of an aircraft carrier, quarter profile, battling the waves. A magazine photograph of Winston Churchill was tacked to the wall above the little corner telephone table.

"Nice place," I said.

"Thanks," she said. She said, "It's quiet."

And it was. Only the hiss of the steam radiators and the slight creak of the windows in their sockets when the winter wind tugged at them.

She said: "They've shut down the steam generating plant. The furnaces. They're gonna take a look inside. Deputy Whitehead called me."

"Well." I didn't know what else to say. I sat down on the couch. I slapped the pillow. It went flat and then filled right back up with air.

"I'm surprised," I said. And I was, too.

"Yeah, well, I told you Bob was a good cop."

She was wearing a pair of tan slacks. High pockets,

wide waistband. The slacks were good to her belly but her backside was a little droopy.

"Whitehead convinced Frank Coad. Told him the town was in an uproar about Kangas. Whitehead said the furnaces were so hot they wouldn't find anything, anyway, but it'd make them look good. So they shut down this morning, when the graveyard shift went off. The furnaces'll be cool enough to search this afternoon."

"I guess that's good," I said.

"I'm sorry," she said, "you want some coffee? I've got some sherry, if you'd rather have a drink." She went into a cupboard and found a dusty bottle of Taylor New York State.

"Coffee'll be fine."

She started her percolator going. While she was fussing with it, she said, "My editor called me this morning."

"Uh-huh." I pulled at the tassels on the pillow.

"He told me to lay off the Kangas story. He said I was 'out of my depth.'"

"Uh-huh." One of the tassels came off and I stuck it behind the cushion of the sofa and kept my hands to myself.

"He wanted somebody 'with a little more experience' to handle it." She looked at me. "Leave the pillow alone," she said.

"Sure," I said. "It's ugly."

"It's my pillow, partner, not yours." She poured the coffee. "It was a gift."

"Boyfriend?"

"That's right. Here."

And I took the cup. The wind creaked the windows. The radiators kept up their hissing.

"Sailor?"

"Yeah. He was. He came back in '44. He'd been

wounded. Burned. I was away at college. It's sad. Here he'd been in the war and all. He'd had all these experiences and a permanent scar all down his right forearm. I'd been kind of hid away, you know. First with all my big brothers on the ranch and then at the sorority at college. He'd got bitter and mean. Mean as a snake. Drinking. I felt sorry for him, sure, but I wasn't going to marry him."

"And how'd he feel about that?"

"He went back to Big Timber and knocked up somebody else."

"Oh."

Her front windows looked out over the chimneys of the roof next door and framed the Highland Mountains: white and nice as a calendar photo. The sky was bright, washed-out blue. Gail's yellow curtains framed the vista, neatly. The stitches in the hems of the curtains were evenly spaced, precise.

I pushed some sounds out from my lips. The sounds were very much like a man whistling the "Butte Polka."

"Well, I quit the mines yesterday." I lit a cigarette.

"What are you gonna do?"

"Hell, I don't know."

"What about the School of Mines? Being an engineer?"

I shook my head. "I haven't been to class in a week. There's other schools. You know what I read in *Life*? I read that winter is going to be so bad in Germany, no food, no medicines, that one guy said no German baby born in 1945 would survive—and only half those under three years of age."

"That's a comfort," she said. "It's always nice to hear about dying babies who are worse off than you are."

"I didn't mean that." I suppose, though, I had.

"Maybe the UN will do something about it."

"Hell, the UN ain't got no power. We've got the power. We're the only country with the A-bomb."

"Sure," she said.

"I wonder if the furnace is cool." I drank the bit of sediment in the bottom of my coffee cup. "I wonder why they killed him."

She said: "Don't ask me."

I put my arm out on the back of the sofa. "Take a load off your feet."

She sat down like maybe the couch was covered with ants. I put my arm on her shoulder. She shrugged it off and said, "No thanks."

Fine.

I put my foot up on the coffee table because I thought it would annoy her. I guess it did.

She said, "I'm not ready for an affair. I'm not ready to get married either. I won't stay with a man with no future."

I'd never slept with a girl I hadn't paid.

"You're very ... modern," I said.

"I want a career, Jimmy. I don't want to end up a poor man's helpmate."

She got right up. She adjusted the yellow curtains minutely. She had real nice breasts. Her legs were nice too. A little plump. She had a difficult temperament. It was close in her apartment. I could smell her perfume garnishing the faint stale scent of cooked cabbage. The telephone rang. We looked at each other.

I picked up the phone.

"Miss Stinson?"

"No. Who'm I talking to?"

"This is Deputy Whitehead and who in the hell are you?"

"Mullholland."

"Jimmy? Is that you, Jimmy?"

"Yeah."

"It was Miss Stinson who asked me to call her, you understand. I already called your father. I woke him up."

"What—?"

"We found him, Jimmy. He was in there. I'm sorry. We were right. I'm sorry."

"Joel."

"I think so . . . yes."

"Uh, does my sister know?"

"Not yet. I'm going to break the news to Kathleen personally. You know, the shock and all. . . ."

"I'll call her. Where's the body?"

"Uh, Jimmy. Those furnaces are real hot, and there isn't anything really like a body. It wouldn't be any use, her, Kathleen, going to see him."

"Where is he?"

"Jimmy, there isn't more of Joel Kangas left than you could fit in a cigar box."

7

"HELL," I SAID. "Maybe it was a dog."

"Sure."

"Or a deer." I pulled one of the chunks of burnt bone out of the shoebox. Corroded, glazed, burnt yellow and gray.

"Sure." Bob Whitehead talking. "If it is, I'm gonna be lookin' somewhere else for work." He spat. The sheriff's office had plenty spittoons.

"They threw a cat in the furnace once," I said. "Ketchel told me about it. Told me about the cat."

Eight pieces of scorched, tormented bone, none of them half the size of my fist. I have small hands.

I stirred through them with my finger. They weren't heavy. They'd had their weight burned out of them.

Deputy Whitehead said, "Ever see a cat with teeth

like this?" He had the teeth in a little candy bag and shook them out on his desktop like dice.

"No. I never have seen a cat with teeth like those," I said. I picked up one of the teeth. Square, blocky. It looked like one of the turrets of the fortresses of Hell. The root had been burned away.

"Is that all?" Gail asked. "Did you find anything else?" She was right beside me. She had hold of my elbow.

"Well," Deputy Whitehead said. He leaned back in his chair and laced his fingers behind his head. I wondered how far back he'd lean. "There isn't much else and I dunno if it even"—he pointed at the heap in the shoebox—"goes with those. Those furnaces are about twelve feet across, each of them, inside. And there's all kinds of junk in there—burned up junk on the floor. The guys who watch the furnaces, I guess they like to open the door and toss in a tin can or something to see how long it takes to melt. Most of it's burned up, you know. Just black lumps. I think we wouldn't have found the bones at all except there's a ring of gas jets around the floor, and we found these under the lip of the gas jet. Everything else was gone. Frank Coad called Duggan's mortuary, you know, and asked how hot they run the crematorium, how hot it takes to burn up the bodies so there's nothing but ash and they said they cremated at 2400 degrees and those furnaces at the generating plant get to 4400 degrees. If these bones hadn't been on the floor and kind of tucked under the lip of that gas jet, we'd still be lookin' for Joel Kangas to turn up in Denver or Cheyenne."

I thought the bones in the shoebox and the teeth on his desk didn't bear much resemblance to any Joel Kangas I'd ever known.

I also thought that Joel Kangas had cashed in his chips.

Where would his smile make him welcome now?

Deputy Whitehead had another candy bag to empty on his desk: three black . . . objects. Small. None of them any bigger than my thumb. He inspected one, clasped it between thumb and forefinger. He said, "This might be a button from a work overall. One of those metal buttons." He shrugged. I looked at it close. Maybe yes, maybe no. "And this thing"—he held up a piece of burnt wire—"it just might be one of the hooks for the shoulder straps, you know." He picked up the third piece of metal. "And I don't know what the hell this is, but it was under the gas jet with the bones so I brought it in."

A flat scrap of dusty metal, an inch and a half long. It looked like the dust had been burned into the metal. It looked like dust metal. The scrap had been rectangular once, but the heat had curled it slightly. There were two little tits, just lumps, on its reverse side.

A wave of sentimentality washed over me so strong and so sweet it was hard to take a breath.

"It's a pin," I said. "A clasp. I've seen it before." I put both my hands down on the desk and leaned because I was dizzy, but my eyes fastened to the little heap of teeth and the scrap of metal and I hated staring at them so I let go of the desk and looked up at Gail's face. Gail's face was white and blank. She'd done a quick job with her eye makeup and one of her eyes seemed bigger than the other. "A clasp. See where the pin used to be?" I wagged my finger at the two metal tits. "Joel usually carried it or wore it. It was enamel, though, green and red enamel. It was a memento."

Deputy Whitehead picked up the pin and inspected it. "Of what?" he asked.

"When he was in Spain. It was the insignia of the Abraham Lincolns. Joel fought in the International Brigade."

"Uh-huh. Reds, weren't they?"

"I suppose they were," I said. "What difference does it make?"

Bob Whitehead lifted his eyebrows. "Makes no difference to me, pal." He wrapped the metal objects in the candy bag and tossed it in the shoebox. He put the teeth in the other bag.

"It was an enamel pin," I said.

"Yeah. Well, maybe the lab will be able to find out if there ever was any enamel on that thing."

"Let me see it again."

So he unwrapped it again and I took it in my hand. It had been very hot. Now it was cold.

There was some tiny remnant of intention remaining in the pin. I laid it carefully back in the box. Neatly on top of the heap of bones. Their badge. Their name. Their intelligence.

"What lab?" Gail asked.

"They're goin' down to Denver," Deputy Whitehead said. "They got a good lab down in Denver. I'll put 'em on Western's night flight and we'll have them back in a couple days."

"I wouldn't want to see them get lost," I said.

"You think I'm real stupid," Bob Whitehead said. "I ain't. And you, Miss Stinson. Front page headlines: Aggressive Deputy Solves Murder. I'll be waitin' for those headlines, I don't think."

"You did a good job," I said.

"Frank Coad don't think so. The Company don't

think so. And the sheriff—he don't give much of a damn, one way or another."

"They got to Coad?" I asked.

"They were on him like stink on shit. There ain't no warrant out for Ketchel, you know."

"Why not?" Gail was indignant.

Bob Whitehead rubbed his forehead. "Don't ask me. I talked to Frank Coad. I said, 'Frank, are you gonna prosecute?' He said, 'How could we prosecute when we don't have a body?' He said he was gonna wait until the inquest. He said I shouldn't go off half cocked. He said I'd made some enemies gettin' the furnaces shut down. He said I broke the chain of command. He never was in the army. He stayed home with the rest of you 4-H bastards."

"I was deferred. All the miners were deferred."

"Yeah. I know."

He went in his pocket and tossed a key to me. I caught it. "You can pick up your brother-in-law's car," he said.

"Was there anything about the car . . . Did you learn anything?" Gail asked.

"Naw. A bunch of Kangas's junk: tools, one glove, some fishhooks, a couple books. No prints or nothin'."

I said, "Uh-huh."

He said, "Did you tell Kathleen? You said you were going to. I didn't call."

"My father beat us both to it. I guess she's all right. It was the not knowing that was the worst. She told my father she was tired and went to bed. My aunt Edith is down at her house now."

"Well, maybe I'll wait a little bit before I stop by. I want to offer my sympathies."

"Such as they are," I said.

We locked eyes. "I found him, Jimmy boy," he said softly. "I found his car and then I found his bones. Now, I know you don't think very much of me. But that ain't gonna stop me from visiting your sister with my condolences at the time of her grief."

"Oh, Jesus Christ," I said. "Gail, let's go get the car."

"Good-bye," he said. "You're welcome."

"What for?"

"I thought you said thanks."

The police garage got me for three-dollars-a-day storage. The car seats were off their tracks and it took me fifteen minutes to get them back on in that chilly garage. The motor turned over when I punched the starter button, but the gas gauge read empty. I bought a couple bucks' worth.

Gail asked me to drive her down to the *Standard* office and that was okay. She said she was going to write a safe story because she liked being a crime reporter and I said that was okay too.

Frankie Coley, the sports reporter, was there and we talked about the Butte High Bulldogs and their chances for a championship next year. Gail typed. Words on yellow paper. She yanked the story out of her typewriter. She was mad at something.

Frankie and I watched her stride into the editor's office. Frankie said that all the other newspapermen respected her for uncovering the murder. He said she was in trouble, that she was a "hell of a good kid." I accepted the compliment for her.

She didn't stay inside long and when she came out, she'd left her color inside. She managed a smile for Frankie, but it wasn't the sort of smile you want to see too often.

Frankie shook his head.

"The . . . the darned idiot said it didn't matter what I wrote," she told us.

"Where we going?" I asked her when I'd started the car.

"Just drive around for a while, okay?"

We drove around for a while. It got dark. She said, "I feel silly."

"Uh-huh."

"What's the sense of surrendering when nobody cares?"

The car smelled like Joel: his cigarettes, his shaving lotion, and soon enough that smell would be gone too.

Her stomach rumbled.

"You hungry?" I asked.

Small voice: "No." Then she got her big voice back and said, "Damn them."

I didn't say anything.

"I'm starved," she said. "Let's pretend. You be Big John and I'll be Sparky, and we'll pretend, all right?"

"The hell with it," I suggested.

"Right!"

The Rocky Mountain Cafe was the bastard child of Maxim's of Paris and the Last Hoorah Saloon. Some said it was the best restaurant west of St. Louis and east of San Francisco.

It didn't look it. A chunky brown brick building adorned with short brick crenellations along the roof, a dangling sign: ROCKY MOUNTAIN CAFE (neon) and in the window beside the front door a leaping trout, also neon.

It'd been a casino once. The gambling floor was now a banquet room: thirty or forty small tables where the wheels had been. The bar ran the length of the room. It was black mahogany, as was the backbar where it wasn't fine beveled glass.

One end of the place was partitioned into tiny dining rooms, for the sports and their ladies. The dining rooms were plain; chairs around tables, some big, some small, and a white tablecloth. In the center of each table were the condiments: salt, pepper, Tabasco sauce, Worcestershire sauce and Durkee's. The rooms were doorless. Sawdust on the floors.

Sunday night. The place was fairly busy—family trade—and as I followed our waitress to our dining room I counted fourteen napkins tied around prosperous throats. (The ladies kept theirs demurely in their laps, the kids lost theirs on the floor.)

I left my coat on when I sat down because I was shivering. "Bring me a whiskey and ditch. Gail?"

Gail wanted a Scotch manhattan and the waitress went off while I was still shivering.

Gail noticed. She said, "I know what you mean."

"That shoebox." The small pile of bones phosphorescing in my mind.

"Sometimes I don't like reality very much," she said. What she said made me mad but I didn't show it.

"Sometimes it gets hard and I wish I was dead just so it was all over," Gail said.

I was quite afloat then, loosed from my moorings, just me in a shoebox with some bones that once belonged to a small, fast prehistoric horse, drifting through the fog, the bones piloting while I rowed, and the bones telling jokes about horses: "My sweetheart's a mule in the mine. I drive her with only one line. All day I just sit/On the dashboard and spit. . . ."

I didn't tell anything of this to Gail because I didn't want her to think I was crazy. The waitress brought our drinks. I drained mine and asked her for another—a straight shot this time, with a beer chaser.

The wall separating the dining cubicles was half-inch plywood. Someone in the next cubicle was talking— a continuous mutter of sound. Some paterfamilias chastising his kid.

Gail didn't touch her drink. "At least they found him," she said.

"Ain't that the cat's pajamas."

"I didn't kill him, Jimmy. I didn't even know him, Jimmy. I'm going to close myself off from it, as much as I can. I'm sorry. I guess you're real angry. I don't need much more trouble, Jimmy. If you want to be by yourself tonight, get loaded, raise the roof, anything, I'd understand."

"No," I said. "I'm afraid of myself right now. Keep talking. Keep me entertained."

She gave it a go. She sang, "Maresy doats and doesy doats, and little lambsy-divey." Her voice slipped all over the notes the way your feet slip on slick rocks fording a stream.

It made me sad, her singing.

She stopped and gave me a shaky grin. She said, "I wish I was the editor of the *Standard*. I would have done an editorial that would have knocked their socks off."

"Yeah. You aren't."

"Someday," she said. "It's a good story. And it'll never get real. A story isn't real until it's printed. Like a play, it's got to be performed. Until then it's just a disgusting piece of paper."

"Why don't you change stations?" I asked. "See if you can get Fred Allen. Or maybe Fibber McGee and Molly. Can you do Molly?"

"I never was very good at imitations."

"Me neither. It's awful to be stuck with yourself."

"Oh, I don't know. There's enough of me to keep me interested. I surprise myself all the time."

"Not me," I said. What I should have said was "Not me, until recently," but I didn't.

She gave me enough time and a quirk in her eye so I could have taken it back if I'd wanted to.

"You loved Joel, didn't you?"

"Hell no. I liked him, that's all. I liked him a lot. He made me laugh sometimes. Nothing could ever get him down. Hell, he knew that all his politics was just whistling in the wind. I told him that once. We were standing downtown on a Saturday night, outside the Board of Trade, and I said that to him. You know what he said to me? He said, 'Well Jimmy boy, then let's go inside and wet our whistles.' "

The waitress brought in the ravioli, the spaghetti, the breadsticks, the sweet-potato salad, the hot and mild salamis, the hot peppers and my drinks.

I ordered dinner for both of us—a couple of good sirloins, medium rare.

And the spaghetti was sort of peppery good and the hot peppers brought sweat to the spot on the very back of my head where I was already starting to get a little bald. I passed up the sweet-potato salad because it was sweet-potato orange with glistening chunks of pale celery peeping out. The sauce for the raviolis was pretty close to the spaghetti sauce, but the filling had elk meat in it and they were just fine.

Gail belched and colored. I wiped some of the sauce off my chin. "You about ready for dinner?" I asked.

Sweet smile. She reached down and loosened her belt. "Sure," she said. "They got wine?"

"We can ask."

Turned out they had French champagne for the big spenders and sparkling burgundy too.

I peeled my wallet open. "You got any cash?" I asked.

She checked her purse. "Fine thing," she said. "I thought you were Good Time Charlie and it turns out you're Charlie Cheapskate." To the waitress: "We'll have the champagne."

The waitress said, "Sure, dearie. You want the caviar too?"

"Caviar?"

"Yeah. Most times people order the champagne they want the caviar too. I don't like it myself, but some people do."

"No," she said. "I think we can skip the caviar."

"Sure."

And the champagne came in its own ice bucket and the steaks arrived on platters ("Watch your hands, honey—hot stuff") and the french fries on another hot platter and the salad—I had blue cheese, she had thousand island—and we started working on the food and the steaks were crisp on the outside and full of flavor and the french fries were cold before we finished the half of them and the champagne had my head whirling and Gail had matched me glass for glass.

I was gnawing on the steakbone, grease at the corner of my mouth, grease dripping down my chin as I tore the last scraps of meat from the glistening bone, when Max came in.

"Everything right?"

Max was a short heavy man with a bland face. He'd won and lost a couple of fortunes. He'd taken a few stupid insults. He ran a great joint. His face was bland like concrete is bland.

"Hi, Max. It's fine."

"Good. Good." He patted my shoulder. "I heard about Joel Kangas," he said. "Jeez, kid, I was sorry to hear that."

"Yeah," I said. I dropped my steakbone back on the metal platter.

He put his heavy hand on my shoulder again. "Dinner's with me tonight."

"Oh, hell, Max."

"No. It's my place."

"I didn't know you knew Joel."

"I didn't, really. He come in a couple times. Him and Sam Curnew from the union. He was okay. He never caused no trouble. I don't want no trouble, all right?"

Did he think I was going to go wild with grief? Was I flattered? His eyes looked right past me. No info there.

"What do you mean?"

"On the house, kid. I just don't want no trouble. I'm sorry what happened to him." He wheeled to go, remembered, and spun around again, delicate as Fred Astaire. He said, to Gail Stinson, "Pleased to metcha." He smiled for barely two seconds and went away, that quick.

And Gail was smiling at his retreating back and had her mouth open to say something, but she converted it into a giggle and said, "Really!" She laughed, and in a moment I laughed too.

"I'll drink to that," I said.

So. Isolated, briefly, in this circle of contentment; drinking coffee, chattering; chirping like the grasshoppers in the first whisper of fall.

I would live better, rarer: something could be done. The hibernating bear also passes the January nights telling himself lies.

I would not share my sister's grief. I was too poor for that.

We talked. We smiled. We lingered until the waitress had cleared everything off the table but our two empty coffee cups. I left five dollars under my cup and helped Gail with her coat because it is a gentle custom. She was embarrassed when she got her arm stuck. She grinned.

Devlin and Kooteney Ketchel were eating dinner in the next cubicle. We saw them. We stopped dead.

They'd come in after us. They'd been served, but hadn't touched their food. The sweet-potato salad glistened. The curled green hot peppers shiny in their juice. The celery sticks with white cheese filling and paprika. Ketchel was playing with his fork. He looked sullen, like he'd taken a licking. I guess Devlin had been chewing him out.

I closed my eyes. Under my breath I said, "Oh, no." I opened my eyes again. My stomach hurled itself at my throat. I threw up on their table.

Devlin was in a twill suit. Kooteney Ketchel wore brown with a Hawaiian shirt. His tie was red and white with a handpainted yellow flower plumb dead center.

Things changed color. The smell got rich beyond anyone's expectations. The heels of my hands set on the edge of their table, and I puked again: thin bitter stuff that scorched my throat and spattered.

Devlin jumped up in time to add a second stripe of vomit to his clothes; just below the first one. Kooteney hadn't moved, so he got a second layer in the same place.

I was choking, coughing, spitting the stuff, snorting it out of my nostrils.

Devlin shouted, "Shit, kid! Oh shit." My eyes were running. Kooteney Ketchel sat and watched.

"Why'd you kill him?" I asked. I dry-heaved. Bile.

Someone very strong had me by the shoulders, pulling me away from their table.

Devlin was peeling out of his jacket.

"You all right, kid?" A voice in my ear. I braced myself against the doorframe. There wasn't much room left over when me and Max were both standing there. "You all right, kid?"

"Yeah," I said. His bouncer was right beside him.

"Sorry. It wasn't anything I ate."

He gave me a smile so quick I wouldn't swear it was one even. "If you'll give me that jacket, sir, the waitress'll take it into the kitchen and clean if off."

Devlin made a couple halfhearted swipes at his jacket before he tossed it to Max.

"Bones," I said. "He wasn't anything left but bones."

Kooteney stood up, pushing the table away from him. He had a lot of puke in his lap. He peeled off his coat, made a neat ball and fired it at Max.

"I told you I only saw him once," Devlin said. "What are you trying to do to me?" He had his fists balled up and started toward me but Max stepped back and the bouncer took his place. The bouncer was chewing gum. Dust Devlin stopped and flashed a look at Ketchel. Behind the bouncer, Max said, "I don't want no trouble, gents." His voice was kind of muffled. He tugged at my shoulder and I came with him. Gail had her fist up to her mouth, worried, I guess, that she was going to upchuck too.

Max got me pointed toward the gents, slipped the two suit coats to a waitress, and as the gents' door hissed closed behind me, I could hear him saying, "Awful thing, awful. You just send the cleaning bill to the Rocky Mountain and we'll take care of it. A drink, can I get you a drink?"

Kooteney and the bouncer glared at each other. Dust Devlin slammed his fist down on the table, disgusted.

I splashed some cold water on my face and blew the puke out of my nose. I sipped the water from the tap and it felt okay in my stomach. When I came back, Devlin was cleaning Kooteney's lap with a napkin he'd soaked in a water glass. The wet spot looked like the Indian had pissed his pants. I guess they'd made up. Max was gone. When I tried to enter the room, the bouncer interposed himself like a wall. I spotted Gail standing at the bar. She had a brandy glass. That seemed like a good idea.

I ordered. She put the back of her hand against my forehead. "No fever," she said. "You feelin' better?"

"Sure," I said. I would have grinned at her but I wasn't all that sure of my teeth.

They made a little cluster at the front door: Max, Devlin, the waitress holding Devlin's coat and Kooteney Ketchel who draped his in front of his groin.

When they left, Max walked through the banquet hall, favoring a few of the tables with a brief explanation.

The brandy was warming my gut. I felt very soft and very slow.

"You got a weak stomach, kid," Max said.

"I never thought so," I said.

"Yeah. I got two swampers cleaning that room."

"You ought to make your meals a little smaller," I said.

There was that fast smile again. "You gotta have a strong stomach kid. No matter how hard it is to swallow, you got to choke it down. It's food. You can eat all kinds of food and get along but you got to keep it down where it can do you some good."

"They killed him."

He rolled right on. "Like those two. They come in pretty often. Couple steaks. The cowboy picks at his and the Indian ends up eatin' both of them. I seen it. I thought about offerin' the cowboy a child's portion so's he could eat all of it, but I figured he'd get pissed so I never did. You got to have a strong stomach. Those two." And he ordered himself a B&B and asked me who I liked for the pennant that year. He asked me did I think there was gonna be a strike. He said some told him yes and some told him no. I told him yes.

He said he hoped I was wrong. He said a strike hurt everybody. He dipped his head in a quick formal nod. I returned it and he moseyed on down the bar.

I drove us to her apartment. We didn't talk. We rode up in the elevator. We walked along the long lonely corridors, past the closed-up dental labs and the chiropractors' offices with the gold lettering on the windows. When she got to her door, she handed me the key. That was nice.

When we had our coats off, I pulled a kitchen chair over to the window and sat down and watched the snowflakes falling into the light. She was bustling around behind me doing whatever it is that women do before bed. I wondered if she didn't really want to get married. The snowflakes whirled and gusted. They couldn't heal anything but they sure could cover it up. I wondered if her figure was real. My mouth tasted horrible. I got up and turned around slow, giving her plenty of time to duck if she needed it. She was doing something to the bedclothes. She was so busy with them she didn't meet my eye.

"Mind if I use your toothbrush?" I asked.

"No, go ahead."

The bathroom was small, but it had a real tile floor. Little octagonal tiles, just like the floor of the train station. Bright red curtains. A bright blue doily on the radiator cover where she'd laid out her hair brushes and combs. I brushed my teeth with Ipana.

When I came out she was lying under the covers reading a magazine and smoking a cigarette. The magazine was the January *Life*. She was wearing pajama tops with the top button buttoned. Her breasts didn't look as high as they did when she was in her clothes. The ashtray was lying on the center of the outside half of the bed.

I sat down in the chair again. A turn to the right. A little white light. We're happy in *our blue heaven.*

I liked the "Butte Polka" better. Gay, insanely fast. If you ever could dance that fast, if ever your body could understand that well how to move—if your body ever became that wise, you could walk through your whole life with your eyes closed.

I took off my clothes and laid them on the chair. I slipped under the covers beside her. She'd given me the pillow with the embroidered aircraft carrier. Blue it was. Gold and red. The back of the pillow was white sateen. She had the ashtray in the hollow of her groin. I reached out and set it on the floor. She put down her magazine. Her eyes on me, frank and curious. I stroked her shiny brown hair but I don't think she felt my hand. As I leaned across her to flick the light off, her breasts tickled the hair on my stomach.

Snap.

The hissing of the radiator. Her breathing. I reached for her hand. "Your fingers are cold," she said, softly.

"I guess they'll warm up."

She chafed them briskly between her own hands. When you pay a woman to fuck you, it's safe. They never chafe your cold hands.

"I only did this once before," she said, more wondering than scared.

I didn't want to talk. I wanted to get inside her because I thought I understood that part of it. I waited, oppressed by timing. "Hello, Gail," I whispered, hoping that would be enough.

She put my hand on her chest, just below her breast. Her heartbeat fluttered her ribs. I hoped she wasn't waiting for me to say I loved her.

I found her lips in the dark and she breathed into me.

Two wild animals, met by chance at a crossroad in the wilderness; we circled, fought and surrendered completely.

When I rolled my knee between hers, she opened to me. She whispered, "Jimmy, I don't want to get married," and her voice was the smallest ferocity I'd ever heard.

But I didn't understand this part either. Since I hadn't paid, she was free to make me pay. I don't know what she did. I don't know what we did. I know she scratched my ass because I found the marks in the morning. I know her cunt muscles milked me and I don't think she had any more control over herself than I did.

Once she tapped my bare shoulder with the tip of her forefinger, like a sigh.

Once she said, "Jimmy," like she was christening me.

Afterwards we slept; curled about each other like two white bears in a white blizzard.

8

INQUEST HELD

A special inquest today determined that remains found in the No. 3 furnace at the Missouri River Steam Generating Plant were of person or persons unknown.

Judge Cogan directed the verdict after Dentist Jack Dritzen testified that the teeth found were too badly burned to be identified from dental records.

Frank Coad, prosecuting attorney, said, "It was probably some tramp crawled in there to get warm when the furnace was down and got caught when they turned it back on again."

Testifying were Deputy Bob Whitehead of the Sheriff's Department, Dr. Dritzen and Mr. Ketchel, a workman at the plant.

Gail Stinson wrote this story to save her job, but she didn't. The day after the inquest, the editor handed her the pink slip. That afternoon, I took my things out of my father's house and moved into her apartment.

9

I NEVER KNEW why the Indian came to Joel's wake. Maybe he was superstitious.

I don't even know how he found out about it. By then, nobody in town was talking to him, except Devlin, and the *Standard* wouldn't print an obituary. They said Joel didn't have a death certificate. Since we had his bones, we went ahead and buried him without one.

The union didn't need a certificate to cough up Joel's insurance, but he only carried five hundred dollars in death benefits and Kathleen had run up a few bills.

Me and the old man went up to Duggan's to buy the coffin. We hired them to do the burying too and we rented chairs for the wake. They said we should have Joel's wake in their fine modern funeral parlors. We said we didn't want to. They hinted we were old-fashioned and said wakes in the home weren't really the mode anymore. My father puffed himself up and told them a thing or two.

We argued about the coffin. I was all for planting Joel in one of the twenty-five-dollar pine boxes Duggan made up for the county. My father wanted something with more dignity than rough yellow pine. "Jimmy," he said, "he'll rattle around in that ugly box like a handful of BB's in a boxcar."

"How about a kid's coffin?" I said.

A hundred dollars.

It was white, about the size of a portable Victrola and lined with blue plush. They had pink plush for the infant girls, but this was no time for a political statement.

We brought it to Joel's house in the trunk of Joel's car.

Aunt Edith and Kathleen had moved all the furniture out of the parlor except for four straightback chairs. Two of them against the wall facing each other like they were having a conversation: the bier. The ladies sat on the other two, side by side, composed, as if the wake was already in progress.

The last time my sister wore black was when mother died and she'd filled out since then. Edith's modifications to her mourning dress didn't work because Kathleen'd had no breasts when she last wore it and she has large ones now.

Quite composed.

My father slipped me the nod and herded them into the kitchen. "Some details to discuss, Kathleen. Just some minor details."

When the door closed behind them, I got the coffin out of the car and brought it in. It looked like hell sitting on the two chairs, so I got a small plant table out of the bedroom and it looked better on that. Kathleen had the damn shoebox beside the bed. I suppose I should have just dumped the remains into the white coffin, but I couldn't. I laid the scraps of bone neatly on the blue plush in the shape of a crucifix. I don't know why. I never thought much about the resurrection of the dead and I don't guess Joel did either, but I suppose I wanted to hedge Joel's bets. If Father McDevitt *was* right, when Gabriel blew his horn and all the coffins all over the earth disgorged their contents, at least Joel'd make his appearance in an appropriate shape. I looked at the cross of bones for a few minutes. I cried. It was cold in the parlor and I could see my breath and I shivered. I wiped a spot off the coffin lid where one of my tears had streaked it.

Simple white, white box. Innocence.

A man's death is longer than his dying and can stretch on for years. So it was with my friend who died one winter night at the Missouri River Steam Plant.

It did not glow, that white box. It gave very little back. It was inward, not outward. It was cold to the touch, except where my hands had carried it. It was as full of life as a beehive on a July day with the honey coming in faster than the nurse bees can put it up.

The boys from Duggan's came. They brought more chairs. They brought black crepe and a wreath to hang over the door. They brought flowers. They covered the bier with crepe and arranged the flowers. They went away.

In the kitchen my father was talking. "Kathleen," he said, "you'll always have your memories. Nobody can take them away from you."

"Yes, Jim," Kathleen said in her new flat voice. "Thank you."

"He had a good life. A wonderful life. He fought for what he thought to be right."

"Sure."

Edith wanted me to drive her home and I was glad to go. Joel's car smelled more like me than it smelled like him.

The kids were dressed in their Sunday clothes. They were listening to *Stella Dallas* on the radio. I wanted to hug them but I'd never done that before and was afraid to start now.

Edith made up a quick lunch for the kids and started packing the baked meats for the funeral feast. A few women friends of the family dropped by and added their contributions. I carried the grub out to the car.

"Jimmy," Edith said, "don't forget about your father."

I didn't get it.

"Kathleen. . . . She's plenty tough," she said. "She'll do what she has to do."

"Jim Mullholland isn't a kid," I said.

"He's a foolish old man," she snapped at me. "You watch out for him."

I said sure, I would. She said she'd bring the children by that evening.

The keeners were waiting on the porch when I drove up to the house. I wasn't overjoyed to see them. The word "vultures" formed in my mind and it was a black word with feathers.

These elderly ladies, so entranced by death, so genteel, so dainty. They drew strength from the funeral feast.

I didn't know any of them. I'm sure Joel didn't either.

But I'd lay a dollar one or two had stayed up half the night ironing the lace on her choicest black linen dress—a little tattered now, one must admit—and traveled uptown all the way from Meaderville, or McQueen, changing buses two or three times to get here. We were a notorious death.

I'm afraid I said, "Hey, would a couple of you give me a hand? I've got all the food in the trunk and without it, everybody's gonna be mighty hungry before Sunday."

Several of them looked up at me, several stopped the clatter of their beads and cocked their ears. But none of them moved an inch. They knew their duty, precisely and to a penny's worth.

As I brushed through them I heard a murmur, no louder than the beat of a moth. "What a pity, he was a dear man, and him so young."

The florist had made another appearance during my absence and the parlor stank. If Joel's flesh had been rotting there, in that box, in that room, it would have smelled like the dying flowers did. I guess that's what they're for.

The keeners followed the groceries into the house. They came single file, beads working. I felt like I was leading the Lenten procession, only, instead of a statue of Our Lady, I was carrying a ham, glazed with honey and stuck with cloves.

A lot of flowers were sent for political reasons. Solidarity forever.

The black ladies filed to the second row of chairs, sat, and began their keening—a low cry somewhere between the cry of a mother grieving over her child and the snarl of a cat in heat. None of them stood by the coffin to pay their respects. They knew their limits.

The keeners were here and until the coffin left the house for the church, they would remain. Their presence eased Joel further out of our lives.

My father helped me lay out the food on Kathleen's blondwood dresser. He didn't say anything. He'd never been too good a talker and consoling Kathleen had used him up. Hams, a turkey, casseroles of tuna fish, and macaroni and cheese. Little Jell-O creations with chicken floating around inside. The dresser had a six-foot top but we covered it and had to put a couple casseroles on the floor.

Maybe my father was trying to puzzle things out. He wasn't very good at that either, though he had the urge. Like me.

We put out a stack of paper plates to reduce the washing up after.

My father's mourning band was redundant on the sleeve of his black suit. It will be, I thought, the suit he'll be buried in. I was wrong—he was buried in a grave with forty others who couldn't be identified—but the thought of his funeral suit made me sad at the time. I thought it strange to see the cloth stretch and flex as his arms rearranged the platters to his satisfaction.

The bedroom was a dark room with only one window facing the winter street and only one lamp beside the bed. It was a little hard to make out what the food was. A mound of nourishment on a bleached slab of wood in a dark room.

"What time you got?" he asked.

"Six."

"I guess I better get out there," he said. "Most of them will start comin' soon. You too, Jimmy."

I didn't want to greet the mourners and told him so.

He said I better learn how to do it, because I'd be head of the family soon.

I wasn't ready for the job.

Kathleen sat in the front row; the family row. Not saying anything and not crying either. She was watching the white coffin as if it might do something.

Later she told me she'd been wondering how many of Joel's bones the cops had returned to us. She'd never opened the shoebox to see and wouldn't open the coffin now. She was afraid someone at the courthouse had kept a piece of Joel as a souvenir.

Edith had borrowed the forty-cup coffee urn from the rectory and it stood, squat, on the kitchen counter, red light glowing. My father had put a couple fifths of Bushmills on the kitchen table. Five more cases out in the garage.

My father's face was ruddy as a heart attack victim's. Red splotches on his dead white cheeks. He stood at the door greeting his old friends, smoothly as he could. "Ah, Mike, good of you to come. And Mrs. Sullivan, it's good to see you tonight. Yes, sorrowful. Will you sign the guest book, please?"

Joel was packing them in. Before eight, the parlor was full, most of the men were on the front porch or back in the kitchen and the women were filing by the dead white coffin in slow turns.

"Sorry to hear, Mrs. Kangas. . . ."

"Sorry to hear. . . ."

"Anything we can do. Anything. . . ."

"So young. . . ."

"Him so young. . . ."

"They'll get the bastard that done it. Excuse the language."

Kathleen hugged her women friends and let herself be hugged by the more demonstrative men. She urged all the strangers to eat.

When Edith brought the kids in, the keeners, sensing drama, upped the forte half a decibel or so. Shirley was alarmed by the presence of all these strangers in her house and began to wail. Carl took her hand and said something to her I couldn't make out and she calmed down. Resolute in his short dark pants, he towed his taller sister behind him to the bier. He crossed himself and knelt. Shirley rather more awkwardly followed his lead. Everybody watched them though nobody knew what they were thinking or understood. Shirley said something with the word "Daddy" in it, but Carl shushed her again. Briskly, duty performed, he rose and the two of them sat beside their mother.

Bob Whitehead excused himself through the crowded room and paid his respects to the little white box. He was a Protestant and didn't cross himself, but just stood there, head bowed, with his hat clutched behind his back like it was his passport out of there. Whitehead was losing his hair right on the top of his skull. Like a tonsure.

Sam Curnew's breath reeked of Sen-Sen and he kept his eyes on the Deputy's back. "When's he gonna put the cuffs on that Indian?" he asked. Sam's dark suit was too tight across his shoulders and his ancient stained rag of a tie had him by the throat.

"He did what he could," I said. I watched the Deputy offer condolences to my sister. I thought she'd not find it too easy to remarry with two children in the bargain. "He found the body, didn't he?" I said.

Sam wore a union button in his lapel. It was the kind of button you'd wear to a convention.

"Yeah, I suppose," he said, losing interest. "Gonna be some bigshots here tomorrow. Just thought I'd let you know."

"Who?"

"From the International. From Denver. They're flying in on Western Airlines."

I didn't care too much.

Shirley started to cry. I guess when Bob Whitehead sat down next to her mother, she got scared.

Kathleen pressed her against her bosom. Her wailing picked up steam and overwhelmed the modest shrieks and moans of the keeners. Edith picked her up and rocked her. "Hush, honey. It's all right." The Deputy touched Kathleen's arm. I felt sick.

Fifty people in the parlor. It wasn't cold anymore—we'd warmed it. Three deep against the back wall, fifteen or twenty in the kitchen at the Bushmills and more out on the front porch having a smoke or getting the air. Plenty union men, my father's friends and even two classmates of mine from the School of Mines. Notorious case.

The ladies ferried more casseroles through the crowd into the bedroom and arranged them along the wall like offerings.

I went outside, stunned by the closeness. It was ten below zero but I didn't need a coat, didn't want a coat, leaned against the porch railing and glared up at the stars.

There was minimum room in front of the house for Father McDevitt's Buick—just a small space behind Joel's old Plymouth. He wrestled the Buick for five minutes before he got the heavy car into the space and when he quit he had his left rear wheel up on the curb.

The men on the porch removed their hats. "Good evening, Father, Father, Father, Father . . ." and he was red faced and puffing a little.

My father took the priest's black hat but didn't quite know what to do with it. Kathleen stood when McDevitt came in and stared at him, her eyes saying nothing. He knelt in front of the white box and went through his moves. He rose, beckoned to Kathleen and she followed into the bedroom. I tagged along.

He'd been to a thousand wakes but the child's coffin shocked him a little. "It's an awful thing," he whispered to Kathleen. "I'm sorry."

"God knows what's best," Kathleen said.

And Father McDevitt gave her a sharp look. Despair?

"We cannot know His ways," he said.

"It was men that killed him," I put in.

He just looked at me. This was between the widow and her priest. "Jimmy," he said.

I was ashamed.

"Father," Kathleen asked, "is Joel . . . is he all there? I wish to bury all of him." Little girl's voice now. Stubborn little girl.

He didn't understand. She explained her fears. I slipped back into the parlor and leaned over Bob Whitehead. He had small white hairs growing out of his ear. "Bob," I said, "uh, Kathleen's worried. She's afraid that one of the courthouse boys lifted a bone or something. You know. Just a small one. For a souvenir."

He turned his face around. He didn't whisper. "What the fuck do you think we are?" he asked.

"Sure," I said. "No offense."

Back in the bedroom I caught Father McDevitt's eye and flashed him the okay.

"Joel is . . . all present, Kathleen," he said. "His remains . . . uh . . . what there is of him . . . uh, child!" He said "child!" fiercely. "Trust God. Can we pray for the repose of his soul?" And we knelt on the cold floor and prayed.

Joel would have laughed at us.

I brushed off my knees thinking just that and when the priest escorted my sister back into the parlor for the rosary, I slipped over by the kitchen door. Escape hatch.

Everyone knelt. The sound of chairs scraping. The grunts as heavy ladies went to their knees. The priest began and the murmur of their voices accompanied him, though not very loud, no louder than the cough of a frightened man on a deserted road.

I stood it as long as I could before I eased through the kitchen door and pressed my head against the door, eyes closed, drifting.

Throat-clearing, the scrape of chairs, a few whispers—done. People relaxing—the odd tentative smile, the social nod. Soon the keeners would line up to get a plate of food.

I took my head off the door so I wouldn't get flattened by the Bushmills crowd. I wasn't hungry. I didn't want to talk. I turned around and looked at the half dozen men who'd got a good start on the second bottle of Bushmills during the prayers.

Papsi Maroni grinned at me. "An Irish wake," he said. "That's where the miners congregate."

"And the drunks," I said. "I didn't know you for any particular friend of Joel's."

Some drunk was sucking on the bottle. White faced. Sweating.

"Oh, my boy," Papsi said, retrieving the bottle and handing it to me. "Here, this'll wash it down."

It did. I coughed. I wiped off the neck of the bottle with the heel of my hand and let it get away from me.

My father came into the kitchen, ignored the other drinkers, bellied me back into a corner between the sink and the wall among Kathleen's brooms. "What's the matter with you," he hissed. "Ain't you got no damn sense?"

"Huh?"

"I don't care whether you believe it or not, God damn you. Kathleen does. You don't walk out on Father McDevitt when he's leading a prayer."

"I'm prayed out," I said. Not being so wiseguy as I sounded, but thinking how cold it had been on my knees in the bedroom.

"God damn you," he snapped. "What in the hell's this family gonna come to once I'm gone?"

And he backed away from me. And wore his stern face of disgust. He slammed the door.

"He givin' it to you, Jimmy boy?" Papsi grinned at me.

"Fuck yourself."

Soon the kitchen was packed with men and the Bushmills was speeding around. The door was open onto the spindly back porch and some men stood around outside.

Most of the mourners came in and took a drink with me and said something solemn or mumbled something and gathered their wives and went home. But there were plenty of others who were there to make a wake out of it, by God, to honor Joel Kangas like they'd want to be honored themselves.

I waited my turn at the bottle with an avidity that scared me. I was determined to drink fullest, deepest, be assured of more than my share. Old Mr. Bushmill didn't mind in the least. After an hour or so, I lost most of my speech and greeted everybody with a sullen stare. Soon enough, most of those who'd needed to speak to me had and the remainder wouldn't get near me with a ten-foot pole.

My father returned to say he was sorry for losing his temper. He said, "All a man can do, Jimmy, is lessen the death he leaves behind him." He asked if I understood. I said I did, but I was lying in my teeth. I didn't want to get his dander up again.

Papsi was hitting the bottle pretty hard. When he saw me watching him, he said, "We're all having a drink on Joel tonight—eh, Jimmy?"

"Sure," I said. "After all the drinks you stood him at Spillum's, I guess he wouldn't mind."

Papsi flushed. He'd never been too quick to order a round.

Bob Whitehead came in and surveyed us with his cop's eyes. "I could use a little something," he said, in the voice of a man who usually gets what he wants. Papsi passed the bottle. Whitehead wiped off the neck and took a deep draught. He held the bottle up to the light, "Damn Bushmills," he said. "Give me good American whiskey any time." That didn't stop him from taking another deep swallow. He looked at me then, differently, not like a cop, like a man. He was nervous too. "I can't get a breath in here," he said. "I'm goin' out to the car. Jimmy?"

So I followed him. The cars were lined up all along Jackson Street, both sides. Whitehead started the motor of his sedan and got the heater going. It blew a lot of

cold air up my pant leg. "Christ, Whitehead," I said.
"Wait until the motor warms up."

Our cold breath froze as it touched the windshield
and soon we were behind a white shiny wall.

Whitehead pulled a pint bottle of hooch out of the
glove compartment, jerked the cork with his teeth and
passed it to me. Bourbon. After the Bushmills it tasted
sweet as soda pop.

He fooled around with the radio dial until he got
Salt Lake City. Tommy Dorsey. The music kept fading
in and out.

I burped. Bushmills and bourbon. I said, "Shit."

I said, "Joel was a Red," to no one in particular.

"Who gives a hairy fuck," the Deputy said.

"Devlin," I said.

"Fuck him too."

"I think I'll go back inside," I said.

"Don't be in such a godawful hurry," Bob said. "Here,
have another."

I washed down the bile in my throat.

"Kathleen looks like hell," he ventured.

"Well," I said, politely, "it's been real tough on her."

"Yeah," he growled. "You hear I almost got canned?"

The defroster was clearing little half moons of visi-
bility on the windshield.

"Fucking Frank Coad. The Company scared him
white. He comes downstairs. I'll bet it's the first time
he's been in the sheriff's office since I been there. I
thought he was gonna have a fucking seizure. He says
to me it's all my fault. I says to him, 'We found Kangas's
bones, didn't we?' and he says he doesn't give a damn,
he's gonna nail my hide to the fence. Well, the sheriff
comes in then. Sheriff Blair don't care very much. He
retires next year and if they fuck with him, he can raise

a shitstorm like you've never seen. He tries to calm Coad down. He says I ain't a wiseguy, I'm just dumb."

"Well," I said, "Kathleen sure thanks you. It was driving her crazy, not knowing."

He lit up a Camel. "Sure."

I said, "More doctors smoke Camels than any other cigarette."

He said, "I ain't no doctor."

I said, "You do all right as a deputy, I guess."

He said, "I get by."

The car smelled like booze, farts, and bad conscience. The cigarette smoke was burning my eyes. I turned the radio dial and picked up a lot of static. I turned it off.

"You too? You a Red too?" he asked.

I didn't much want to answer him. Maybe I wouldn't have if Kathleen hadn't had the kids. "No," I said. "I ain't interested in politics."

"Me neither," he said. "It just ain't worth it."

"Thanks for finding Joel," I said. "That's from me."

"I try," he said. "When I was in Germany I saw things—starving kids, women who'd do anything for a pack of butts, doctors stealin' penicillin out of their own hospitals. I learned."

"Learned what?"

"Keep your eyes and ears open and your mouth and asshole shut. I do my job. I don't make trouble."

"Well, you stirred it up this time."

"Like the sheriff said, I'm real dumb." He barked his laugh. "Maybe if the Reds take over they'll make me the sheriff, I don't think."

"Yeah," I said. The Deputy said he had to get to work, that it was nice talkin' to me, that I wasn't a bad kid. "Thanks a whole lot," I said.

Inside, the crowd had thinned some. Thursday night.

One A.M. Half the keeners had gone home until the morning. They ran a two-shift operation. Edith had the kids at her house and my father had gone on shift. I sat down beside Kathleen. She gave me a quick, tired smile. I patted her hand.

Most of the drinkers had quit too; only a few hard cases trying to finish the rest of the Bushmills before it finished them. They thought the booze was all right. I did too.

My co-drinkers were dressed in a range of fashions from hand-me-down to down-and-out. They were glad to see me. I couldn't say the same.

My brain was working fine, if the brain's an old cogwheel with a couple teeth missing. It spun around and around, making the same lurch at the same spot each time, wearing itself into smooth pot metal.

"Hey, don't hog the dew, Jimmy boy."

"He was my brother-in-law," I said. "Not yours." And my eyes were enough to drive all but the most resolute out of the room. These men were the most resolute: survivors of a thousand insults, ten thousand slights. Grins all around. Somebody slicked the bottle from my grasp.

I thought: "Joel Kangas was my brother-in-law," and that relationship seemed very special to me. "Brother-in-law" was shorthand for all the marvelous things Joel meant to me that I couldn't really remember. I knew I'd remember later when my head was clearer; and I thought the four men in the kitchen were taking advantage and of course they were.

And I thought I'd created this wake and now I was its attendant. Of course that wasn't true but it made a phrase to go around in my mind which satisfied me by its ironical flavor. "I created it and now I'm its attendant," I thought, and for some reason that made me feel better and the phrase went pretty good with the other phrase, "You don't have to be a Commie to be a Red."

"You don't have to be a Commie to be a Red," I said.

"That's right, Jimmy boy. You just wait your turn now. Papsi's cracking another one."

And my eyes started to water and my thoughts melted into such a great radiance that I wanted to cry out and I knew, I *knew* that these poor sinners would understand because isn't that the reason that Christ went to the outcasts first? Because they'd understand?

I choked. "How's the food?" I asked.

"Oh fine, Jimmy boy. First rate. Here, have a little slug of this. It'll bring you around all right. Tragic."

"What'd you say?"

"Tragic. It sure was tragic about Joel. He was a fine man. You won't find his like again."

"Unless you turn over a rock," I said. I knew I had to lie about Joel to these men or they'd ruin him for me.

"Haw, haw, haw. You always was a joker."

"Sure." And I took my memories of Joel and my shaking legs into the other room.

I made up some kind of sandwich, ham and roast beef and pickles and a scoop of sweet-potato salad and ate it with my face to the bedroom window because I was crying and didn't want anyone to see. I took a cup of coffee like a draught of medicine and took another cup of coffee and a third. I looked at the flowered wallpaper that Kathleen had picked out for her bedroom and remembered helping Joel scrape off the old wallpaper, cursing it, the pair of us sticky with old paste and water and not dreaming that each one of those layers was somebody's life we were removing.

I sat down in the back of the viewing room. Murmured prayers. The rattle of the beads from the keeners at their duty. Kathleen sitting by herself. I fixated on the coffin and tried not to pass out.

It was a near thing. There was still booze in my stomach ready to enter my blood in turn and one sandwich and three cups of coffee wasn't much of a defense.

I won't describe my efforts to keep my eyes open— the biting of the inside of my cheek, the discreet head shakes—because you've been there yourself and there's no need to.

I was sweating like a pig. I tightened my necktie until I felt the pressure in my eyes. Kathleen rose finally, about four o'clock, and looked at me, a little worried, and I managed a ghastly smile which she answered with a sad one before she left for my father's house for some sleep.

Just before dawn, I got convinced I was struggling for the soul of Joel Kangas, which was ridiculous but the lie helped me until I was more sober and knew with the dawn pressing on those curtained frosted windows that it was my prissy little soul at stake. Ain't we something?

It got light. It took a long time, but it got there and when I went outside for a cigarette, the old snow on the ground was crusted and dirty. I walked back through the parlor, past the remaining ladies. The kitchen was wrecked. Somebody'd puked into the sink. Somebody else had dropped a bottle and there was glass all over the floor. Papsi Maroni was unconscious in the corner. Judging from his shirt front, he was the one who'd puked.

"Up and at 'em, Papsi. Time to go home."

I got him to his feet and scrubbed his face off with Kathleen's dishcloth and found his hat and his coat. He was saying about what you'd expect, "Oh, Jaysus, oh,

Jaysus." I took him to the door. He could find his own way home and I guess he did.

It felt pretty good cleaning up the mess though I couldn't help wondering why the stomach continues to go about its business, digesting food, when the stomach's boss is off on a drunk.

I splashed some water on my greasy face. I put some of my sister's Ivory soap on a dishtowel and scrubbed.

Kathleen had taken Joel's car so I walked over town. Jesus, it was cold and crisp and clear.

When I walked into Gail's apartment, I nearly stumbled over her overnight case. She came out of the bedroom, all duded up in a severely tailored green suit and a little pillbox hat attached to her hair with pins. "Oh," she said.

"G'mornin'." I knew I looked like hell and probably smelled that way too. "You on your way out?" Since her coat was draped neatly over her overnight case, my question was just marking time.

She nodded. She tried out a smile that was too small for her mouth. "Missoula," she said briskly. "I've got some good friends on the faculty of the journalism school. If there's an opening for me on another paper, they'll know about it."

"Uh-huh." I sat down heavily on a kitchen chair. "Good luck," I said.

"How was the wake?" she asked, brightly.

I shrugged.

"Well," she observed, "from the look of your eyes, you must have really tied one on."

I shrugged again. I looked at the oilcloth that covered the table. There was a tiny crusted lump of something she'd missed during her cleaning attempts and I picked at it with my fingernail.

She came over and put her hand on my shoulder. It felt very light. "Jimmy, are you mad at me?"

"Why should I be mad at you?"

She removed her hand like it was burnt. She set her face like a sad concrete mask. She said something I could barely make out that might have been, "God knows why. I don't." And picked up her coat.

I thought about getting up and hugging her but I smelled too bad. "Good luck," I said again, but I doubt she heard me because she'd slammed the door behind her.

I stood up and addressed the spot where she'd been standing. "You didn't even come to Joel's wake," I said. Then I put my hands on my hips. "Some Mullholland you'd make," I said.

I didn't sleep very long, just until noon, and I woke wide eyed, my heart pounding. I had one other clean white shirt. I thought it'd probably last me through Sunday if I didn't do any more drinking.

Kathleen and I sat alone in the parlor all afternoon. The dusty silence as the sunlight drifted across the bare floor. The flowers were wilting.

You sit with the body so spirits don't enter it while it's unmourned. If the spirits get in, they won't let the death progress toward forgetfulness.

The wake was quieter tonight which was a good thing because we'd gone through three of the five cases of booze and I was damned if I was going to buy any more.

The keeners were back in force—five of them—and Father McDevitt came by to say the rosary again. With Jim Mullholland's eyes on me, I went down on my knees with the rest.

Bob Whitehead showed up about eleven and stayed

an hour. Sam Curnew never made an appearance and the two union bigshots he'd promised didn't show up either.

I walked home again at dawn. I thought that I liked walking around in the very early morning. Maybe I should get on the graveyard and I could walk home through the crisp streets every morning. Maybe, in a week or so, I'd go talk to Walker and get my job back. Fuck him.

Gail's bed was empty. I folded my clothes carefully.

I woke up Saturday noon, full of purpose with nothing to spend it on. My mind wouldn't let go of that damn white coffin until it was in the ground, but any thoughts I had now were just crazy. Can't get a grip, can't let go.

I spent the afternoon with Joel. As I sat there, alone, Joel gradually let go his hold on my heart and gave me peace.

Kathleen and Bob Whitehead arrived about six thirty. Bob had a case of bourbon—Old Crow—which he put in the kitchen. I helped him stash a Bushmills and an Old Crow behind the kids' breakfast cereal. Like Bob said—tonight was the last night of the wake and we needed a little something in reserve.

Bob sat down in the front row between my father and my sister.

Gail came up on the porch just as Father McDevitt was trying to push Frank Bick's Pontiac out of the way with the Buick's massive bumper. Frank must have had the Pontiac in gear because the Father had to rev the hell out of the Buick to do any good.

Gail had parked up the street somewhere. I couldn't see her car anywhere. She wore the same severe green suit. She wore ladies' high rubbers. She watched the priest bang Frank Bick's car around.

I leaned against the porch railing and lit up a smoke. Finally Frank's Pontiac skidded back on the ice and Father McDevitt began to nose his Buick in. "Glad you could make it," I said to her, with a big false smile. "I was wonderin' where you were."

Her face was tight. "We're not married, you know, Jimmy," she said.

"No shit."

"I'm not family, Jimmy."

I dropped my eyes before she did. "Yeah," I said. "How'd it go in Missoula?"

"Not so good. Every newspaper has men reporters coming back from the war. I heard the Great Falls *Tribune* has a vacancy in their Sunday edition—a homemaker's column, but that's only one day a week and they pay by the inch. The Deseret *News* needs a society reporter."

"Salt Lake."

"Yep."

"What kind of society they got in Salt Lake?"

"You're real smart," she said. "But not smart enough to keep me from getting fired."

"I never told you you had to help."

"Seems to me you never say much of anything, Jimmy. But you're real good at trying to make me feel bad."

She put on a nice smile for the priest puffing up the walk toward us. "I'm sorry," she said to me, quietly. "I guess I'm upset. My rent's paid until the end of the month. Then I'm going to Salt Lake. You can tag along if you want to."

"Maybe," I said. "Maybe I will. Come on. Let's go inside."

After the prayers I brought her over to my sister. I hoped they liked each other. Each of them hoped that too. "Thank you," Kathleen said, "for trying to find him."

"Sure," Gail said. Awkwardly, she patted Kathleen's black shoulder.

"I understand from Old Jim that you lost your job on our account."

Gail made a funny face like a comedienne. "Well, maybe I didn't like the job anyway. I've just heard about a better job."

My sister looked at me and I looked right back.

"I'm sorry if you're leaving Butte," she said.

I thought they'd talk better without the presence of yours truly so I mumbled some excuse.

The kitchen was full of men, but everyone was on best behavior since Father McDevitt was there, peering rather unhappily at a bottle of Old Crow. I went up behind the cereal boxes for the Bushmills.

"Ah, Jimmy," he said when I handed him the bottle of Irish. "Ahhh." He took a good swallow. "Phew. Here's to Joel Kangas, God rest his soul. He worked hard for his family. He was honest. He wasn't of the Faith but he let his two children be reared in it." He took another swallow and when he passed the bottle on, we all took a nip.

"To Joel."

"Here's to him."

"He was a friend to every workingman," somebody said.

Just the two slugs, that's all the Father allowed himself in our company.

The fellow who came in the front door with Sam Curnew was about my age, dark haired, wearing a cheap black suit right off the rack. The suit had been meant for a big chesty man, not for him. His eyes were dark too and they ranged over everyone, alert to sudden moves.

Sam tapped his elbow, whispered in his ear and they both went over to speak to Kathleen. Sam talked to her for a minute or two but the dark-haired fellow kept his condolences brief.

Respectfully, his head lowered, Sam passed down the rows of chairs toward the kitchen. Sam wore a blank face and sad eyes. The fellow behind him walked with his head lowered too, just like Sam. The fellow wore a union pin, much like Sam's, only his pin was more discreet, and while Sam's pin was tin, the other fellow's was silver.

Following in his wake, I got a whiff of his aftershave. It was the same Old Spice I use.

Inside the kitchen, Sam shed his stiffness and went for the bottle. The fellow rested his back against the kitchen cabinets and faced us. He nodded to me because I'd been watching him but his eyes slid right off mine.

"Men," Sam said. "I'd like to introduce an official of Mine Mill International. He's come to Butte on this tragic occasion on behalf of the union. His name's Mike. Mike Rostov."

Most of the miners lined up to shake his hand. He gave a long-faced crooked smile and a handshake to each one of them. I whispered in Sam's ear. "He's two union bigshots?"

Sam's eyes closed down a notch. "At least they sent

somebody, Jimmy. Who the hell else did? Mike!" he called. "Come on over here, comrade. I got somebody I'd like you to meet."

So I took his hand, saying, "Jimmy Mullholland," and "Glad you could come."

He dipped one shoulder briefly. "The president was going to come, but, at the last minute, he decided his presence might be misinterpreted. We don't want to heat up the strike talk Sam's been telling me about." He had a smooth, honey voice and it surprised me coming from him. Except for his voice he was all sharp edges.

"The miners want to go out," I said. I didn't say I wasn't a miner just now. "As soon as Sam here schedules a strike vote, the men'll go out."

And the fellow just smiled and nodded, not like he agreed with me—he'd heard me, that's all.

So we all had a couple. Sam offered a toast to Joel and then somebody else did too. The fellow took a swig out of the bottle just like the rest of us but I think he'd rather have had a glass.

The fellow spoke about the strike and as he warmed to his subject, his cheeks lost some of their pallor. His voice was his instrument. He said much the same sort of thing Sam said: that Mine Mill would never win this strike and that a failed strike would be an excuse for the Company to bust the union. He also said there wasn't much money in the strike fund, which was news to all of us. My father came into the kitchen to meet the union bigshot and listened quietly. Finally he said, in his soft voice, "But what about Joel Kangas?"

"A hero of the working class."

"He's dead," my father insisted. "What are you going to do about it?"

"There's nothing we can do about it," the fellow snapped.

"None of us'll get out of it alive," someone remarked from the kitchen doorway. It was Burke.

And his pal, Walker, was with him. Walker made a grab for the bottle and he got it.

I hadn't seen the Company men come in. I wondered if they'd bypassed the coffin to come directly to the kitchen. But afterwards, Kathleen told me they hadn't, that they'd talked to her about Joel and that "they were nicer by a long sight than that kid Sam brought in."

Sam wrinkled his nose like they were dubious meat. "This is a worker's funeral, Burke."

Walker: "I heard it was Joel Kangas's wake. We thought we'd lend the proceedings a little class."

"Aw, fuck, Walker," Burke said. "Come off it." To Sam: "Kangas was a good man. We're both sorry he's gone. He was just a man we worked with, that's all."

"He was a *Red*," Sam said. I don't think Sam would have put the issue in those terms if the fellow from the International hadn't been at his side.

"Yeah," Walker said. "We heard that he was. I think we heard something about that." He took a hit of Bushmills and offered me the bottle. "Forget about the other day, Jimmy," he said. "Come back to work on Monday and we'll fix you up a new rustling card. I'm short of good machinists."

Nobody else was talking. Walker and Burke had the floor to themselves. Burke said they'd come to say how damn sorry they were. A couple miners nodded but kept mum. Walker grabbed for the bottle again, though it hadn't made a full round.

"Oh, hell," he said. He spotted the dark stranger,

stepped up and stuck out his paw. "My name's Walker,"
he said. "You must be new in town. I ain't seen you
before."

Real quick, Sam identified them. "Company men.
They scabbed in '34."

The dark-haired fellow gave the two of them his long-
faced crooked smile but put his right hand in his pocket.

Walker looked us all over, like he would remember
every man's face. More than a few miners looked at
Kathleen's floor. "Fuck you then," Walker said. "And
the horse you rode in on." He passed the bottle to Burke,
who took it like it wasn't completely welcome. Walker
rocked back on his heels and pushed his thumbs into his
belt. "Actually," he said, "we come here lookin' for a
little action. The Vargas-Ketchel fight is on. The date's
set for next Saturday at the 1,2,3. Now how many of you
dumb bohunks want to put money on Vargas."

"Walker," Burke said. "Maybe this ain't the time for
it. Skip it."

Walker gave him a look. "Hell," he said. "We got
money on Ketchel to take Vargas. We say Ketchel's the
better man. I got a grand ridin' and you got better'n
four hundred. I don't talk to Ketchel or tell him what to
do. I ain't bought him a drink in my life, even."

"Once," Burke said. "Once we gave him a bottle of
Scotch."

"And I don't know if Ketchel killed Joel Kangas or
not. I know there's talk he did. Maybe Ketchel is a little
nuts and maybe I shouldn't have bet a grand on him.
But I did. Jim Sly is backin' Vargas so there's gonna be
a fight no matter what I do. I ain't just tossin' my money
away, you know. I'm backin' my assessment."

The fellow from Denver was behind Sam Curnew
now. I hadn't noticed him move, but he had.

Sam said, "And the bones of the man Ketchel murdered in the next room. It's the Company's doin', Walker. You know it is."

"Sure," Walker said. "That's all they do downtown in the offices. They sit around and try to figure ways to knock off wiseguy miners."

"You boys gonna be shooting any strikers this time?" Sam asked.

Burke picked up a glass and held it up like he was looking for a fly. He didn't find one. "I never shot nobody," he said. "They don't own me, you know. It's just a paycheck."

"They own every one of us," Sam said.

"Except Jimmy," Papsi Maroni said. "He's free as a little birdy in the sky."

"Oh yeah," Walker said. "I heard something about that."

"Lucky Jimmy." Burke was grinning.

"You're better off than these other stiffs," Walker said. "Sam's gonna take everybody out and nobody'll be drawing a check."

"Except you," Sam said. "And the rest of the scabs."

Walker started to throw a pretty good punch, but my father got between them and intercepted the punch and got knocked into the wall and got the air knocked half out of him.

"Decent," he wheezed through the hole in his white face, "this is a decent house, and it's a dead man's house, and it's his booze you're drinking. Take your damn hooligan brawls out of here."

"Hey, hey. What's this all about, now?" Bob Whitehead came in behind Burke and Walker—big and legal —flatfooted on the floor. "The ladies are complainin' about the noise. Keep it down, for Chrissake."

"Sorry," Burke said.

"Get that bastard out of here!" Sam pointed a shaky finger at Walker. Whitehead looked at me for instructions. With my father hurt I guess I was man of the family.

"Why don't you boys go into the other room for a while," I said. "I know you didn't come to make trouble."

"Sure," Burke said, and Walker nodded right along with him and they favored us with twin grins and Walker said, "Sorry, Jim."

Everybody cleared out of the kitchen.

I brought my father a drink of water. "Where's it hurt?"

He tapped his bony ribcage and gasped and I could see he didn't want to start coughing and couldn't talk. After a bit, he nodded at me and took a drink of water.

"Who do you think you are?" I asked. "Joe Palooka?"

A little cough escaped him, like a peep. "It didn't hurt me," he said. "It's nothin'."

"Sure."

He took another sip of water.

"You ought to go home and get some sleep," I said. "You were up all last night."

"I didn't think you noticed. I won't be workin' much longer," he said. "And the social security will barely keep me."

"And I'm not workin' at all."

"The union will pay for the funeral. And they'll pass the hat for Kathleen."

"I've got a few bucks," I said.

"You'll need 'em, Jimmy boy." He shook his head. "Your girl friend too."

I said sure. I said Gail was thinking of leaving town

and I was too and he just looked at me, neither aye or nay.

When we came out into the parlor, the union guys were gone and the Company guys too. My father was still shaken and he took a chair in the back. Bob White-head craned around to check us out and I gave him a nod. Welcome to the family.

Kooteney Ketchel turned in at the gate of the small house. The gate had a black wreath on it. He wiped his snowy shoes carefully on the mat before he came into the house. A couple of mourners were just inside the door putting on their coats. He waited for them to move and when they didn't, he said, "Please."

They don't connect.

Kooteney is wearing a new suit that's been torn pretty badly and mended, clumsily, with carpet thread.

The mourners, I'm afraid, just stare at him.

I connect.

Kooteney's suit was pressed. The strings of black thread were pressed flat against the greasy fabric.

A timid smile. He inspected all the walls of the room except the front wall. His hat. He had his hat in front of his groin.

Whispering. Other people connected. Glanced at him once and looked away.

My father breathed in my ear, "Holy Mother of God."

Bob Whitehead stood up, but stood still.

Kooteney's face shone with sweat. His eyes fluttered around the room like moths.

A slight hiss from the keeners. Like snakes disturbed in their winter den.

I was watching the back of Kathleen's head and I couldn't swear that some breeze didn't ruffle her hair, brush the nape of her neck just above her stiff black lace collar. Her head came around smoothly, deliberately, like the gun turret of a great ship swivels, locked to the target. In the same motion, she rose.

She put her eyes on him.

He ducked his as long as he could. Contact.

Two poles of a battery. Burning the air between them.

You'd think I'd remember seeing her start to move, but I do not. She moved toward him.

She held out her hand, palm uppermost.

Twenty seconds later, his hand slipped into hers, flew into it like a sparrow flees into a dark cave.

He came with her, easy as a bride.

The bier. She lifted the lid of that child's box and he looked within.

She kept her eyes on his face.

That little crucifix of silent burnt bones.

Kathleen drew from his face everything she wanted to know.

10

GAIL WAS PASTING CLIPPINGS on the black pages of her leatherbound scrapbook with rubber cement she'd lifted from the Montana *Standard* when she'd cleaned out her desk. The editor had promised her a good reference. He was sorry and better luck next time.

Shoes off, I was curled up on the couch with a copy of the *Information Please Almanac*. "There's a half million people living in Salt Lake," I said. "They mine salt out of the lake. Maybe I can get on there. They got a couple colleges too: University of Utah and Brigham Young. It don't say if they have night classes. Probably be a lot of vets enrolling. It won't be easy to get in."

"Uh-huh," Gail said. "You'll get in if you want to. How 'bout some tea?"

She put the water on and returned to center another

clipping in what she called "her sample case." The radio was playing: Bob Wills and the Texas Playboys singing about "Daddy's Little Fatty." The radiators hissing. The wind shaking the windows. The Highway Department announced that the road to Anaconda was closed. Ditto the nineteen-mile pass. The radio played Dan Hicks and His Hot Licks.

I felt like a householder. I liked the feeling.

The radio said it was eleven P.M. and that we were listening to Butte's Best on KBOW.

Gail was flipping through the pages of the scrapbook noting the place of each story but not reading them. "I don't know," she said. "I just don't know."

"You'll get in if you want to," I said.

She flicked me a nasty look.

I got off the couch and turned the scrapbook toward me. "Looks fine to me," I said. The first pages were all society events: big weddings, benefits, the golf tournament at the country club. People's names; names of their clothes; a few lonely verbs.

In the middle, she had an article on the Mesopust Festival—the annual Croatian blowout—and her crime pieces. She put her longest crime pieces in the back where a prospective employer would get to them if he was real, real interested. "You don't show your best quarterhorse to a man who's come to buy a cow," she'd said.

I didn't really remember seeing any of the articles though I read the *Standard* fairly regularly. She explained that nobody really read newspaper articles, they just noted them, like a man counting votes.

"You've got really pretty eyes," I said.

She said she had to get some resumes typed and I

should turn loose of her ass. So I sat down on the couch again, miffed.

"Why don't you send some of those off to the other Montana papers?" I asked.

She was inspecting her carbon paper. "I've no reason to stay in Montana," she said. "And you don't either." She flipped her carbon paper over. "How many carbons do you think I should make?"

"I never learned to type. I never wrote no resume."

She laughed, "Sure. You're just another empty-headed mucker. Now why don't you read something, or something, and let me get this done."

"I'm tired of reading."

She said "Tssk" and started to peck on her typewriter.

I drank my tea in twenty seconds. I got up again and paced.

"Jimmy, please. You're nervous as a cat."

"Well. Hell. When you're done, let's go out some place and have a drink. Johnny's Hot-Shots are playing at the Acoma."

"Jimmy, it's late. It's snowing. I've got work to do. If you're bored, you go ahead and go out. I'm happy here."

I looked at her and wondered how she'd look when she got old. Her skin already had wrinkles it didn't need and her dandruff was bad. I thumbed through *Life* magazine, looking at the car ads. I wondered what the new cars would look like once they were old enough for me to buy. I tossed the magazine down. "Why don't you want to get married?"

She kept her eyes on her resume but she stopped typing. "I told you already. I grew up with three brothers and a father. I'm tired of picking up after men."

"I don't understand you."

She looked at me, eye to eye, and shrugged.

"What if you get knocked up?"

Her yellow Faber pencil pointing at me like a pistol. "That's what the diaphragm's for, Jimmy."

"What'd happen if you got swept away one day, and forgot."

"Jimmy," she said, laying down a principle, "you'd better hope and pray that never happens. I'd take care of it. I'd find some way to take care of it."

"God damn it! Why? What harm would. . . ."

"I'm not gonna lose my life for you, Jimmy. Not for you or any man. We'll be partners." Her voice got softer. "Okay, partner?" She tried on her sunny smile but it didn't fit.

She said we could rent a place together and split expenses. She said that we could both use her car. "What have you got to lose? One day at a time. We'll play it one day at a time."

"Yeah," I said, unhappily.

"Don't be so scared," she said.

I said I wasn't scared, I was just nervous. I got out of my clothes and got into bed. For half an hour I laid there listening to her type. Twice she tore her resume out and started over. Then she spent a long time in the bathroom. I wondered what she was doing in there. I thought she might be waiting for me to fall asleep. When she slipped under the sheets, I covered her breasts with my hands. She said she didn't feel like it.

11

THE 1,2,3 SMELLED like horsepiss. It smelled like twenty stud racehorses had been quartered inside, soaking the sawdust since the ground froze hard, last November. It was smoky too. It made my eyes water.

I slipped through the crowd, careful to maintain the short formal distance from all the other males packed in here.

There might have been two hundred men inside the bar and fifty still braving the weather out in front. The room was warm and I wanted to take off my coat but we were packed too close. The men sitting at the tables looked like they were sitting in holes.

The 1,2,3 had come down quite a bit since Stanley Ketchel's day. The back bar mirrors had been replaced with 4 x 8 sheets of unpainted plywood, and the street window too. The only natural light that came into the place filtered through the transom over the door. Dim in the daylight, presently black.

Most of the furniture couldn't be broke. The booze was kept under the bar. Beer and shot glasses cost management five dollars per gross.

Neil Murphy, the man who'd first discovered Stanley Ketchel's purpose in life, had sold the place years ago to more realistic owners.

Old Jim Sly had a place for himself at the end of the bar. He'd cleared a three-foot space around him by shin-kicking any man who came any closer.

The room was real loud: fight talk, strike talk, some talk about Kangas. Until I was right at the edge of Jim Sly's charmed circle I couldn't make out a word Sly was saying. He said something about Ketchel but I couldn't tell which Ketchel, Kooteney or Stanley. Jim Sly's eyes were scanning the bettors in the middle distance. Tonight he was dressed more like a tinhorn than a pimp. He laughed at me. I didn't think I was that funny. "Kooteney Ketchel's the toughest man in town," he said. "Do you know the quickest way to toughen up your hands?"

I was looking around for a bartender.

"You piss on 'em. The first couple days they'll turn yellow, but they get tough as boot leather."

"I'm puttin' my money on Vargas," I said.

Jim Sly giggled. "Why, Jimmy," he said. "So am I." His voice changed; he opened his eyes wide like an adult telling a fairy tale. "Stanley Ketchel was the toughest man in Butte. And he fathered this boy. And so Kooteney, he's the toughest man too, hah, hah, hah."

I thought Jim Sly had a poor sense of humor. I told him so. He said I shouldn't take it seriously and that life was a joke. He'd heard that I was shacked up with some dame. He said I'd be comin' back down the Line soon enough when I wanted a taste of the strange. He said he was going to make some real dough off Kooteney Ketchel tonight.

I wondered how much money had been made off the Ketchels, father and son. I wondered how you'd figure it up.

Burke's blond fat face swam above the crowd like a balloon.

"Where's your sidekick?" I asked.

Burke moved his mouth around like he was chewing on ashes. "You may have noticed he ain't here." He drew back from the bodies pressing him, "It's tighter'n a sheepherder's asshole in here," he said. As an afterthought he added, "How you doin', Jimmy?"

"I'm gettin' by."

"Uh-huh." Burke wasn't real interested. "You ought to show up for work tomorrow. I think you'd find a job waiting for you."

"Yeah," I said. "Well, maybe I don't want to go back. Maybe I'm sick of going down the hole."

"Makes no difference to me."

"Me and my girl are going to get the fuck out of here. Maybe you'd like to grubstake me."

He lowered his eyes long enough to decide that he didn't know me from Adam. "I'm tapped out," he said.

"I ain't askin' for no handout. I got three hundred fifty dollars, Burke. And I'm bettin' against you and Walker and Devlin and Ketchel."

Sour look. "Yeah. You and every other damn mucker in this town. I ain't bettin' no more."

I caught the bartender's sleeve. "Beer and a shot

down here, Mac." Their beer was lukewarm and had a lousy head. "I thought you was all hot for Ketchel," I said.

He opened up then, wide enough for a complaint: "I got every damn dime I own bet on that fucking Indian and he's done nothing the last week but try to drink himself to death. It's pitiful, that's what it is."

He smacked his fist into the palm of his hand, but not hard enough to sting. "Go on. Go on out back. See for yourself. Hell, maybe Devlin's got some money to bet."

And he turned away from me and wouldn't talk anymore.

So I eased through the crowd as quick as I could without stepping on anybody's toes. I'd come here to watch a rumpus, not to star in one.

The back door swung open as some fight fans went out into the alley. I followed.

Ice-crusted snow in the alley, except for two ruts where the garbage trucks went through. It was slippery and the ice was sharp enough to tear your pant legs if you fell down. There was a big light over the back entrance of the cafe next door. One of those lights with a wide metal hat.

Kooteney Ketchel was running in place. The same crusty brown suit. The same greasy black bowler. His arms rigid along his sides like he was running at attention.

A dozen miners standing around in a loose semicircle. A couple were smoking ten-cent cigars. They were watching Kooteney's knees pumping effortlessly—his breath even and slow. Kooteney's cheeks twitched, his nose ran snot, his eyes were big white things with tiny, tiny pupils.

Devlin was hunkered down beside him, murmuring, speaking low, "Now, you got to do it, Kooteney. I don't want you to be letting me down. You're twice as tough as the Mex. Sweat, Kooteney. Sweat it out."

The miners watched Kooteney's knees. They listened to his slow, even breathing.

"Three hundred fifty on Vargas," I said. Kooteney never faltered. He was in some other place and didn't hear me. I held up the sheaf of bills I'd taken out of the bank that afternoon.

One miner eyed my money. "Good luck," he said.

Everybody watched Kooteney Ketchel's legs. The guys with cigars smoked them. I came under the conical light beside Devlin and riffled the bills. "Joel Kangas's wife and kids want to put some money down on Vargas."

Devlin came up off his hunker then, turning fast. Next to the Indian, he looked smaller than he was. His balled fists relaxed. "Christ, Mullholland," he said. "Don't ever sneak up on a man that way."

Ketchel's knees were rising and falling: sophisticated hinges.

"He ain't lookin' so good," I said.

Devlin said, "Oh, I dunno." His face was cut into sharp sections by the light.

I asked was he backing Ketchel or not?

"All the way, Jimmy. I got to back him all the way. Ketchel can beat him, too. But he's had an awful week. Ol' Dust's got to admit it."

I don't think the jogging Indian heard him any better than he'd heard me. Up went the knees. Down they came again.

"Three fifty on Vargas," I said.

I swear he flushed before he said, "Your seven, my two."

"You're back of him all right," I said. "Way back." I hated to bet the whole of my savings when I only stood to make a hundred bucks but I didn't see any way out. So I bet and went back inside and got myself a stiff one.

The waiters were still hustling their trays through the crowd, but trade was slacking off. The head bartender was pulling the punchboards off the bar. One of the other bartenders was slipping bottles of whiskey back in their cases.

The joint still smelled like horsepiss. Mean horses.

The air was very tight and an outgoing breath could ruffle a man's hair all the way across the room, and cause offense.

A grunt at the door, a flurry, and a path appeared in the crowd like Moses' path across the Dead Sea.

Vargas.

Him and two retainers. Both retainers were Mexicans and both were taller than Vargas. One of them was chewing on a matchstick and the other wished he was.

Somebody finished his drink and left the bar. Nobody moved to claim his place. Vargas stopped at the edge of the open space. The air was blue and smoky. Vargas leaned over to whisper a joke in a retainer's ear. Retainer smiled. Vargas clapped him on the back which sounded like a meat axe smacking a carcass.

When Vargas sat down on the bar stool, his buttocks hung over and it looked exactly like somebody had stuck a chrome pipe up his ass. He glanced up and down the bar. If he was surprised Ketchel wasn't there, his face didn't show it.

He raised a finger. The head bartender smiled real quick. Not one of your believable smiles. The head bartender was trying to get out one more round of trays but he stopped long enough to bring Vargas a draft. He continued setting out trays.

Vargas stared at the beer for a little while and sort of flicked it. The beer glass smashed against the back bar. A little explosion of glass. The bartender stopped with his trays. Again Vargas raised his finger in the air. The bartender reached into the cooler and brought out a bottle of Schlitz. He discovered a pilsner glass. He poured very carefully, maintaining a perfect head.

A waiter grabbed for a ready tray but Vargas put his hand on it. The waiter was in a hurry, was already looking for his customers and didn't see Vargas's hand land on the tray like a quarter of beef. He started off with the tray but the tray didn't go anywhere and he stumbled and Vargas let him pull the tray over on himself.

New rules.

Now you could hear the jukebox. The "Beer Barrel Polka."

You could hear two hundred men breathing. Carefully, politely, the waiters hung up their aprons. They drew themselves a beer or a shot, very careful not to brush against each other behind the bar. The head bartender crossed his arms and leaned against the backbar. It was a shit smile, but steady.

I could hear the whirring of the electric clock. Somebody lit a match. Vargas took a sip of beer. When he set the glass down, everyone strained to hear the very slight clink the glass would make on the bartop.

The "Beer Barrel Polka" stopped. The record lifted and went back to its place with a great whirring and ticking.

Time passed. It is hard standing around doing nothing. We aren't built for it. Maybe the Hindoos are, but we're not. Nobody'd come down here tonight to watch a fat Mexican drink a bottle of beer.

Some miner elbowed another miner. A muffled yelp. One of Vargas's retainers went over and stood in front of the injured party. The retainer chewed his matchstick. The rebellion was quelled. But in about three minutes, chairs were going to be flying all over the place.

Kooteney Ketchel plowed through the crowd toward the bar, Devlin following on his heels.

Papsi Maroni barely had time to get off his stool before the Indian got there and some said, later, Papsi hadn't managed it very well. Insufficient grace—unseemly haste. Others said it wasn't Papsi's fault at all, with that damn Indian just appearing like that with no warning or anything.

Vargas was wearing a bright plaid sportcoat over his normal Saturday work-fight clothes.

Later, some said that Ketchel's shabby attire showed insufficient respect and should have warned us.

Kooteney put his hat on the bar. He settled himself beside Vargas. Vargas, of course, paid him no mind.

Shortly, the other men at the bar finished their drinks and decided to stretch their legs. Nobody else wanted to sit down so Vargas and Ketchel had the bar to themselves.

"Yes, sir," the bartender said brightly, "what'll you have?"

"Shot." His voice sounded like the cough of a distant shotgun. When the bartender brought his shot, Kooteney left it on the bar.

He turned his head toward Vargas. Little gasp in the room? Not me, I didn't gasp. Besides—surely Kooteney Ketchel didn't have anything to *say* to Vargas.

Vargas let his eyes roam right on by Ketchel. A stranger sitting next to a stranger. Vargas knew all the moves. We approved.

Vargas stood up, hitched his belt and went over to the jukebox.

"Dime," he said. And one of his retainers flipped him a ten-cent piece.

Vargas studied. He played "Goodnight Irene, goodnight Irene. I'll see you in my dreams."

When he sat down again, we were again treated to the sight of two huge backs side by side with not much space between them. I think Vargas was a trifle heavier than the Indian, but Ketchel had very heavy legs and maybe Vargas didn't outweigh him by that much after all.

A whisper, "Ten on the Indian." Somebody else was grading the meat like I was.

After the song finished—after a decent interval— Kooteney went over to the jukebox. He fumbled in his pocket for a dime. He played the "Butte Polka." And the bright, driving music bounced around the room and got lost in everybody's winter clothes.

Vargas spun around on his stool and inspected the crowd. His elbow coincidentally came around and smashed into the Indian's side. Vargas left it there. He stared emptily at the crowd. He chewed on something, meditatively, his elbow still buried in Ketchel's ribs. Ketchel didn't do anything about it. The "Butte Polka" ended. Vargas turned back to his drink. He looked at the bartender, whose smile got brighter and dimmer like a DC lightbulb in an AC current.

Vargas took Kooteney's shot and drank it. "Thanks," he said. Ketchel stared at his hands.

The bartender put another shot in front of Ketchel.

After a decent interval, Vargas's big hand brushed against the drink and dumped it in Ketchel's lap.

"What the fuck you mean, spilling my drink?" Vargas said. "Barkeep. Another!"

A few drops of booze ran off Ketchel's lap into the sawdust.

Ketchel seemed to sigh. Some air leaked out of him. He stood up. Vargas stood up too. A couple feet apart. Ketchel was wearing the sort of dreamy expression young poets are supposed to wear; vague, narcissistic, lost in the moment.

Vargas put out one hand and pulled at Ketchel's coat. He tore half of it right off him. The Indian had big holes rotted out of the armpits of his shirt.

Kooteney sighed again. He stopped, picked up the torn piece of coat and went through the pockets. Little stir from Vargas's retainers. Kooteney brought out a beer-can opener. I glanced at Vargas's boys. Mr. Matchstick had a gun out and it was kind of hanging from his hand like it was surprised to be there. Vargas, of course, just kept on chewing.

I knew what Ketchel was going to do. I didn't want to know. The opener was a hunk of thick ugly metal, a quarter inch thick and four inches long, with the prong at one end and the cap lifter at the other. Ketchel raised his fist. He squeezed his fist closed. He bent the opener into a U shape. He dropped the opener on the bar. It went "clank."

Vargas stopped chewing and stared at Ketchel. He stared for ten-twenty seconds.

Ketchel sighed again. He got down on his knees in the sawdust. He wrapped one huge hand around the leg of a bar stool. He lifted it effortlessly, swiftly. He got up from his knees and lifted the stool over his head.

Vargas slapped him. Open-handed slap. Wham. Kooteney set the bar stool down where he'd got it.

Later we agreed that Vargas did right slapping Ketchel. Vargas had been provoked.

The fight was on. Some fight. Vargas hit Ketchel in the gut, two or three times, hands flashing. Kooteney didn't raise his hands. The two men eyeballed each other. Vargas started in again. Great grace, speed and power. Three or four more shots to the belly. Kooteney didn't give an inch. Vargas kept working. Though Kooteney didn't budge, it got so every time Vargas hit him, his eyes bulged a little and Vargas was trying to chop him down, swinging close and hard, his little hands bouncing off Ketchel's iron diaphragm. WHUP, WHUP, WHUP, WHUP, WHUP, WHUP, WHUP, WHUP— Vargas must have got off twenty shots before the bruised belly muscles began to go slack and the fists went in deeper and finally Ketchel gave a little "oof" and took a breath. His belly muscles were shimmering like jelly.

Vargas turned to the bar. "Shot," he said. And the bartender poured a shot. He handed it to Kooteney. The Indian drained it. Tidily, Vargas returned the shot-glass to the bar before he started in again. WHUP, WHUP, WHUP.

Another couple minutes and his blows began to take effect. Reluctantly, like an injured plant, Kooteney bent forward, making a little pocket for Vargas's fists. WHUP, WHUP, WHUP, WHUP, WHUP, WHUP. And Kooteney's leg muscles buckled and he went down on his knees.

Vargas stopped and stared at us and he was so pissed we wouldn't meet his gaze. Lots of eyes examining the sawdust.

Vargas stuck out his hand and helped Kooteney to

his feet. He got a beer and handed it to the Indian. Kooteney said, "Ough. . . ." He tried again but it came out a wheeze. He said, "Tough." He threw the beer at Vargas, though most of it missed him.

Well, Vargas finished the job. He hit Kooteney again and again until the Indian's great body couldn't absorb the blows anymore and Kooteney reeled and stumbled through us, wrecked and punished. Each time Vargas knocked him down, he offered his hand, and Kooteney took it and Vargas helped him to his feet and knocked him down. Vargas was shining with sweat. Kooteney was gray and mottled. Vargas never touched his face— kept his fists working the soft places.

It was bad to watch. It would have been worse to leave. In a while Ketchel went down and we could all breathe again.

He lay there. Slumped up against the wall. And his shirt was gone and he was lumps and welts and blood. And he tried to give Vargas his hand. He did try. He lolled his great head over and stared at his arm. The arm wasn't going to come up anymore. And he said, "Huh," like he was surprised.

Vargas wiped the sweat out of his eyes. He wheeled around and marched out of the 1,2,3. His retainers had to run to catch up to him.

Everybody seemed to want a drink. Me too. The bartenders were filling a dozen shot glasses at a crack and the waiters would get half a dozen steps into the crowd before their trays were empty except for the silver coins tossed there.

Old Jim Sly was crowing as he collected his bets.

A few men stood around Ketchel. They didn't touch him but they murmured and pointed at the spots where Vargas's fists had done the most damage.

Burke was paying off one man after another. He was saying, "I'm not holding for Walker. You got bets with him, don't come to me. Talk to him."

Devlin was still against the wall, where he'd been since the fight started. He wasn't alone. Maybe a hundred men wanted to have a word with him.

Devlin had his Stetson in his right hand. He was rubbing his thumb over the brim. "It wasn't no fight," he said to the men who'd bet against him. "I bet Ketchel was tougher than Vargas. Ketchel never fought, so it ain't no fight."

A hundred men became dangerous. They didn't answer him but a nice sort of tingle started in everybody's nerves.

"All right," Devlin said, "All right." He took out his wallet but kept it closed. Probably he didn't want us to see his badges. He plucked a thin deck of currency out of it and said, "Dust Devlin's my name. I always pay what I owe." He set his hat square on his forehead and tugged the brim a quarter inch down. "Come on if you love money, boys. Come and get it till it's gone."

So men filed by him and every man announced the sum and Devlin checked his notebook and counted out the cash without a word.

He'd paid about a third of us, breaking hundreds to do it, when he ran out, except for a lone five-dollar bill. He pulled a couple silver dollars out of his pocket and shouted, "Anybody here I owe seven dollars to? Speak up."

One man took the five. The man who got the two silver dollars was in his seventies.

Devlin was broke. That didn't sit too well.

He raised both his arms. That faint tingle of excitement went through us again. The oldster who'd got

Devlin's silver yelled, "He can't raise the money from a hospital bed." He also spat to show he thought as we did about Devlin, even though he'd been paid off.

I didn't want my drink but I drank it anyway. It didn't taste like anything.

Devlin said, real loud, "Monday. I'll have it Monday, every damn cent." He waved his notebook like a flag. "I got all your names here. Every man. Monday. You got Dust Devlin's word on that."

Nobody punched him when he walked through us toward the door but nobody spared him their elbows either.

12

I NEVER FIGURED to see Devlin's money. You always pay for your education and I'd been educated about a hundred dollars' worth.

It started snowing Monday late afternoon and never let up. Me and Gail Stinson stayed indoors, working out our new life. It looked like a pretty good one. Maybe the timbering wouldn't hold the weight but, to tell the truth, we weren't looking too close at that.

Gail'd cooked up some corned-beef hash and some cabbage too. While we ate, I said we were foolish to stay here, just because her rent was paid up. She said something about how I was getting on her nerves too, lying around all day with nothing to do. I made some crack about how I had something to do, but most of the time she didn't want to.

She said, "That's not love, Jimmy. That's not even lust. That's bored. Real bored."

"I'll do anything for a thrill," I said, dead earnest.

At first she didn't know how to take that but finally she laughed and I laughed too.

I talked about wanting to be an engineer. I said I wanted to have the things engineers had; the money and respect. Maybe I'd get a half-time job in Salt Lake so I could get my engineering degree quicker. She said she wouldn't want to stay in Salt Lake if she got an offer from a better paper. Salt Lake, she said, was a "stopgap measure."

"I could probably transfer schools," I said. Then I said, "Let's cross that bridge when we come to it."

"When do you want to leave?"

"No sense moping around here, eating up our grub-stake." I turned on the radio for the ten o'clock weather. The snow was supposed to fall all night and ease up by morning. "Salt Lake's about five hundred miles. We can make it in a day if we leave early. Day after tomorrow morning. That'll give 'em a chance to get the highways clear."

"Jimmy, you sure this is what you want to do?"

"Damn betcha!" And I felt my face get real happy. Maybe I wasn't exactly sure where I was going but I was surely going somewhere and now there was a date stamped on my ticket. I wondered if me and Gail Stinson would ever learn to love each other.

Somebody started banging on the door and I guess I knew who it was before I got up from the table.

Devlin had his wallet in his red, rough hands. He wore the same suit he'd worn Saturday night, but burrs clung to the back of the jacket and he had what looked

like a rope burn on his left sleeve. He'd found the time
to shave but he'd nicked himself a couple places. The
thin blood was a brighter red than the red in his eyes.
"I wasn't five minutes inside the city," he said. "Not five
damn minutes. I been burnin' a little oil lately and was
pulled up at this Texaco when I looked in the mirror
and there they were. My God, I never been so tired.
When I saw the cops pull in behind me, I wanted to
puke."

He stayed in the hall doorway, straddling both spaces.
Deputy Whitehead was just behind him with a big
grin pasted across his face, like a happy poster on top
of a sad one.

"Jimmy? Who's at the door?" Gail called.

I told her not to worry because I couldn't think of
anything else to say and didn't want to invite them in.
Devlin held his wallet like he was going to give it up.
"I come to pay you what I owe," he said. "The Deputy
said that'd be all right."

When he shook his wallet open, I saw that both his
badges were gone. I stared at the pinholes in the leather
while he counted out twenties. "Welcome to private
life," I said.

He didn't get it. I took the money and waited for him
to back up so I could close the door. "I got to leave
town," he said. "I wanted to pay my debts before I left.
You're last."

Bob Whitehead moved in on Devlin like a gray shark.
"That's that," he said. "Cowboy, it's time for you to
ride." He had a hard grip on Devlin's elbow.

Devlin shook his arm impatiently but the Deputy
kept his hold. Devlin stayed in the doorway, neither
here nor there, his bloody eyes making some demand.

Gail came out of the kitchen, coffee cup in her hand. "Deputy Whitehead," she said. "Mister Devlin," she guessed.

Bob Whitehead coughed modestly. He let go of Devlin's arm to touch his hatbrim. "Miss Stinson."

"What do they want, Jimmy?" She was asking me but would take an answer from anyone.

Deputy Whitehead coughed modestly again.

The words rose past Devlin's bulging throat and puffed out his cheeks, before he squawked, "I want to say good-bye to Kooteney."

Gail's puzzled eyeglasses turned to me and Whitehead in turn. She thought for a moment before she said, briskly, "Why don't you both come in for a moment. We have coffee, or I have some sherry if you want. How bad's the snow? Don't mind your boots, I've had muddy floors all winter."

Whitehead checked me over for the okay. I didn't get a chance to give it to him before Devlin marched right in. Whitehead no more than a leash length behind him.

Gail paused with her coffeepot angled over a couple big stoneware cups. "We've only got Carnation canned milk."

"I'd take a little of that sherry," Devlin said softly.

He slurped the coffee down an inch or so and poured the glass of cheap sherry into the mug. The hot aroma of sherry smelled like a metal fruit-tree blossoming.

Whitehead hung a cigarette on his lip. "I'm not a bettin' man myself." He spoke to me like I was the only person at the table. "Devlin here must have made fifty stops this afternoon, all over town. Passin' out money like he owned the mint. Some places the man was home, some places nobody was home and he just stuffed the money under the door. Some places, only the old lady was home and he gave the money to her. You got a few men in trouble this afternoon, Devlin."

Devlin had his raw red hands wrapped around his coffee cup, warming them. "I said I'd pay off Monday. This is Monday."

"Your hands look terrible," Gail said. "I have some hand lotion." I don't think she would have made the offer if she'd met Devlin at the courthouse, but this was her kitchen. Devlin turned it down anyway though the skin was split at his finger joints, open and sore. "I been too long away from cows, oh my." He laughed.

"Oh, I been between the silk sheets too long. My cousin quit me once I had the cows on the trucks and on top of it I lost my damn gloves somewhere. Ma'am, I got to tell you, sellin' those black cows like to broke my heart. I never *seen* a market like that one. It's the winter. Jimmy, don't you think it's the winter?"

I looked right back at him but I didn't have anything to give.

"I drove to my ranch Saturday night. Loaded cows all Sunday. Got 'em into Helena for the regular Monday sale. Six damn buyers. Just six! The roads are so bad only the railroad's moving cows. They gave me twenty-six dollars a head for those cows. Slaughterhouse buyer got most of 'em."

Gail laid both hands palm down on the table. She drummed her fingers, "What's the story, Bob?" she asked, softly.

Bob Whitehead rubbed his face like he was trying to erase away the last scraps of a grin. "Seems Mister Devlin isn't welcome in Butte anymore," the Deputy said. "Seems like Mister Frank Coad thinks Devlin's a mite noisy. Seems like the Company never heard of him and would like to hear less. Sheriff Blair, he was tickled pink. He gives me the job to run him off. Gail, you know the sheriff. Well, he said that maybe I ain't dumb. Maybe I'm just crazy. I took that as a compliment."

Devlin never looked up from his coffee. "And they lifted my tin. The man from the Cattleman's Association caught me at the market and said that since I didn't own no cattle I couldn't be a member no more."

Gail took slow sips of coffee. She fished out a cigarette and lit it herself, ignoring Devlin's Zippo.

"Bob," she said, "why not let him say good-bye to Ketchel?"

"I already bent things lettin' him cruise around town all afternoon. I should have turned him around the first time I seen him. Besides, I ain't heard nothin' about Ketchel since the fight. When the ambulance got down to 1,2,3, he'd already got off and I don't know where he is. Hell, he probably skipped town."

It slowly dawned on him that he'd used the same words to describe Joel and he looked away from us, pursing his lips.

"We don't know," Gail said.

"You ain't on the paper no more. Why do you want to know?"

"And curiosity killed the cat," she said sweetly. "Right Bob?"

Devlin had forgotten his coffee. His hands were still folded around the cup. His eyes were blinking, fighting sleep.

"Look for Ketchel until morning, Bob," I said. "If we don't find him, we'll turn loose of it." To light his grin, I added, "Besides, like the sheriff said, 'You're crazy.'"

So the four of us clattered down the five flights of marble stairs to the street. Whitehead wanted to know about the fight. I told him. He said he'd had the jail-house duty that night and missed it. He'd heard that Vargas felt so bad about the fight he'd left town. Vargas had a brother or a cousin or something in the mines at Bisbee.

Gail wanted to ride with me in Devlin's car but the Deputy gave her a sharp look which meant, "Bad idea."

Devlin's hat was already dusted with new snow. He kept his hands jammed deep in his pockets. "You drive," he said. "I ain't had no sleep since Saturday mornin'."

The Buick started ragged. The oil pressure wasn't anything to brag about either. The chains were on, but one of the links was broken and slapped the fender wheel every time it came around.

Downtown was almost deserted; quiet except for the streetlights swinging and clanking in the wind. The night was pressing hard against the all-night cafes. In-somniacs huddled along the counters with their one more cup of coffee.

Devlin said, "I never meant for it to turn out this way."

I didn't see how that made much difference.

The Deputy's headlights kept fifty yards behind us. He coasted up closer and switched them off when I parked in front of The Big Ship. In summer the old wooden three-story's long front porch would be lined with miners having a sociable pipe. Now it was a wide, untracked corridor of snow.

Devlin opened his eyes long enough to say, "It don't look like he's here. His light ain't lit up."

"Maybe." The minute I turned the wipers off, the window started to fill in with soft fat snowflakes.

When we started across the street, Gail got out of Whitehead's car but hesitated and finally didn't follow.

The sign beside the door read: Beds: 50¢. Rooms: $1, Board.

Inside, I took a broom and brushed off my overshoes. Partway up the hall, one dim light showed above the stairs. The house was plain but solid and the stairs never made a sound. Devlin stopped before Kooteney's door, raised his knuckles and lowered them again. "I know he ain't here," he said. "Even before the fight, he wasn't makin' it home most nights." He inclined himself and pressed his ear against the door. "Kooteney," he called out. "Kooteney, it's Dust. You in there?" He rapped three soft taps. "He ain't in there," he said.

"You can bet your boots he's not." A clear woman's voice from the top of the stairs. It was Kooteney's landlady, hair in curlers, hands on hips. She looked like she'd been eating hornets. "Mister," she threw her voice at Devlin, "get your damn ear away from that door! Get away from there!"

I said, "Jimmy Mullholland, ma'am. We've met. I'm lookin' for Kooteney Ketchel."

She was all charged up and it took her a minute to remember. "You were here before. That fellow you were lookin' for. He was your brother, you said."

"Brother-in-law. I'm Mullholland. He was Joel Kangas."

I guess she didn't know Joel's name because she bristled up again and said, "Well, he don't live under my roof and that damned Indian don't either."

When Devlin removed his hat a few scraps of snow fell onto the hallway runner. "I'm a friend of Ketchel's," Devlin said.

"Then you'd be wantin' to pay on his back rent," she came right back at him.

Maybe he would have but she didn't give him a chance to reach for his wallet. "No, of course you don't," she snapped. Angrily she pushed past us, produced a key and swung Kooteney's door open. "Just junk," she said. "I cleared his junk out of here. The Mister's going to repaper the room. It's one of our nicest rooms. There's plenty of light." The window was a black square in the wall. The bed with its mattress rolled up on the spring skeleton. "Junk," she repeated. "Whiskey bottles and rags of clothes. I asked the Mister and he said, 'Don't even bother to call St. Vincent de Paul. Garbage. Put it all in the garbage.' "

Green linoleum floor. Cigarette burns around the lip of the bed table, like serrations. The room smelled of disinfectant.

"Look at that," she said, pointing at a couple dark splotches on the wallpaper. "He was throwin' bottles at the wall. Throwin' 'em! I must have hauled four trash-baskets of glass out of here. Broken glass all over the floor. I ask you, what the hell. I ask you."

"So you threw him out," I said.

"He threw himself out. That's how the Mister puts it. Now, I ain't too crazy about Indians, but I take in all kinds. I keep the house clean. Linen change, Monday and Thursday; beef on the supper table except Sunday when it's ham or chicken. And I'm no prude either. I've seen mining men drunk a time or two." She stopped for drama. "Murder," she said. The word came out like air leaks out of a tire.

Devlin mumbled, "Nobody proved he did it," but her eyes were hotter than his and he had to look away.

"So?" she demanded. "So?"

Devlin twanged one of the bedsprings.

"I was the one had to carry the broken glass out of here and it's a nice room too. He used to keep it nice. Four years he lived under my roof. Quiet. Never said much. Rent on time. Then, last fall he seemed to come out of himself. Like he'd got himself a girl or something. He bought a couple real nice suits. And I don't mind admitting, I like to see a man look swell. But then, he just seemed to fall apart. I never seen a man go downhill so fast." It was her eyes' turn to wander. "I kind of felt sorry for him, but when we heard what he'd done . . ."

"You threw him out," I said.

"He threw *himself* out," she came back, like a child repeating a lesson.

"The Mister was going to get the sheriff down here Monday to run him off, but he didn't have to." She paused, and in a much softer voice said, "I kind of felt sorry for him, he was beat up so bad."

"He was in a fight," Devlin told her. "It wasn't his idea."

"Sunday mornin'. He had all those lumps in his chest where his ribs was broke. Nothin' wrong with his face. Oh, I mean it was a little puffy, but he didn't have any real marks on it. He looked so bad hurt, I wouldn't have done anything on my own, but the Mister. . . ." Her eyes had some sad wisdom in them. "The Mister saw him crawling up the stairs Sunday morning. It was almost six and we were just goin' out for early mass. We was in the hallway, ready to leave, when we heard this noise up the stairs, more like the mewlin' of a cat than anything, and, in fact, that's what I thought it was, but the Mister runs up the stairs in two bounds, and there's the Indian, curled up on the stairs, where, I suppose, his strength had failed him." She took a breath. "Well,

I'd be the first person to admit, the Mister's got a temper. Most of the time, he's gentle as a lamb, but he's got one of those hair-trigger tempers. And before I knew it, he was up on the stairs, shaking Mr. Ketchel. Shaking him and kicking him with his shoe. The Mister was yelling about the rent. Six weeks' back rent he owed us."

I let my eyes wander around Kooteney's bare room. Already it was half scrubbed of him. Only the splotches on the wall where he'd thrown his whiskey bottles were eccentric enough to earn him a history here.

"The Mister got Mr. Ketchel on his feet. He wanted him out of here, he said, and he was shakin' like he does when the temper's comin' off of him. The Indian pulled all his change out of his pockets and dumped it on the floor and then he went down the stairs again. He didn't take any bags with him either. I followed him downstairs because the Mister was feelin' a little unwell, you know. The Indian didn't have a coat and it was terrible cold outside so I got an old coat of mine, old green thing. I was gonna just throw it away, anyway, and gave it to him to put over his shoulders."

When we stepped outside, the landlady rattled the door and locked it behind us. Devlin clutched the porch post like he needed it.

Bob Whitehead turned on his lights and rolled his window down when I trudged toward his car. "He ain't there," I said. "His landlady gave him the bum's rush Sunday morning."

"The bars?" Whitehead suggested.

"I guess so. Gail, why don't you ride with us. I don't like Devlin enough to get anything out of him. Maybe you'll have better luck."

Devlin had a bottle clasped between his thighs but

he leaned forward graciously enough to let Gail into the back seat. While I drove over to the east side, he practiced on the bottle.

"We're leaving town too," Gail said, so brightly I winced.

The snowflakes dove at our windows like fat moths. The headlights weren't showing me much.

"Yep," Gail said. "No more snow and ice for me. Me and Jimmy are going south. You ever been in Utah, Mister Devlin?"

"No," he said. "I never." He let the silence spread for a minute before he said, "I been in Canada plenty times, but never in Utah." As an afterthought, he added, "I wish you every happiness and success."

"Thank you," Gail replied, like a bride-to-be. "I'm sorry this didn't turn out better for you. I know how you feel about those cows. My dad's a rancher too."

My breathing. Gail's breathing. The gurgling as Devlin took a drink. "I been up in Kooteney's room before, you know. God, I hate like hell what happened to him."

The broken chain link was setting up a steady drumming in the fender well.

"Kooteney must think the world of you," Gail ventured.

"So what if he does? So what business is that of yours? I think the world of him too."

I thought he had a hell of a way of showing it, but I held my tongue. The Yellowstone Bar didn't look like it was doing much business on a snowy Monday night, but me and Devlin went in anyway. Only four customers, all male. A pair and a couple solos. The bartender was a Finn I'd seen around a couple times. He wasn't in any big hurry to get to us, but he did, wiping his hands on his bar towel. "Beer," I said. Wordlessly, he drew us two. When I asked him if he'd seen Kooteney Ketchel, he stopped short, a beer glass in each hand. He stared at me for a second and flicked his gaze to Devlin.

"No, I ain't." He poured the two beers into the sink. "We're out of beer," he said, calmly. He picked up a bung starter and let it dangle from his hand. His eyes on Devlin.

One of the customers was up and heading for us. Somebody was about to perform an unpleasant chore.

"My name's Mullholland," I said. "Jimmy Mullholland. Joel Kangas was my brother-in-law. I'm looking to talk to the man who killed him."

The bartender gave me a disgusted look. "Why didn't you say so in the first place. Jesus." He put the bung starter on the bar but didn't draw us a beer. And his eyes never left Devlin. "Why don't you get him out of here," he said. "A lot of the boys knew Joel."

"Go on," I said. "Go on out to the car."

When the door closed behind him, the bartender drew me one and said it was on the house. The customer sat down again. The bartender hadn't seen Ketchel since the fight, Saturday, and nobody else had either. He noted that Ketchel had quit the generating plant. I drank my beer. It was pretty poor.

"Why don't you try the joints on East Park," the bartender said. "They don't give a damn who they serve."

When I got in, Devlin was scrunched around, leaning over the seat. Him and Gail were having a tête-à-tête.

"I'll bet it was awful, leaving him there like that when he was hurt so bad." Gail's voice was very kind.

"I had to get the money to pay my markers, didn't I?"

he said. "Man's only as good as his word. I had to get my cows to the market, Monday morning, nine A.M. sharp. His choice. It wasn't my choice, it was his choice."

The Buick's oil pressure never came above twenty pounds, even when I revved it. I drove east looking for a bar that was poor enough.

Devlin ignored me. I was the taxi driver or chauffeur and heard no evil. "I kept tryin' to get him into shape. Every night I'd track him down and try to get him sober. I should have locked him up somewhere, that's what I should have done. He wouldn't take no help. 'A silver dollar,' that's all he wanted from me. And when that was gone, he'd want another one."

I swear I felt warmth from the back seat where Gail was cranking out the sympathy. Me, I kept my mouth shut.

I left Devlin in the car next time I stopped. The bartender knew Ketchel and said I should try the next joint up the street.

When I passed the Buick, Devlin and Gail were hard at it. I guess he thought he had the right to explain.

The joint was a wino joint and I got panhandled twice before I reached the bar. No jukebox. No tables, or chairs. Everybody pressed up against the bar communing with their spirits. I didn't give up any money to the panhandlers because the bartender was watching me. "Gimme a shot," I said. "And one for yourself, while you're at it."

He took my two bits for the shot. "I own the place, Mac," he said. "Anytime I want to, I drink for free."

I asked him if he'd seen Ketchel. He walked away, strutting down the bar. "You been workin' that beer for an hour now, Charlie. Come on, come on, order up!"

When he returned he inspected me until I tossed another two bits on the bar. He produced another shot. "He's supposed to be so goddamned tough," he said. "Well, he don't look so tough to me."

For another two bits, he said he'd bounced Ketchel earlier tonight. He said, "Anybody can drink in here who has the price of a drink." Kooteney hadn't.

I turned around and addressed the bar. "I'm buyin' for any man who can tell me where to find Kooteney Ketchel."

Some didn't hear. Some hadn't for years. Some were singing inside their minds. A whisper came from somebody, I couldn't tell who. "A railroad man always has a woman waiting. . . . Wet. . . . A railroad man. . . ."

For him, I left a buck on the bar.

The snow had quit. Powder snow over rough snow over icy snow over ice over the dead earth.

I gave Whitehead a friendly wave. I didn't want him getting impatient.

Devlin was faced front again, quiet. The space between him and Gail was almost palpable. I turned the Buick south toward the Northern Pacific yards.

I cracked the wing open. Devlin smelled bad. Not high, exactly. More metallic than that.

"It was a mistake, Jimmy," Gail said.

We passed a couple gallowsframes. Their straight religious lines weren't much softened by the snow.

"The last morning he saw Joel. . . ."

"I only met him the once," Devlin interrupted, setting the record straight.

Gail kept her voice low, impersonal. "Ketchel thought Mister Devlin was mad at him because Joel hadn't backed down. Joel was still fighting for the strike. Mister Devlin said some things to Ketchel he now regrets."

"I called him a 'teepee creeper,'" Devlin said, surprised at himself.

The two cars bumped over the tracks beside the NP freight depot. I got out of the car. Devlin folded forward to let Gail by but stayed himself.

I slipped in beside the Deputy, and Gail crowded in right next to me. I liked the warmth of her. I told Whitehead that Ketchel was probably around here somewhere if he wasn't dead.

"You're a real forgiving bastard, aren't you, Jimmy."

"No. I'll talk to the trainmaster. Do what you want."

So we all ended up asking the railroad men about Ketchel. Some of them remembered him but nobody'd seen him tonight.

They were making up a westbound freight for Spokane. I asked did they mind if I searched it before it rolled and the brakeman said him and me'd take a looksee.

Gail and me stood under the freight depot overhang and waited while the Deputy checked the yard.

Gail said, "What do you want from him? You know Ketchel knocked Joel on the head and put him in the furnace. You aren't doing it for Joel anymore."

"I never was. I just had to know."

"And now?"

I shrugged.

We checked the westbound freight car by car. Me, Whitehead and the brakeman. No luck. Beside an equipment shed, Whitehead found a refrigerator carton that somebody'd used for a bedroom. Lots of big, dragging footprints and a couple places where somebody'd pissed blood in the snow.

The brakeman swung his lantern and the westbound's wheels spun and squealed as the big ten-wheeler put its back into the load.

It was going fifteen, twenty miles an hour when Kooteney made his play. He'd been hiding behind a tool shack down the track and he popped out from behind the building and ran for the train. He was easy to see. His landlady's coat was streaming from his shoulders like a cape.

I suppose his brain had bad information about his body because he ran like he was going to catch the train but he never had a chance. He was still twenty feet away when the caboose whipped by his outstretched fingers. He chased it a hundred yards down the track. He stopped. He was going to turn around but he got his foot caught between two ties and dropped to his knees.

"He never was able to get out of this town," I said.

"At least this time he was smart enough to try the westbound," the Deputy said.

Down the line, the train was hooting at a crossing.

Devlin was coming down the tracks between us. He was walking funny, like he was reluctant, but he stopped walking funny when Kooteney fell. He broke into a dogtrot and ran by us. I don't think he saw us. His voice was coming in little puffs, huh, huh, huh, but he probably didn't notice that either.

He stood by Kooteney's head. He kneeled down in the snow. One of his shoes slipped off his heel and dangled, pinned by the toe.

Kooteney's chest looked like someone had shot a deer close range with Double-ought buck and left the skinned carcass in the sun for a couple weeks. It was black in places, white where the frostbite had got him and some of his bruises were bright blue as a bottle fly.

We didn't get too close, me and the Deputy.

"I never meant. . . ." Devlin said.

Kooteney raised his head. We couldn't see much because Devlin was blocking us, but Devlin put his hand over his eyes and I guess Kooteney's face was why.

With one hand, Devlin reached behind him and got his shoe on again. "I had to leave after the fight," Devlin said. "I had to get money for my markers. Jesus, Kooteney, you know how much money I lost? Thousands of dollars, Kooteney."

"I couldn't no more," Kooteney said.

"Hell," Devlin said, mock cheer. "That's all right. Nothing wrong with that. You gave it your best, Kooteney."

Devlin's shoe slipped off his heel again. He put it back again. He said, "I never meant for you to do it, Kooteney. You know I never meant—"

"I ain't right," Kooteney said. "I ain't . . . right."

The wind was starting to whirl the surface of the snow and it was pretty cold. The Deputy took Ketchel by the shoulders and got him to his feet and tried to wrap the coat around him. It covered him like a thin, tatty scarf.

We got him inside the freight depot and sat him on a bench beside a radiator. Closed, his eyes looked like walnuts.

Devlin got down on his heels, his face close to the Indian's. "They got me too, buddy. They got me good. Took everything and told me never to come back here no more."

Except for the rise and fall of his chest, you would have thought the Indian was dead.

"I told you about my spread, Kooteney. Oh, it's a hell of a pretty place. When you get to feeling better, well, my cousin just quit me and if I'm gonna get back in the beef business, I'll be needin' a good hand. What do you say?"

The depot walls were brown. I wondered why they used such an ugly shade of brown.

"Well, you look me up, Kooteney," Devlin said. "We'll tie one on together." He came up off his heels with a certain weary grace. His hand found its way to his hat and straightened it. "So long, amigo," he said, and was gone.

"Ketchel called him up in the middle of the night," Gail said. "It was the two of them moved Joel's car down to the dogtrack. Devlin said they were laying a false trail."

Bob Whitehead peeled his own coat off and spread it over Kooteney's shoulders. Between it and the green one, he was almost covered. "What are we gonna do with him?"

When the mine searchlights came on, I didn't pay attention to them, though I was standing by a window and they were plain enough to see. Every single mine on the entire hill had switched on its lights and they were waving around the sky like piss-colored lances. I guess I was lost in my thoughts.

The sirens started to wail. Then the mine whistles. One mine got started whistling a few seconds before the other ones: TOOT, TOOT, TOOT, TOOT. I noticed the lights, then. Like New Year's Eve when they lit up the whole sky.

Bob Whitehead ran outside to his car radio and ran back real fast.

All the sirens—all the whistles in Butte.

Bob said, "There's a fire at the Spec." His eyes were on me and they were pleading for something. He said, "Jimmy, it's a big fire. A helluva fire."

My father worked the graveyard at the Spec. He was a firebug. He'd been a cowboy before he was a miner. He used to say, the only thing dumber than a dumb miner is a smart cowboy.

13

MY FATHER'D BE EMBARRASSED. He hated to need help. He was, as I am, inconsolable.

Bob Whitehead floorboarded it up Anaconda Road. The road up the Hill was narrow, steep, washed with glare ice. We were passing ambulances and police cars and I was thinking how embarrassed my father'd be if someone had to haul him to the surface from the guts of a burning metal mine. There's worse things than shame.

Kooteney and me in the back seat. The back end of the car whipping like a cat's tail. Whitehead was steering for the occasional dry spots and doing his abrupt corrections when his wheels were off the ice. The two of us in back gave him five hundred extra pounds over the driving wheels. He probably appreciated that. The car'd lurch; I'd slide into Ketchel; and it was like slapping your hand on a well-aged steak. He'd been tenderized.

On my sister Kathleen's wedding day, my father slipped on our front walk and tore his hands on the concrete, trying to catch himself. He'd ripped the sleeve of his new blue suit and popped the second button off his white shirt too. The cab stood waiting for us. We were to pick up Joel and were late. We climbed into the cab.

"God damn fucking hell. God damn it to fucking hell," he'd said.

I pulled the handkerchief out of my breast pocket and he said, "What the hell you think you're doin'? Don't get no blood on that."

His hands had been badly scraped; nothing fatal, but a fair amount of blood, and he was holding his hands over the floor of the cab so he wouldn't get blood on his pant legs. The blood dripped into the dusty floormat and it seemed like the dust sucked it up as quick as it fell.

He wouldn't let me touch him. "Straighten out your snotrag, Jimmy," he said. "One sloppy Mullholland's plenty. There don't have to be two of them."

A few people running up Anaconda Road. Ghosts. We swept by them.

Kooteney had his eyes open but I don't think he saw where we were going. I don't guess he cared.

A few flakes of snow in the air, swirling around. Caught in the searchlights, diving into the pillars of light.

Fifty or sixty mine whistles blowing at once. I couldn't hear very good but nobody was talking anyway. Bob Whitehead's fingers drumming on the steering wheel. He'd slowed to forty or so, backed up behind two ambulances. One was white. One was white and green.

The searchlights were bouncing off the low clouds. The Hill was glowing and Bob could have killed his headlights if he'd wanted to.

The two cops at the Granite Mountain gate waved the two ambulances through but flagged us down.

So soon, the families were gathering outside the mineyard: men with pants pulled over their nightshirts; women with heavy men's coats over their bathrobes. One of the young men looked like he was barefoot. But that couldn't be.

A cop stuck his head in the window. "Jeez, Bob, I'm glad to see yuh. We need some help. It's a fuckin' mess. It's a shaft fire. The Speculator shaft."

"Yeah, sure," Whitehead said. He drove into the mineyard and parked next to a stack of heavy timbers.

I stepped out of the car into the stench. Copper sulphide burning, rotted dirty timbers burning, hose burning, electrical cables burning. The stench coated my face and took my breath away.

Gail said, "Oh God," and put her hand over her mouth. Bob Whitehead was running back toward the gate, slipping on the ice, running awkward.

We left Kooteney in the car. At least he'd be out of the weather.

As I ran toward the shafthead, I was trying to get a prayer through for my father but all the lines were jammed. I guess there were too many people calling at once.

The two-decker cages were shuttling up and down the Granite Mountain shaft, fast as they could. And the bell signals in the shafthouse setting up a clamor: "200, come and get me; 1500, Jesus, hurry!; 3100, hurry, hurry along!"

And the mine whistles blowing. And the sirens. And the whine of the cables, whipping around the sheaves on top of the gallowsframe.

The cage clangs to a stop at the shafthead. All I can see is the miners' dirty boots and the tops of their hardhats. The steel cage-door swings open. Two rescuers, wearing MSA airpacks. They're carrying another guy with them and there's many willing hands helping to take his weight and a couple more guys in airpacks are in the cage and one yells, "Cut the rope," and the cage hurtles down, down, and the whine of the cables and the jangle of the bells.

One of the rescuers lifts up his face mask and sucks in gulps of plain air. "Jesus," he says. He wipes the sweat off his rubber face-plate. Somebody's tugging at his harness, wanting his turn with the airpack, but he says he'll be okay in a second and he knows the 2600; he was working the 2600 yesterday and there's twenty men he knows of still down there. The new guy says yeah, and pulls the airpack off his back anyway.

The miner they rescued can walk but his face is beet-red from the carbon monoxide and he's sucking in tiny breaths like a landed trout.

We sit him down with two or three other guys on a wooden cable drum and they all have their heads thrown back, and their breathing is like the beating of butterfly wings.

The first-aid crew's loading a stretcher into an ambulance. They give the driver the "take off" and his siren blends with the rest as he scurries off down the Hill.

In front of the ambulances, they've laid out a dozen

bodies, covered with a big black tarp except their red faces and their mouths pursed like they wanted to kiss something.

I look into each dead face. Not my father.

Five hundred yards up the Hill, the Speculator gallowsframe is lit up like a cold Christmas tree. A few men standing in the yard. A few wisps of smoke slipping out of the shaft. I can hear the bell signals ringing from here. Like distant streetcar bells. The cages aren't doing a thing. They just hang there high above the shafthead.

The Granite Mountain cages dropping and rising. But they aren't moving so quick now and the signals aren't as frequent.

Walker's got four machinists unbolting the heavy steel cover on the Granite Mountain fan.

"Walker," I say, "who's keeping track of the men who come out?"

"Burke was, last I heard." Walker has his hawkeye on his crew. "Come on, you dim bastards! Get that fucking housing off there!" Walker sees who I am. "Good. Jimmy, I want you. Burke's down the hole closing the fire doors." Walker's wearing a heavy red-checked lumberjack jacket and sharp pointy-toed shoes. I guess his work clothes are still in his locker. He points at the Speculator. "I got two men over at the Anselmo, pulling the hoist clutch. They got an Ilgner system, same as the Spec. I want you standing by when they get here. The smoke's hanging low in the Spec. Below the 1600. I want to get those cages moving again."

Impatiently, Walker snatched a heavy wrench from one of his men and attacked the housing bolts himself. They were trying to reverse the fan. Since the fire was at the bottom of the Speculator shaft, normal fan action was drawing the smoke into the Granite Mountain workings. That's what was killing them down there: gas poisoning.

I said, "You seen my father, Walker?"

"Oh shit, Jimmy. I forgot. Jesus, kid. No, I haven't." He grunted as he jerked on the two-inch steel bolts. "Uhhh. Son of a bitch!"

His hand was streaming with blood. That quick he passed his wrench to another man. The guy wiped the bloody thing on his coveralls before he set to.

Walker was doubled over his smashed hand. "Aw, fuck."

He turned his face to me and spoke through his teeth. "It don't mean he's dead, Jimmy. Some guys got out. Some came up at the Emma. They smelled smoke and made it through the manways." He sucked on his hand and spat out the blood. "I heard there was a crew got into the Black Rock workings. Ben Tregonning led 'em out and he's gone back for more. Shit, there's men poppin' out all over the damn Hill."

"Unless they run into a bulkhead," I said, softly.

"Yeah," he said. "I know about the bulkheads, Jimmy. We all know about the fucking bulkheads." Then he said, "Forget what I said about the hoist clutch. I got enough men to handle it."

"Who's keeping track of the men who got out?"

"I dunno. Burke was gonna give the list to the mine clerk. He's over there." Walker pointed at the Dry. "Handing out airpacks."

"I might want one myself."

"You on the first-aid team?"

I didn't say anything about my father.

"All right," Walker said. "All right. Tell him I said

it's okay. If you run into Burke down there, tell him to get his ass back up here."

The airpacks were dangling from a long wooden rack in front of the Dry. Each had a number painted on the regulator box. The mine clerk was an old paddy, name of Harrington. I knew him slightly. He had a list. He marked down the airpack number and the name of the miner who took it.

"Is Jim Mullholland up?" I asked. "Old Jim Mullholland. He's a firebug. He works this shift."

"I'm signin' out airpacks," he said. "They're switchin' them around at the shafthead, so God knows who's got one now. They're signed out. Every manjack on this list. They're responsible. It can't be helped."

"How many men got out?"

"I don't know about that. There's some that got out and some didn't. Mister Burke asked me to check on the men but I told him I was checkin' out these airpacks so I couldn't check men too. I ain't Superman."

I lifted one of the airpacks off the rack. It was heavy—forty or fifty pounds.

"You on the first-aid team?" Harrington asked.

I got my shoulders into the harness, leaned forward and snugged the straps. It rode high on my shoulders; the compressed-air bottle just about in the small of my back. I cracked the regulator valve and felt the little shot of air against the palm of my hand. "Who's checkin'?" I asked. "Who's checkin' the men who got out?"

"The hoistman," he said. "No use puttin' that on if you ain't a member of the first-aid team."

I pressed the mask over my face and snapped the rubber straps that bound it to my skull. I covered the airhose with one hand and tried to suck air. It was a good seal. I stuck the airhose into the regulator box and cracked the valve again. Good air. I pulled the mask off. I said, "Jimmy Mullholland. You spell it with four *l*'s."

I took a hardhat and an electric lamp too.

I guess he would have chased me to reclaim the gear, but he got distracted. Kooteney Ketchel came out of the Dry and he wanted an airpack too.

I don't know where Kooteney found the strength to climb out of the car. I don't know what he understood. He'd borrowed some coveralls, too short for him, and six inches of shin was showing.

An ambulance churning slush toward the gate. The cops had a few wooden barricades up to hold the crowd. Behind them, the women were craning their necks to see if their man was inside the mercy wagon.

Kooteney didn't have a shirt, but he'd picked up a hardhat and a carbide lamp somewhere. He was pushing toward the airpacks and the clerk was pushing him back. It was a draw. The clerk was yelling and a couple miners came over to help out. They wrestled Kooteney back into the Dry. He dropped his carbide lamp.

The survivor list was tacked up inside the Granite Mountain shafthouse. The hoistman was running the cages and trying to explain the list to a big Italian miner. "No, the list ain't complete. How the hell could it be? I know there's more than forty-three men come up already but forty-three's all I got on the list. God knows how many got out and just went home."

The Italian miner looked like he hoped the list was incomplete. I hoped so too. My father's name wasn't on it.

So I got on the cage with four other men and I

cinched my air mask as tight as I could and we dropped into dark like a stone.

I couldn't see sweet fuckall at the 1600 shaft station. In the light from my lamp, I could just about make out my hands in front of my face. Somebody'd been signaling at the 1600—we'd heard it topside—but when we opened the cage, nobody came aboard. We fanned out in the shaft station, walking carefully as the blind, and I kept the faint glint of the next man's lamp at the edge of my vision.

The steady hiss of the compressed air in the mask. My short breaths.

We swept through the big room and a couple shift-bosses went on further—a ways down the 1600 main tunnel—but we didn't find anybody. Not even a corpse.

We dropped down to the 2400. When I pushed the cage door open, somebody fell onto me, grasping like a drowner. He was a thin guy and not too much life left in him, but he got one hand under my airhose and hugged me and pulled my mask down and my lamp was twisted so it shone up at the ceiling someplace and he was gasping, gagging in my face, and most of his weight was on me and I was holding my breath and my eyes were flooding and somebody else peeled him off and dragged him into the cage. I tugged the mask back in place and blew the smoke and the air was cold and smelled like the inside of a musty airtank and sweet, sweet.

The thin guy was collapsed in the back of the cage.

I straightened my lamp and followed somebody onto the station. I wanted to cough but was afraid of blowing my seal. When the other guy's lamp stopped moving, I came over. He'd found a live one; sitting down, arms locked behind him like a brace and his head thrown back.

Two dead men lying beside him. I rolled them over. Not my father.

We hooked the seated man under the arms and dragged him through the black, swirling smoke.

The cage rose into the noise and the light. My regulator gauge said I'd used eighteen minutes of my half-hour air supply. My knees were scared and weak. We got the two men out of the cage and over to the medics. It was hard work.

When I lifted my mask, the air smelled pretty good except it had too much pepper in it like one of my aunt Edith's salads.

We set the two men on the cable drum. One of them—the thin guy—couldn't sit up because he was dead. The other one locked his neck back like he was blowing a trumpet at the stars.

I walk the dead man's row again but don't find him. I see Gail Stinson talking to a foreman inside the shaft-house. She's writing in a notebook.

I don't want to go back down the hole so I tell myself I don't matter much; the world will go on just fine without me. That cheers me up.

The air compressor's mounted on the back of a flatbed truck. Three workers recharging the airpack bottles, though the job only needs one. I sling my airpack up on the truck. They say it'll be a few minutes.

Over by the Granite Mountain fan, Walker and Sam Curnew are yelling at each other. Sam's face looks strange, but maybe that's a trick of the light.

I wish they'd kill the sirens. A man could scream and scream and never be heard.

A couple of Walker's men are hanging around, trying to eavesdrop the argument. The rest of his crew is hurrying toward the Speculator engine house. I guess Walker got the clutch repair parts he wanted.

Sam was pleading, "For Christ's sake, Walker! Reverse the airflow. All you got to do is connect the motor. You already got the fan turned around. Come on! What the fuck you waitin' for?"

Walker's eyes darting around like a worried tomcat. Walker's remote voice. "The Speculator fan pushes thirty-three-thousand cubic feet of air down the shaft every minute. The fire, as far as I know, is confined to the lower levels."

"You're killin' 'em down there! The fuckin' gas is spreadin' into all the workings!"

Walker continued his lecture. "When I reverse the airflow and push air at the bottom of that fire, the Speculator shaft'll be a blowtorch. Curnew, nobody below the 1600's still alive, unless they barricaded themselves up. It isn't any use caring about the dead. If anyone's still breathing, he's on the upper levels where the smoke isn't so bad because the fans are holding it down. When I decide that all the men on the upper levels are dead, I'll hook up this fan and reverse the Speculator fan. We'll blow the gas back and fan the fire." He added, almost dreamily, "I've never seen a 3700 foot blowtorch, have you?"

He was looking at me and Sam. I didn't know what he wanted.

"No," I said.

I don't think he heard me. "Then we'll send rescue teams down the Granite Mountain to reach the miners who sealed themselves off. We'll move spare air bottles down to the shaft stations. We'll have crews working until everybody's out of the hole. Alive and dead."

Sam's voice was white. "We'll strike you, Walker. You know we'll strike you now. It ain't gonna hurt you as much as it'll hurt us, but we got to hurt you some."

Walker squinched up his face like he was puzzled. He shook his head. He got mad. "You cocksucker! You sayin' I caused this fire? You sayin' I wanted it? Fuckin' Burke is still down the hole. He had thirty minutes of air and he's been gone forty. Burke went down to close the fire doors *your* men left open, Curnew. They ran through and left the fire doors open and the gas came right on after 'em and killed everybody. Burke's down there and he's dead, you son of a bitch. He was tryin' to save a few of the dumb muckers that pay you to lay around the fuckin' Miners' Union Hall all day and whine."

"I'm sorry about Burke," Sam said. Sam's face wasn't strange anymore, just sort of weary. "I guess, Walker, you're sorry about all the men who died today. You always are. Every year, you kill twenty, thirty men in your goddamned holes and I'll bet you're sorry about them too. Walker, this year's gonna be a bumper crop. There's four hundred men on the Speculator graveyard and . . . and . . ." Sam's lips were working and his eyes were wide open but he was having a little trouble. "And . . . many . . . most have cashed in their chips." Sam took his eyes off Walker and talked like he was talking to himself. "I ain't much of a Red, Walker. I ain't Joel Kangas." A gust of smoke took Sam wrong and he was coughing and he was choking. "I don't kill nobody, Walker," Sam whispered. "I never killed nobody in my whole life. Every year you kill twenty, thirty guys. Just like you took a gun and shot 'em in the head." Sam turned his back and walked away. He was crying.

I think I heard Walker say, "I mine metal, Sam. That's what I do."

The same three guys working, refilling the air tanks, getting in each other's way. My airpack was next in line.

Gail Stinson spotted me. "Jimmy," she said, "you look awful."

"You don't look so hot yourself."

She touched my hand with her pale hand and we hugged each other hard. Protection.

And the men running through the mineyard were brown blurs.

And I couldn't hear the sirens because of the noise in my ears.

And we were melting into each other, and my heart jumped.

When I could see again, I was looking at the lights on the Speculator gallowsframe. The cages were going up and down again. I guess they'd got the clutch fixed. They'd be bringing bodies up the Spec as long as they could.

I said, "I ain't heard anything about Old Jimmy."

She shook her head against my chest.

I said, "I saw you writin' something over there. You were talkin' to that foreman: Sullau."

She wiggled her head in my chest again.

I pushed her away from me a little, and said, "Come on, Gail. Talk to me."

She was hanging her head, but she brought it up sharp and there was something fierce in her eyes and she said, "I'm doing a story on the fire, Jimmy. I'm going to write it and sell it to the *Saturday Evening Post*. I've hired Jeffers, the photographer, to take pictures. The *Saturday Evening Post*, or *Life* magazine—that's where it'll appear. Millions of people will read about the Speculator mine fire."

"That won't bring anyone back," I said, and regretted saying once it was too late.

"I got something, Jimmy," Gail said. "It's mine. It's what I do."

"Yeah," I said. I lit a cigarette but it tasted like dogshit and I dropped it into the slush. "What time is it?"

"Nearly six A.M."

"Sun'll be up soon," I said. The Speculator corpses were coming down the Hill in the Company armored cars. I guess they'd run out of ambulances.

I said, "I'm not going to Salt Lake. I want to, but I can't. I'm head of the Mullhollands now. I got to stay in Butte."

"Why? So you can go on strike with everyone else?"

"I got some money. There's Kathleen and the kids."

"I see," she said. Her body was set to take a punch. She relaxed it. She said, conversationally, "Do you want to know how the fire started?"

I didn't care but, conversationally, I said that I did.

Some electricians had been lowering a couple thousand feet of electrical cable down the Speculator shaft. They had it tied to the chippy hoist. They didn't use cable clamps because they didn't want to smash the lead sheathing. At the 2800, it slipped and started to run free, smashing and slamming its way to the bottom of the shaft. The electricians were real glad it hadn't taken any of them with it and said the hell with it and went off shift. A foreman went down to inspect the cable and it was heaped and mangled in the bottom of the shaft like a ball of lead spaghetti. When he leaned over to inspect the broken cable, his carbide lamp caught the exposed, tar-soaked insulation on fire. He couldn't beat

the fire out and it caught the dry-as-bones shaft timbers
and he ran through the manways to warn the miners.
He never made it out.

"He went deeper in the mine to warn them, Jimmy.
He could have got out but he didn't."

"Yeah," I said, "I suppose he's better off dead."

"It wasn't his fault. He wasn't guilty of anything."

"You don't have to be a bad man to be a murderer," I
said. "God's made a lot of murderers. Some of the best
people. All sizes, all shapes, every religion."

"Jimmy," she said so quietly, "I want to stay with you
but I can't."

My airpack was ready so I shrugged it onto my shoulders and gave her a good kiss and walked up the Hill to
the Spec.

I knew the Speculator workings pretty well, though
not so well as my father did. I knew where he'd be—if
he was me. He would have run and run and crept up the
manways connecting the levels and when it got too bad
for him, he would lay down beside one of the compressed air lines and cut it and pull his coat over his
head to make an airpocket and he'd be snug there, listening to the shrieking stop, the cages stop, the bell
signals stop, the mine losing its life; and him, lying with
his airhose, praying nothing caved on it or the fire didn't
burn it through somewhere further on in the dark.

The cage was at the shafthead but it wasn't going
anywhere. A dozen tired miners standing around sucking on cigarettes and coughing. They were men who'd
done what they could.

Kooteney Ketchel was there too. He still didn't have
an airpack but he'd got hold of an electric lamp somewhere.

The hoistman didn't want to let me on the cage. He

said all the rescue crews were out. In ten minutes, Walker was going to reverse the fans. He said I could help men moving equipment away from the shafthead because once the fireball came rolling up the shaft, everything up here'd melt, even the steel gallowsframe.

I said, "My father's down there. He never once let me do anything for him."

And maybe the hoistman's father was like mine because he said he'd drop the cage and hold it there for nine minutes and then he'd haul it up, with me or without me.

"Any of the compressed air lines down there still good?" I asked.

He shrugged. "Maybe on the 900. They were okay ten minutes ago."

Kooteney Ketchel got right in the cage with me.

He wanted me to meet his eyes so I did. I wanted to flinch but I didn't. He put his hand out to me: partners.

For some reason, I noticed that the hair on his forearms was soft and brown.

"No," I said. "Fuck off."

He wouldn't do me any good without an airpack.

He got off. The cage dropped me out of reach.

At the 900, I could see the fire through the floor gratings.

Far, far below me, it was a presence as much as a fire, a gleam like the headlight of a train deep inside a tunnel.

That gleam was just death, taking his own sweet time.

I opened the cage door. My clothes didn't fit right. I itched in my armpits and the crack of my ass. I was dirty.

I couldn't remember his name, I couldn't remember

mine. I tried to think and there was smoke inside my mind, curling slow and mean, like the smoke in my lamplight.

I could see maybe thirty feet into the shaft station. I was waiting for a call, but nothing, nothing. Just the shifting gray curtain and the bodies it licked and washed. I don't know how many dead men there are. I don't want to count them. Most of the fingers on both hands. I would call out but who would hear me over the hissing of air in my mask? I tried to speak, but my voice filled my mask like a balloon and scared me.

The back of my legs itched. I scratched them. I was looking at the dead men's legs, never their faces. My father is bowlegged. He was a cowboy once and that made him bowlegged. This man is too short. This one is too fat—unless it's the way he's lying like he's trying to press himself into the earth, so eager to be buried. A puzzle: A man's under the ground and he's trying to get under the ground.

I do not want to go into the main tunnel because I am afraid. Gray is very much like green and the tunnel is a forest path, overhung with mossy trees and all the light comes from my headlamp.

I do not wish to go. I deserve more or less than this. But I walk forward, helpless as a magnet.

The air line runs beside me down the tunnel. It's canvas, about eight inches wide.

I pass a couple of bodies, face down, lips pressed to the last shallow pools of good air.

They were right beside the air line but hadn't thought to cut it.

The hiss of the air in my mask. My frightened breathing. I am hurrying, hurrying.

Another corpse, a little man sitting with his back to the wall. I wave at him. I say, "Good luck, old timer." My voice crashes around inside my mask.

Perhaps he is the guardian. Perhaps I should have given him some token or coin.

Suddenly the airhose is flat, limp. I didn't notice the cut that emptied it or the rock that fell and tore it open. I don't notice enough. I don't have my wits about me.

Somewhere down this tunnel is the connection to the Black Rock Mine. I'll just keep walking forever. I'll come out in the Black Rock.

Jim, it's so peaceful here.

The tunnel stopped.

At first, I thought it was a rock fall, the shape was so irregular. Some rock fall that'd closed the tunnel. I was wrong. The concrete bulkhead had stoppered the tunnel like a cork.

The dead men.

I am the barbarian standing outside the gates of your brilliant cities. I am the cry that sounds just like a victim but must be the wind.

Dead men hunched up against the base of the wall. Dead men sprawled up against it with their hands raised like they could scratch their way through. Streaks and smears on the concrete that point to broken bloody fingers and hands. One dead man is lying on top of another and his boots are in another man's face.

Apart from the rest, two miners are sitting peacefully, holding hands.

Friends.

Thus they went into the dark.

I don't go close. I remember what Jim looked like but if I find him here I will forget.

I know enough. I don't want to know.

They want me gone. This is their place, not mine. They have the special knowledge of the dead.

I think I say, "Good-bye," but maybe I'm dreaming.

The signal cord at the cage, dangling like a scrap of forgotten material. I tug it and tug it though I'm afraid it's going to come apart in my hands.

The cage starts with a jerk and I rise out of my father's grave, scorched by tears of joy.

Somebody helps me out of the cage. Somebody helps pull the airpack off me.

The sun is coming up.

The ambulances idling in the mineyard. The searchlights switching off, one by one. The sirens die; grumbling. The mass of people outside the gate, silent as a dazed animal. The stink. The dirty snow. A couple men loading bodies into an ambulance. They don't need space for the live ones now. Gail, over by the Speculator engine house, talking to Sam Curnew. He's waving his arms around like a middle-aged man doing morning exercises.

Ketchel's helping the crew clear everything portable from the shafthead. He has no strength. He's slashed some of his bruises open. The red blood trickling from the black puffy skin. He's shoving an orecar and it takes everything he has to move it.

I sat down. Bob Whitehead came over and sat beside me.

I was very light and my throat was full like there was a ball inside it, and I didn't want to talk to him because I didn't know myself anymore and didn't know what I'd say.

His eyes were red and tired. He tossed me a pack of

Luckies and scratched a match with his thumbnail. We watched the people filing past the bodies and the wisps of smoke and the sun coming up.

"I ain't seen him, Jimmy," he said.

I didn't trust myself to talk. I nodded.

"Maybe he's down at St. James. He might have got out. Maybe he got out the Black Rock."

My throat was too full. I croaked something. I wanted to say, "No, no hope," but there's always hope: it's constant.

"I liked him," he said. "He always treated me right."

I'd got dirt on my cigarette and it sputtered and tasted foul. I wiped my hands on my pants and gestured for another one.

The Speculator cage was poised and ready. The Granite Mountain cage poised too. Like well buckets. Nobody was ringing the signal bells and the first-aid teams were taking a break, drinking hot coffee.

"What about you, Jimmy?" he asked. "What are you gonna do? Are you and Miss Stinson goin' off to Salt Lake?"

"No," I said. "I'll stay in Butte. Why should I leave? It ain't no different anywhere else."

"If you're worried about Kathleen . . ."

I didn't want to talk. The weight of my unspoken words was all the ballast I had. Empty, I would float away like a tumbleweed.

"I got a little saved up," Whitehead said. "And the job pays enough for a family."

"You ain't gonna buy her," I said. "Not so long as I'm alive."

Jesus. I sounded just like my father.

He looked off. Softly he said, "I didn't know Kathleen was for sale."

And I said I was sorry and maybe I was.

I wondered if Gail would stay for a couple days. She would, I thought. And when she left, I'd have that too.

The bitterness of my love cleared my throat and I got my voice back. "I'll get hired on again. I can wait out the strike and when it's over, Walker'll hire me on again."

"I'm a little sorry to hear that, Jimmy. It'll be fine for Kathleen, but what about you? You ain't cut out for the holes."

"Yeah. Everybody's got daydreams."

The sun, very small and pale over the snowy Highland Mountains. Cold as hell and clean. No men lived in those mountains in winter.

I heard the fans start up. The smoke was sucked right down the Granite Mountain shaft. Walker ran into the Speculator shafthouse. He was yelling, "Get the hell out of here, she's going up!"

Bob Whitehead started moving men back.

Gail's photographer had his camera mounted on a tripod. Big Speed Graphic.

Kooteney Ketchel was heading for me.

Maybe he wanted to explain.

Maybe he wanted to tell me about Joel.

Maybe he wanted to tell me how much his body hurt.

And the snow lay round about. Deep and crisp and even.

I wasn't his priest. I ducked into the shafthouse. Walker was grabbing reports and forms out of the desk. He was telling the hoistman about Burke. He said Burke was a fucking hero. I took a clipboard off the wall. Production figures. I put it back. Let it burn.

The hoistman was sweating. "Come on, you guys. Let's get our asses out of here!"

Sure. We'd already turned to leave when the bell signal rang. "Dang, dang, dang."

Somebody alive at the 300.

Somebody lucky. Some lucky miner who'd outrun the gases, traversed them, snuck around them, prayed his way up through the manways, made it almost to the surface of the earth. Someone lucky.

"Dang, dang, dang." Summoning the cage.

Just a lousy three hundred feet and the ball of flaming gases rolling up the shaft below him, picking up speed.

"It's a short circuit," Walker cried. "Ain't nobody alive down there."

"Dang, dang, dang."

Kooteney Ketchel opened the cage and got aboard. He waggled his fingers to get our attention.

He still didn't have an airpack.

We could hear the roar. The floor of the shafthouse was shaking. Like a train was coming into the depot. The hoistman was already into the doorway, ready to run.

Kooteney Ketchel was so big I could see his face above the steel cage door. His boots weren't laced.

"Dang, dang, dang." The signal was very faint in the roar.

Kooteney had his father's crazy eyes. He said, "Cut the rope."

My face. Walker's face.

"Cut the rope," I said.

And somebody threw the hoist lever. And I believe Kooteney Ketchel waggled his fingers again before he descended.